STEEP AND DEEP

Also by Catherine O'Connell

The Aspen Mysteries

FIRST TRACKS *

The High Society Mysteries

WELL BRED AND DEAD

WELL READ AND DEAD

Standalone Novels

THE LAST NIGHT OUT *

* *available from Severn House*

STEEP AND DEEP

Catherine O'Connell

SEVERN
HOUSE

First world edition published in Great Britain and the USA in 2026
by Severn House, an imprint of Canongate Books Ltd,
14 High Street, Edinburgh EH1 1TE.

severnhouse.com

Cover and jacket design by kid-ethic

British Library Cataloguing-in-Publication Data
A CIP catalogue record for this title is available from the British Library.

ISBN-13: 978-1-4483-1858-2 (cased)
ISBN-13: 978-1-4483-2099-8 (paper)
ISBN-13: 978-1-4483-1859-9 (e-book)

All Severn House titles are printed on acid-free paper.

Typeset by Palimpsest Book Production Ltd., Falkirk, Stirlingshire, Scotland.
Printed and bound in Great Britain by TJ Books, Padstow, Cornwall.

The manufacturer's authorised representative in the EU for product safety is Authorised Rep Compliance Ltd, 71 Lower Baggot Street, Dublin D02 P593 Ireland (arccompliance.com)

Praise for Catherine O'Connell

"This compelling, Scandinavian noir-style thriller should appeal to readers of both Ruth Ware and Arnaldur Indriðason"
Booklist on *First Tracks*

"A superior mystery . . . O'Connell tells this intricately plotted tale with verve"
Publishers Weekly Starred Review of *The Last Night Out*

"Brimming with witty observations about the well-heeled and the machinations of greedy businessmen, this sophisticated romp takes the daring amateur sleuth all the way to Thailand and Vietnam"
Publishers Weekly on *Well Read and Dead*

"The surprising denouement includes a last line that's laugh-out-loud funny. Fans of Nancy Martin's Blackbird Sisters mysteries will enjoy Pauline's escapades"
Publishers Weekly on *Well Bred and Dead*

About the author

Catherine O'Connell divides her time between Aspen and Paris and sits on the board of Aspen Words, a literary center whose aim is to support writers and reach out to readers. A graduate of the University of Colorado School of Journalism, she is also the author of the High Society Mysteries.

catherineoconnell.net

For Zuzuna

PROLOGUE

Evie

Her pace was steady, her arms and legs moving in perfect symmetry over the skis. Despite the calf-deep snow, she climbed with little effort, her skis floating on the surface as they were engineered to. She was determined to distance herself from the parking lot as quickly as possible, as if distance was the cure. Soft fat flakes of snow caressed her face, icy fingers to wipe away her tears, and after a while a soothing calm came over her. Wilderness and solitude held comfort.

The kids had been beyond challenging this morning. Her hangover made it worse. Thankfully, she had two volunteers helping out or she might not have made it through the day. Ten preschoolers were a handful when you were on your game, worse when your head was throbbing. Making things more problematic, these preschoolers came from wealthy families and were spoiled far beyond the typical perfect child. Of course, this was no fault of their own and they were still cute. There was no way children of that age could be anything but cute, even in their designer play clothes, even when they went into meltdown every morning when she took away their iPads. But underneath all the excess, they were like every other child, wanting more than anything to be loved and to know where home was.

Her thoughts turned to Buzz and their fight last night. She'd never seen him so angry and unreasonable, and thinking about it had weighed her down all day. She'd even broken into tears twice during today's nature walk and run into the woods, glad the volunteers were there to keep an eye on the kids, hoping they hadn't noticed her red-rimmed eyes when she rejoined the little group.

She'd gone back home this afternoon after work, determined

to straighten things out, to convince him that his suspicions were wrong. But no matter how she professed her innocence, he refused to believe her and wouldn't let her back in the house. So she had driven up the pass where she could turn to nature to assuage her misery. It was looking like she'd be spending another night away from home. She wondered if leaving her sleeping bag at Greta's this morning had been an oversight or prescience.

The effort of the climb was catching up with her and she was relieved to be nearing her turnaround point. Weller Lake was five miles from the parking lot, and with the road closed for winter, it was the perfect destination for a winter outing. Her throat was raw from the dry air, so she stopped to drink from her water bottle. She was putting the bottle back into her pack when her ears pricked at the sound of a snowmobile. Not only was it annoying that someone was breaking the white blanketed silence, it was illegal. Motorized vehicles were prohibited on the pass once the Winter Gate closed for the season.

She turned to see headlights coming toward her through the curtain of snow. In the graying light, she could barely make out the silhouette of the driver riding upright with one knee on the seat. She wasn't overly alarmed, though she did reach down to pat the Leatherneck knife she kept in her boot when she went out alone in the wilderness. She held her ground and stared the snowmobile down.

The machine drew up beside her and the driver cut the engine, greeting her with a familiar smile.

"Jesus, you scared the shit out of me," she said, her eyes shifting to the back of the snowmobile. "What on earth are you dragging that sled for?"

ONE
Greta

Day one

I parked the Wagoneer at the snowbank, where the county stops plowing the road, and killed the engine. The Goner—as I fondly called my forty-year-old Wagoneer—sputtered in appreciation and the world fell into backcountry quiet. I sat still, taking in my surroundings. On the other side of the snowbank, a snow-covered meadow opened into a valley banked by forest and white-capped peaks. Farther up the valley rose the alluvial fan, a chute of pure white from top to bottom, benign in appearance until you noticed it was devoid of trees. There was a reason for that. Periodic slides took down the trees, but that didn't concern me since the valley was wide and my plans didn't take me anywhere near it.

Floyd sat beside me on the bench seat, his lean furry body quivering in dog anticipation. His excitement was rooted in experience. Long car rides usually precipitated an unencumbered romp in the wild, and there was nothing he liked better than being let loose in virgin wilderness. It was his opportunity to let his freak flag fly, the dog version of it anyhow, an expression stolen from the Woodstock album my mother played ad nauseam when I was a teenager.

"Stay," I commanded in no uncertain terms, bringing his expectations to a rude halt. He was used to being let out to run while I got ready for whatever adventure was to follow. He lowered his head in a silent whine and watched me climb out of the car and walk around to the back. In a rare show of obedience, he remained rooted to the front seat while I opened the hatch and took out my gear.

It wasn't until I slammed the hatch shut, and he saw me

putting on my skis that he realized he wouldn't be joining me. He sailed over the front seat into the cargo area and started barking his disappointment. I glared back at him through the glass, giving him an 'I mean business' look. He stopped barking and his mug turned into that of a child who has just been told there will be no Christmas this year—or ever again for that matter.

Floyd plopped down dejectedly onto the pile of "just in case" equipment that lived in the back of my car. Just in case the weather changes. Just in case I need different boots. Just in case I'm snowbound and have to sleep in the car. Survival type gear. He buried his muzzle in Evie's sleeping bag laying on the top, untouched after a month, and gave me one last pitiful look in an attempt to win me over.

"I know. I know. Just stay put. I'll make it up to you later," I promised.

I put on my pack, grabbed my poles and started across the meadow. Floyd started barking again, but I ignored him until the noise faded into the winter wind. The valley that stretched before me went as far as the eye could see, a bucolic ocean of white in the shadow of the unforgiving mountains. It was a savage landscape, awesome in the true meaning of the word, and my spirits were buoyed as always at being the only human for miles. Wilderness is nature's opiate, and I'm a devoted addict.

A jab of selfish satisfaction flowed through me as I revisited my earlier run on Ajax this morning. One of the perks of wearing a ski patrol uniform is the privilege of jumping the line the morning after a storm. There is nothing like getting in the first tracks through the virgin powder, working with gravity to part the feathery flakes, riding the mountain like a surfer rides a wave. There isn't anything that beats it. Well, maybe making love. On second thought, not really.

I'd traveled about a mile into the valley before stopping to check behind me. The Goner was nowhere in sight which meant there was no chance of Floyd seeing me. A hole broke in the overhead clouds and a ray of sunshine peeked through. With the spring sun in the southern sky, the shortest days of winter were past, and the thin air warmed rapidly like stones to a fire. Even more than downhill skiing, cross-country is hard work, and sweat streamed between my shoulder blades and down my chest. I rolled down my neck gator and unzipped my jacket to let off some steam.

Deciding this was the perfect place for my purpose, I looked around for a landmark. I was rewarded by two sharp rocks resembling giant arrowheads jutting from the ridge to the south. I skied across the meadow toward the rocks and stopped just shy of the woods. The storm the night before had driven snow to the edge of the meadow, creating tufted drifts like waves on a frozen sea.

I stepped out of my skis and sank into snow to my thighs. Wanting to waste no time, I unstrapped the plastic shovel from my pack and started digging. The snow was light and kept collapsing in on itself, so I had to work fast to keep ahead of it. Once the hole was deep enough that the sides held, I reached into the pack and took out the clothes I'd brought along for Floyd's K9 avalanche training: an unwashed T-shirt from my last hot yoga session, a pair of dirty socks, some worn jeans. I dropped the bundle into the hole and filled it back in.

I had just strapped the shovel back onto my pack when the hole of blue overhead closed and the sun disappeared. The temperature dropped as if a switch had been flicked, and within seconds the air turned raw. Fresh snow started to fall, heavy wet flakes turning my blonde braids white. Mountain weather can change at any minute, and any respectable mountaineer knows it's essential to be prepared. I rolled my gator back over my chin and zipped up my coat, tightening the collar around my neck. Then I fixed the flaps of my wool cap over my ears and headed back to get my dog.

Floyd entered my life at the end of last season, after enough time had passed that I could finally bear to replace Kayla. Though Kayla could never truly be replaced. Letting her go was the hardest thing I've ever done. Aside from being one of the finest recovery dogs ever, she was my best friend. But typical of goldens, her hips went bad, and it became insufferable to watch her struggle onto her feet whenever she needed to go outside to do her business. The day she fell down three times on her way to the door was the day I loaded her into the Goner for our last trip together.

That last ride with Kayla was nearly as painful as watching my mother draw her last breath. Except Mom's death wasn't my decision and Kayla's was, though that didn't make the doing of it any easier. Sometimes when I think back to the way my mother suffered, I wonder if it wouldn't have been better if I could have made that decision for Mom the same way I'd made it for Kayla.

It wasn't until after the lifts closed last spring that I headed back to the shelter for a new dog. My mind was dead set on another golden and another female. After all, we girls have to stick together. My experience with males thus far has taught me they pretty much like to do things their own way. Since avalanche rescue requires complete obedience to the handler, it was imperative that I be boss. Which meant my new dog was going to be a female.

Maeva at the shelter gave me the green light to look around, so I wandered down the rows of rescue dogs looking for Kayla's clone. That's when I made the mistake of pausing in front of Floyd's cage and glancing inside. The moment he saw me he jumped to his feet and wagged his tail expectantly. He was a mix of Labrador and Bloodhound, officially a Labhound, with dark gold fur, black markings around his eyes, and ears that stuck straight up from his head. Cute enough, but he wasn't a golden, and he most definitely wasn't a she. I smiled at him and moved on.

Unbeknownst to me, Floyd had chosen me. Like it or not, I wasn't getting out of there without him. He let out a howl that turned me back on my heels and fixed his soulful brown eyes on me saying, *I'm your guy. You need me. And I need you.* I decided to give him a test drive.

"I'm giving you a head's up, Greta, this guy is a bit of a rascal," Maeva warned when I asked to take him into the yard. "He's only a year old and has a mind of his own. He belonged to a widowed rancher down valley who died when his horse fell on him."

Well that was a good thing, I thought. Not for the rancher, of course, but for me. If Floyd came from a ranch, it would mean he was trained to take orders. Another thing in his favor was his large floppy paws. They were ideal for avalanche (or avy, as we called it) work, good for both digging and staying aloft in the snow. I drilled him in the kennel yard, giving him simple commands like sit and shake, and was impressed by how quickly he responded. Even better, his eyes stayed glued to me as he awaited my next command. Surely loyalty and obedience were to follow.

I signed the adoption papers.

It wasn't until we got home that I found out I'd been played. Floyd's entire performance at the shelter was a ruse. The moment that I let him out of the car, he took off. After running halfway down the road, he turned back to taunt me with a quick yip before taking off again. *You knew I was a snake when you picked me up.* Then he disappeared from sight. Maeva had warned me, and I ignored her.

It took nearly an hour of slushing through melting snow before I found him and was able to lure him back. And that was with a steak. Floyd was laying the ground rules, letting me know who was really in charge. He had me so aggravated, I was tempted to take him back to the shelter. But being a true player, he sensed my change in attitude and came up to lick my hand, regaling me with those soulful eyes. Damn if he didn't have me suckered.

We'd been a team ever since. I worked him super hard last summer to get him ready for avy work, burying things in remote places for him to dig up. If you could say one thing about Floyd, he had one hell of a nose. He found everything I buried no matter how hard I tried to trick him. His shortcoming was he only obeyed when he wanted to and he tended to bolt when something more exciting, like a rabbit or a squirrel, came his way.

Which brought me to our mission up Gulch Creek today. With Floyd's certification as an avalanche dog scheduled for tomorrow, I didn't want him to screw it up. With just the two of us in this isolated wilderness, this would be the ultimate test.

He was lying in the cargo area pretending to be asleep when I got back to the Goner. I rapped on the window, and he opened one lazy eye and then closed it like he couldn't be bothered. It was all a ploy. As soon as the hatch was open, he bolted from the car at Mach speed and raced off into the meadow. He made several large circles before stopping to stare at me in "you deserve this" defiance. When he felt he'd punished me sufficiently, he trotted back to the car and sat down at my feet.

"All right, Floyd I get the message," I said. "Let's go."

The skies had turned threatening again, and the snow was heavy as we headed into the meadow. By the time we arrived at the two arrowhead-shaped rocks, they were barely visible and my previous tracks were obliterated. Which was ideal for Floyd's test. I had him hold his ground awaiting his release. He obeyed. This was a good sign.

"Vas-y," I said, releasing him with a phrase I'd picked up during a fling with a visiting patroller from Chamonix years before. "Let's go. Find the victim."

His nose tested the air, hovering in the wind for a few prolonged seconds. Then he shot across the meadow like an arrow honed in on the target, and my heart swelled with a mother's pride as he headed straight for my buried clothes. But, just shy of the goal, he stopped abruptly. His nose went back into the air, and he sniffed for a long second. Without looking back, he sprinted to the edge of the meadow and disappeared into the woods through a fence of pines and Aspens.

"Merde," I swore, putting yet another French word to use. I skied after him and stopped a few yards into the woods. A slope rose steeply in front of me.

"Floyd!" I shouted in my most authoritative voice. "Come!"

My voice echoed through the trees and was swallowed by the wind. "Floyd!" I repeated sharper, disappointed at his disobedience as well as the failure of our training mission. After shouting a good ten minutes, it was time for the move every pet owner and ignored wife plays as last resort. I pretended to leave.

I was well into the meadow when he came bounding out of

the woods farther down the valley, across from the alluvial fan. He had something in his mouth and was running like his tail was on fire. As he drew closer, I could make out that whatever was in his mouth looked like a black ball. He screeched to a halt in front of me and dropped it at my feet, his tail wagging in expectation of praise.

"You are not getting rewarded for this. That was not the game plan," I reprimanded him, irritated at his disobedience.

It wasn't until I picked it up that I realized it wasn't a ball. It was a ski mitten. Which didn't strike me as unusual at first. We were standing in the world's largest outdoor playground, and people were always losing things on the trails. But when I hefted the mitten in my hand, I was surprised at how heavy it was. A nylon mitten should be practically weightless. An empty one anyhow. This one was the weight of an orange. I turned it around and looked inside the cuff.

I've never been a screamer, but I suppose there's a first time for everything. I dropped that mitten like it was a hot iron and let out a horrified shriek. There was a reason why the mitten was so heavy.

There was a human hand inside.

TWO
Dan

Sheriff Dan Nichols' belly was pressed against the edge of his desk as tightly as his phone was pressed to his ear. That belly just kept getting larger every year with the waistband of his pants tightening at the same pace. It was getting to where he really needed to stick to his diet. Sometimes it hurt to remember how slim and fit he'd been when he landed in Aspen forty years ago. Now he'd gotten so big that he'd switched to snowmobiling instead of skiing, and even that was tough.

He bent forward to listen to the caller, his bald head glowing beneath the fluorescent light. His aviator-shaped eyeglasses slid further down his nose, their thick lenses making his blue eyes appear smaller than they actually were. He was rubbing his chin with his free hand, a sign that he was agitated, a habit developed back when he was a young bond trader on Wall Street.

The rough week was getting rougher. Tourist season always was a nightmare with so many knucklehead drunks getting into bar fights and women plying their wares to male tourists in the manner of the world's oldest profession. That is when they weren't practicing the world's second oldest profession, stealing. He couldn't begin to count the number of fur coats and top designer purses that had gone missing from luxury boutiques in the last weeks.

Then you had the spoiled kids of the second homeowners. There was sure no shortage of stupid out there. Just the night before a young woman had rolled a Land Rover on Main Street where the speed limit was twenty-five miles an hour. He was still trying to work out the physics of that one. Luckily she and her passenger were both wearing seat belts and emerged unscathed. You couldn't say that for the Land Rover.

And now with pot legal, stupid was in even more abundance, making the season an even greater challenge. People were constantly turning up at the hospital sure they were going to die after eating too many gummy bears or brownies. And hard drugs were still in play too, if the number of cocaine packets the local dry cleaner fished out of customers' pockets every week was any indicator.

There were the avoidable thefts. The Erté poster disappearing from a street-level gallery where it sat in clear view for the taking. A $100,000 diamond bracelet walking out on the wrist of an assumed customer. His personal favorite was the fur coat ingeniously stolen after a man and his 'wife' entered a luxury fur store and set off the security alarm. The man explained that metal in his knee caused this to happen every time he walked through any kind of metal detector. He proved it by walking in and out of the store several times, setting off the alarm every time. When he and 'wife' left an hour later without making a purchase, the staff ignored the alarm and waved goodbye to them and a $75,000 sable coat.

Violent crime was rare in Aspen, but grand theft . . . well that was workaday.

Then there was this other thing that really had him scratching his bald head. In the past two years there had been a half dozen unexplainable break-ins at doctors' offices in town. Nothing was ever stolen, not even drugs, but the doors had been jimmied and the security cameras disabled. Was it some kind of a prank or someone wanting to get even with their health provider? Only the perpetrator knew the answer to that question.

Today his stress level was off-the-charts dealing with Mayor Berthe Dunne. A newbie who had lived in Aspen a grand total of five years, she landed in the valley and decided she was going to right everything wrong in the town, from too much affordable employee housing to not enough parking. She was the polar opposite from previous mayors who looked out for the locals instead of the new landowners. Dan and Berthe didn't particularly see eye to eye, which made him glad that the county sheriff was an elected position and not an appointed one.

Mayor Dunne was reaming him a new asshole about not keeping her in the loop about complaints that Marynell Hennings was keeping chickens in her backyard. He tried to explain that Marynell had been raising chickens in that yard long before he, the mayor, and just about everyone else moved into town. Nobody ever had a problem with the chickens until some Los Angeles couple overpaid for their house next door. Evidently they wanted to turn the West End into Beverly Hills. Dan had treated their complaints thus far the same way he handled most nuisance complaints. He ignored them. After getting no fawning response from him after four calls, the couple did what any respectable mega-millionaire would do. They kicked it up to their attorney. Who rang the mayor's office right away with threats of suing the city for non-compliance of zoning.

"You know they're trying to push her out," he said to the mayor. "They just want to get her land. They'll take that landmarked house of hers and slap Versailles on the back."

"They're taxpayers, Dan, so I've got to listen to them. Land grab or no. Anyhow, why don't you go and have a little talk with her. Tell her the chickens have to go." Her authoritative voice softened a bit. "I'd do it, but she's not too fond of me."

Dan stifled a laugh at the understatement. Any fondness Marynell Hennings might have had for Berthe Dunne dried up when the lady mayor shut down her late husband's metal workshop two years ago for not paying city taxes. Chickens were one thing, but revenue? That was an entirely different creature. Marynell blamed Clive's death two months later on Berthe, saying the stress of losing his livelihood killed him, even though he already had stage four lung cancer from the pack plus a day he'd been smoking since he was fifteen.

"OK, I'll pay her a visit," he assuaged the mayor, his pawlike hand rubbing his jaw ever harder. "But you know she's not going to have any of it." His hand moved to his belt. He was really trying to watch what he ate, and any visit to Marynell was guaranteed to wreak havoc with his diet. You couldn't pay a visit to her miner's cottage without being plied with a tray of boulder-sized cookies and more often than not leaving with a to-go bag.

"Great," said the mayor, appeased. "Now I've got one other thing to discuss. Hopefully not as daunting as Marynell Hennings. Have you heard about this new virus?"

"I heard something about a cruise ship, but I haven't really paid it any more attention."

"Well, maybe we should put it on our radar. It's our responsibility to keep our tourists safe."

"Right, Mayor. Will do."

Nichols hung up and scratched the back of his neck. Talk of some virus didn't particularly disturb him. He'd been around a long time and these seasonal things came and went, especially in a packed tourist town. He remembered when everyone got all riled up about the swine flu. Hell, he'd caught it and survived to tell the tale.

But the very thought of going up against Marynell Hennings disturbed him a hell of a lot more than some rogue virus. She'd been a part of Aspen since time began, and even though he was committed to uphold the law, you had to be flexible when it came to dealing with a long-time local like her. That gal had one iron backbone.

He decided to pay Marynell a visit at the end of the day. That resolved, he turned back to a noise complaint from the Miami couple who owned a ten-million-dollar condominium over a downtown nightclub. They said the club ruined their sleep and they wanted it shut down. What in hell were they thinking anyway buying an apartment over a bar? And what did they want him to do? Close down all the bars in a tourist town? It wasn't his problem if they'd paid way too much for the joint.

Aspen was changing . . . had changed since that day he pulled into town as a young man. The small town character it fought so hard to hold was diminishing by the day with big money bringing in big city ways. Hell, it was a miracle to find any locally owned shops anymore. Everything had gone the way of luxury chains due to the exorbitant rents landlords charged in the commercial district.

And the way he felt about all these baseless complaints from newbies? He'd listen, but damn if he was inspired to do anything about them.

THREE
Greta

By the time Floyd and I got back to the car the snow was coming down so hard you could barely see three feet in front of you. It was a good thing we were out of the meadow where a whiteout without anything to focus on can get you in real trouble. Wander too far off course and you can end up in the next county before you figure it out. That or your body will be found in the spring. I loaded my gear into the back, along with the backpack that now held the hand of a human being. I closed the hatch and went around to the driver's side with Floyd trailing behind me. When I opened the door for him to jump in he sat down and refused to move.

"C'mon, boy. Let's go," I said. Floyd was always eager to ride anywhere, so I couldn't understand why he was being so stubborn. Maybe he was traumatized after finding the hand—hell, I was traumatized—but with the snow coming down harder every minute, I wanted to get down the mountain before it was a total whiteout. In the interest of not losing any more time, I pulled a treat from my pocket and held it out. I wasn't usually one to give food as reward, preferring to go the praise and play route. A quick game of tug of war can get you far. But Floyd loved treats and I always kept a few on hand for emergencies. Which this was becoming. He snatched the treat and swallowed it in one gulp.

"Goner in," I ordered.

Bribery will always get you somewhere and this time he hopped onto the front seat. We headed down the snowy road with Floyd resting his muzzle on my thigh. He was still acting strangely. I wanted to rub his head to assure him all was OK, but the road conditions called for both hands on the wheel. And though I was itching to punch down on that accelerator to get into town as quickly as possible, it's not a good idea when you're at the wheel of a forty-year-old, two-ton vehicle. Especially in a blizzard on a winding road with significant drop-offs and no guardrails.

It was work to concentrate on driving and not slip into dark thoughts about the contents of my backpack. Having that package on board was as unnerving as having a rodent running loose under the seats. After ten plus years of ski patrol, it's no stretch to say that I've seen my share of gruesome. I've witnessed injuries that would give most people a run of sleepless nights. Bones protruding from shattered legs. Faces bloodied after smacking into a tree. Feet facing in the wrong direction. Such encounters are not for the timid, but it's an accepted fact that people get injured skiing, and I've developed a pretty thick skin when it comes to the gruesome. But to find a human hand? That sure wasn't anywhere in my training.

The snow was still coming down hard and traffic crawling bumper to bumper when I finally hit the edge of town. I had a hard time keeping my cool as we inched into the roundabout. My thoughts were ruled by the desire to get rid of what was in the backpack. After a painful eternity, I rounded the corner onto Main Street and drove directly to the sheriff's office.

The building that houses the new sheriff's offices is situated next to its former home in the old county courthouse. It's nothing like its previous digs or any of the other vintage buildings that line Main Street. The old courthouse is stately and imposing with a red brick façade and a gabled green tower that hails back to the 1800s. It speaks of times gone by. The new building has contemporary written all over it.

I pulled into a spot marked 'official vehicles only' and practically leapt from the car. When I went around to the back to grab my backpack, Floyd jumped into the cargo area with his usual expectations of coming along, his tail whipping the air in anticipation. I slammed the hatch shut on his long face for the second time that day.

"Sorry, boy, no dogs allowed," I said.

He proceeded to bark his disappointment, the sound

following me across the brick courtyard and through the glass doors. It felt cold inside the building, not in temperature but in design. It was hard to shake memories of the old county courthouse with its red-carpeted halls and thick brown doors and heavy weight of history. I'd visit Dan there from time to time, back when things were looser and everyone wasn't so rule-abiding and there wasn't so much wealth to look after. I hurried through the building past glass-windowed offices with people performing their duties and wondered if they longed for the time when they worked in privacy instead of on display. A dark-haired deputy sat in the reception area behind yet more glass, staring at her computer screen. I tapped on the glass, and she slid it open.

"Hey, Greta."

"Hey, Yvonne," I said, working to sound normal. "Is he in?"

"In his office," she replied, giving me a long second look "Are you all right? You look really pale."

"Must be the cold."

"But wouldn't the cold make you red?" she asked, clicking a button to allow me in.

I propelled myself past her without answering and headed to the sheriff's office at the end of the hall. 'Dan Nichols, Pitkin County Sheriff' was artfully stenciled on the frosted glass door. I walked in without knocking.

Dan was seated at the same heavy wooden desk that had been in his former office in the courthouse, along with an equally heavy leather chair. Even though the furniture was out of place in the modern surroundings, it was nice to see some of the vintage stuff had made its way over with him. His chair was pushed back far enough to allow for his ample girth, and his round head was bent over some papers. I hadn't seen Dan in a while, and my first thought was he should start taking better care of himself. However, with a more pressing matter at hand, no pun intended, that lecture would have to wait for another time.

Dan straightened up at the intrusion, ready to be annoyed. But when he saw it was me, a gap-toothed smile stretched his bushy moustache to his cheeks. He got up and walked over, his six-feet-four-inch frame towering over my five eight. Before I had a chance to stop him, he'd grabbed hold of one of my braids, an annoying practice started when we first met.

"Hey, Trouble," he teased. "Boy that's a whole lot of hair."

"Obviously not one of your problems," I said, tugging my braid from his paw. "And don't call me 'Trouble'. You know I hate that almost as much as you pulling my hair. What are you, teenager?"

"Don't I wish?" he replied. "You know I just like getting a rise out of you." He laughed a deep-throated laugh and walked back around his desk. The chair squeaked painfully as he sat down. "To what do I owe the honor of this visit?"

I'd known Dan since I moved into Aspen at the turn of the millennium. He was a regular cop back then and a lot thinner with a full head of hair. We dated once, but I'd really only gone out with him to get out of a speeding ticket. He clearly had the jones for me, but the same didn't hold true on my part, so I ended up giving him the 'let's be friends' treatment. I knew he was still fond of me in more than a platonic way, but I managed to keep him at arm's length. Why ruin a good friendship.

Not many people know that Sheriff Dan was once a Wall Street trader who busted out in the eighties when the market went one way and his bets went the other. He loaded up his car and headed west to escape the wrath of his angry clients, landed in Aspen and never looked back. Like just about everyone in that era, he worked nights so he could ski days. It wasn't long before he became an expert, and he was thinking about getting into racing when he blew out both knees on a missed landing jumping over Cloud Nine. It was the ski patrol shack back then. Now it's a restaurant where people spend hundreds, make that thousands, of dollars to douse each other with champagne at lunch. Go figure. But Dan lives in infamy there, a picture of his jump pre-explosion pasted on the door to the men's room.

His ski career cut short, Dan decided to try his luck at something he was totally unqualified for. He became a cop. He applied for the job because the cops drove Saabs and wore shorts. He figured what could be easier than keeping the peace in a mountain town with hip people, stunning panoramas, and a high tolerance for drugs. Forty years later he was sheriff.

Dispensing with preliminaries, I took the mitten out of my pack and placed it on the desk. "You owe the honor of a visit to this."

He smiled at me curiously and picked up the mitten. He hefted it just as I had and turned it around to look into the cuff. His right eyebrow shot up and his massive face turned dead serious.

"There's a hand in here," he said.

"No kidding."

He put the mitten down on the desk and reached for his cowboy hat on the cabinet behind him. He fixed the hat on his head in an official manner and leaned back in the chair, away from the mitten as if it might start crawling across the desk toward him. He exhaled loudly.

"Want to tell me where you found this?"

"Up Gulch Creek. A little over a mile from the road. I took Floyd up there for some avy training this morning, and instead of obeying my orders, my wonder dog disappeared into the woods and came back with this."

Dan rubbed his chin. "You know you shouldn't have touched it. You could have destroyed evidence."

"What do you mean evidence?" I asked, sidelined by what the word implied.

"Until we know more about this hand, we have to consider this a criminal event of an unknown person. Where you found it is considered a crime scene until proven otherwise."

The term 'criminal event' had me rattled. Though parts of my life have been no Saturday afternoon picnic, I can actually be Pollyanna sometimes. I've come across so many deer bones and skulls in the wilderness that until Dan mentioned a criminal event, it hadn't occurred to me that anything other than a wild animal was responsible for the severed hand. The very suggestion that the human animal might have something to do with it put me in a spin.

"You don't think some animal chewed it off—like a bear?" I challenged him.

"Bears're hibernating, Greta."

"Tell that to the guy who was beating on my trash can last week. You know how whimsical they can be. Sometimes they just come out of hibernation for no reason. Or maybe some other animal like a wolf or a cat?"

"That'll be for the coroner to say. Criminal event or animal attack. First we have to find out who this hand belonged to."

I lowered my voice and put words to a thought that had nagged at me ever since Floyd dropped the mitten at my feet. "Do you think it could be Evie's?"

He looked blank for a minute as if he were trying to place who Evie was. Then he appeared to have a revelation and sat up even taller in his chair. "Evie Kearney? She went missing up Independence Pass. Not Gulch Creek."

"Evie didn't 'go missing'. Evie vanished."

Evie Kearney was one of my best friends. She went cross-country skiing up Independence Pass the month before in a blizzard and never returned. Her car was found in the lot with her phone on the front seat and the keys on the rear tire. While it wasn't unheard of for backcountry skiers to get lost in storms, Evie's disappearance defied explanation. She was an inveterate outdoorswoman, a naturalist who could identify any bird or flower, an athlete who could climb fourteeners without stopping to take a breath and then ski back down. For her to get lost in terrain she knew inside out seemed unfathomable, even in the worst of whiteouts. When it comes to the whims of Mother Nature, no one of us is truly invulnerable, but still, Evie falling victim seemed highly unlikely.

There had been a massive search for her in the days after her disappearance. Aside from the regular search and rescue teams, nearly half the town's locals turned out to help, combing the pass up and down, risking their own lives searching gulleys and slopes covered with loose rock. Nothing had turned up. Not a trace of her. The search was finally called off to await the spring thaw. If this was her hand, it might solve the mystery of what had happened to her.

"What makes you think this is Evie's hand?" he asked, shaking his head like he wasn't really buying it.

"That's the brand of mitten she wore."

"Greta, everyone around here wears this brand." He was right. The brand was popular and there had to be hundreds, if not thousands, of mittens like it all over town, in cubbies and lockers and the back seats of cars. But while my rational mind was telling me no way, my intuition was telling me that the mitten, and the hand inside, belonged to her. He shook his head again. "It's over twenty miles from Independence to Gulch Creek."

"Not as the crow flies. The way I'm seeing it, some animal attacked her on the pass, chewed off her hand and carried it over to Gulch Creek. Or maybe she froze to death first, and a bear chewed off her hand after the fact. Or a cat or wolf. They all have large ranges."

He gave me a hopeless look until he read the anguish on my face. His expression softened and he reached for the phone.

"What are you doing?" I demanded.

His hand stopped mid-air. "I'm calling for an evidence tech. We'll get some prints so we can identify whoever this is."

"Wait," I commanded in a voice that shocked even me. "What if Evie was never fingerprinted?"

"If she had a driver's license, she was printed. We'll know if it's her soon enough."

"How soon?" I asked.

"Should know within a week."

"A week?" I cried. "I can't go a week without knowing."

"Greta, sometimes the wheels of justice turn slow and all that. You've got to be patient."

Patient. That was easy for him to say. Patience wasn't one of my attributes. My mother used to say I came out of the womb in a hurry. I was born a whole five minutes before my twin, and I've never stopped hurrying since. I hate waiting almost as much as I hate wasting time. Especially when there's a way to get things moving faster. Why be tortured with the unknown when there's a way to make it known.

"Wait!" The words poured from my mouth. "I know how to find out if it's her. Evie wore a Claddagh ring that her grandmother gave her for her high school graduation. Her grandmother was her only anchor to normalcy in her whacked-out childhood. She loved her so much she never took it off. If this is Evie's hand, that ring will be on her finger."

Dan stared at me like a hole had opened in the back of my head and my brain was pouring out. Then he turned back to the mitten like it was a piece of a jigsaw puzzle he was trying to place. His fleshy cheeks tightened and he tugged at the corners of his moustache with his thumb and pointer.

"You're asking me to tamper with evidence?" He said it in a way that sounded like I wanted to violate a dead body. Which maybe I did, but not a whole body. Just a hand. I clamped my lips shut and pleaded with my eyes in a poor imitation of my dog.

"Just a little peek," I begged. "It'll only take a second."

"You are going to owe me big time for this," he said, picking up a tissue from the box on his desk. There was a zipper on the top of the mitten where a skier could insert a heat pack, and he pinched the tissue between his fingers and pulled the zipper open. Inside the opening, a black nylon liner covered the fingers. He flicked his eyes at me to say 'here goes' and took out his pocket knife. After making a small slit in the nylon over the ring finger, he used the blade to hold the fabric aside. A sliver of gold could be seen through the narrow opening. He stared at me over his glasses and then made the slit a little larger. My heart skipped at the sight of gold hands clasping a crowned heart, the Irish token of friendship, love and loyalty.

I fought hard not to cry. What could have been closure was overshadowed by the question of how the hand got severed. Dan put down his knife and closed the glove's zipper. Then he picked up the phone. This time I didn't stop him.

"Yvonne, will you send Investigator Roark in. And tell him to bring an evidence kit." He hung up and gave me the kind of look my mother did when she really meant business, like when she told me not to open the door to strangers while she was out with one. "This has to stay entirely between us. What I just did is highly unprofessional, not to mention unethical. They'd have my ass big time for this. You cannot tell anyone."

"Not even Buzz?"

"Especially not Buzz," he said firmly.

Before I could ask what he meant by that, the door opened and a tall clean-shaven man entered the room. He was hatless, with a head of wiry dark hair and a pair of green eyes that would have suited a leprechaun. A smile warmed his freckled face. Dan introduced the newcomer as Deputy Sheriff James Roark.

"Jim, it seems Greta here found a human hand up Gulch Creek this morning." He filled the investigator in on what I had told him. When he finished he asked me if I'd left anything out.

"Only that where Floyd went into the woods near the two arrowhead-shaped rocks was about a quarter mile from where he came out. I can go out there and show you," I volunteered.

My offer was met with silence. Dan pointed at the mitten and started giving out orders. "Let's get this into the freezer ASAP. Let's have the ME to do the pics and prints, because I want you out in the field with a search team ASAP, before the weather gets worse. Six investigators and a few cadaver dogs. Usual protocol. Cordon off the area. Let's see if we can find any more of whoever this is."

At the word 'whoever,' he turned to me with a look that demanded silence.

"Will do, boss," said Roark, already on his feet.

"Don't you want me to come along?" I begged. "To show you where Floyd went into the woods?"

Roark looked to Dan and said, "I don't think that's necessary. Arrowhead rocks about a mile in. That's pretty straightforward. Shouldn't be too hard to spot them."

"But Floyd . . ."

Dan broke in and was firm in a way he'd never been with me before. "Greta. This could be dangerous. Let's leave it to the experts. Those dogs are trained to find cadavers and if she's up there, they'll find her." Realizing his slip in saying 'she,' he added, "Obviously, this is a woman's mitten."

"Right. I'll get right on it," said Roark, seeming not to notice

Dan's gaff. He dropped the mitten into an evidence bag with a gloved hand and gave me a nod before leaving the room. There was no further conversation.

Dan turned back to me in the ensuing silence. "I know you're upset, Greta. This has to be really emotional for you. But it's best if you go home and put your feet up. You'd only be in the way at the site. I'll call you if we need you for anything."

"I'm sure Floyd can take us to where he found the hand," I insisted.

"We will call you if we need you," Dan repeated with unmistakable finality.

"But . . ."

"No more buts, Greta. It's handled. Now go home. You've done enough."

I stood in defeat and gathered up my pack. Then I remembered the clothes I'd buried up Gulch Creek for Floyd's training were still there. In an act of rebellion, I decided to keep that piece of information to myself and walked out the door without pleading my case any further.

FOUR
Greta

I stopped at City Market for groceries on my way home: Triscuits, Jarlsburg, bagged salads. The staples. As I drove past the open space at North Star Preserve on the edge of town, my mind traveled back to the day Evie, Judy and I dropped from the sky into that field. The three of us had been talking about parasailing forever, and one day, after smoking some ganja one of the customers at the Deep Powder Lodge left us as a tip, we finally pulled the trigger. Even though that virgin flight was a tandem ride with an instructor, the joy of being disconnected from the earth was a thrill I could never forget. After landing intact, we locked arms and crazy-danced around the field like the witches in *Macbeth*.

I've envied birds ever since.

The sweetness of that memory was broken by the thunderclap of Dan's insinuation that Buzz could be involved in Evie's disappearance. There was no way Buzz could ever harm Evie. Buzz loved her more than anything and probably hadn't had a good night's sleep since she disappeared. My frustration with this possible 'criminal event' was starting to boil over. I wanted to be in the field searching for answers, not sitting at home waiting for an update.

Floyd's pretty dialed into my moods, and sitting on the bench seat beside me, he sensed something was disturbing me. Then he did something he's never done before. He started tugging my sleeve the way he does his chew toys, pulling so hard I had to fight him to stay upright.

"What is wrong with you?" I said tersely, pulling my sleeve out of his mouth. He looked at me and whined. Then he jumped into the cargo hold and started barking out the back window like we were being followed. But when I checked the rear-view mirror, there was no one there. He kept it up, alternating between barking and whining, until I got the message. He was telling me to turn around.

"You're right, buddy," I said after considering it for a half second. I swung the Goner around and started back toward town with the ultimate destination of Gulch Creek. I'd been part of the search for Evie from the beginning and damn if I wasn't going to see it through to the end. "This is a free country and they can't tell us what to do."

It was noon when I pulled back up to the snowbank where I'd parked with Floyd earlier this morning. This time there were five Pitkin County Sheriff's vehicles parked there as well, their presence announced to the mountains by a circus of wildly flashing lights. A group of men and women in winter gear were assembled around Jim Roark who was giving out orders. Three cadaver dogs sat at the ready beside their handlers.

Roark stopped talking when he saw me pull up. He raised his hand to the group in a 'give me a minute' gesture and came over to the Goner. I started to get out of the car, but he blocked the door with his body before I could get it fully open. A heavy wool cap was pulled low on his forehead, and the friendly open face of earlier had been replaced by a frown. His green eyes were as frigid as the air.

"How'd you guys get out here so fast?" I asked as an icebreaker. "You shot from a canon or something?"

"Time is of the essence in situations like this," Roark replied in a none-too-happy tone. "Didn't Dan tell you to stay away?"

"Yes, but I thought about it and I know Floyd and I could be of some help."

"We're trying to assemble the team here, and to be honest, Greta, you'll just get in the way."

I was arguing my case when all conversation was cut short by four paws scrambling across my lap and out the partially open door. A moment later, I watched all hell break loose as Floyd pushed his way into the group of cadaver dogs and got into it with the largest one. The other two dogs started going crazy and the handlers were having a hard time restraining them.

"Somebody come get this mongrel!" one of the handlers shouted.

I jumped from the car past Roark and, after a couple of missed starts and a nip on the hand, managed to get Floyd by the collar. He was so determined to better the other dog, it took all my effort to pull him away. I'd never seen him so territorial, behaving as if they were intruding on his personal turf. I dragged him back to the Goner and shoved him inside, slamming the door hard to make a point.

"I'm sorry, he's never done anything like that before," I apologized. The assaulted dog sat obediently at his handler's side, staring up meekly as if to plead 'it wasn't my fault.' One look at Roark's face told me any chance of me taking part in the search had just been skunked.

"This isn't going to work, Greta," he said. "This is police work. You're welcome to sit here in your car for as long as you want, but there's no place for you and your dog in the field."

I pouted in the front seat, watching the team click into their skis and start out across the open meadow, trailing dogs and yellow tape behind them. They melted into the falling snow like ghosts on a movie screen. It took me a while to realize that sitting in the car with Floyd wasn't doing anyone any good. Especially me.

"I know you thought that was your job," I said to Floyd. "But I'd appreciate you practicing a little more diplomacy next time."

I started up the Goner and headed back down the winding mountain road in tail-between-the-legs defeat.

FIVE
Greta

It was nearing three when I turned onto my street. My A-frame sits on a cul-de-sac at the end of an unpaved road with no street sign and only one other residence. The altitude is 8,800 feet, an elevation that can often send flatlanders scurrying for oxygen. That makes things quiet up here, and that's how I like it.

I had the good luck to find my home ten years ago after responding to a classified ad in the Personals:

> **Free housing to appropriate candidate. Must be willing and able to pick aging ski bum up off the floor and show good humor tolerating stories of how much better things used to be here.**

Housing in Aspen has always been difficult, and I was stuck in the end-of-season shuffle when the place where I'd been living for two years got sold. When I saw the ad in the *Daily*, it was a godsend. I jumped on the opportunity and called right away. A gruff voice answered the phone and asked me what I did for a living. I told him I was a ski patroller.

"Ski patroller is good. I like ski patrollers. You don't have a cat, do you? I hate cats," he said.

"I have a dog," I replied holding my breath. Kayla was three at the time and still had a lot of life left in her.

"What kind of dog?"

"She's a golden."

There was a pause and then: "Come on up. Bring the dog too. I love goldens."

He gave me directions and I piled Kayla into my old Toyota and headed up the pass. I nearly burnt out the engine, gunning it uphill in first gear, but I wanted to get in the door before anyone else. The moment I pulled onto the gravel circle and laid eyes on the A-shaped house snuggled in pine trees, I felt like I'd come home. An ancient yellow Wagoneer parked on the side of the house and a thin old guy with a scraggly grey ponytail smoking a joint on the deck completed the picture.

Sam and I were kindred spirits and hit it off from the start. He'd come to Aspen with the first wave of ski bums in the '60s, after traveling around the world on a Vespa. He'd lived one heck of a life ever since. With the exception of a short-lived marriage that produced two offspring, he'd always marched to the beat of his own drum. He was the kind of guy who did things when and how he wanted.

He confessed that taking on a boarder was a big decision for him. It was like saying goodbye to the independence he'd cherished his entire life. But being so remote at his age had him worried. He ran the ad after his third 'I've fallen and can't get up' experience—when he missed a step coming down from the loft and the rest of him followed. It had taken him a couple of hours just to pull himself over to the phone. His body was worn out from too many on-hill crashes and too many off-hill parties. Sam confided he didn't want to die up there all alone, and that's why he'd run the ad.

He told me being a ski patroller worked in my favor for two reasons. The first was patrollers worked most days which meant he'd have his precious solitude much of the time. The second reason: patrollers were trained in first aid.

I moved in that day. The arrangement worked out perfectly. Not only did I get a home, I got a dog sitter. Sam moved from the loft into the downstairs bedroom, and I took over his former sleeping quarters. We shared the house for five glorious years with me keeping his refrigerator filled and listening to the same stories over and over again. I really only had to pick him up a few times. Then one March evening while I was working my coat-check shift at the Bugaboo, Sam took his last run during the Avalanche game. I came home to find him in the Barcalounger, fully reclined with the television blaring. He'd only taken a sip from his ever-present can of Coors when his heart gave way. Maybe it was the way the Avs were playing that night that did him in, but, whatever, his time had come.

In a move that surprised me more than anyone—well, maybe his two grown children were a little more surprised—he left me the A-frame in a life estate. It was a gift I'd never asked for or expected, and an even greater gift because it meant I would never have to do the seasonal shuffle again. I had a permanent place to live.

Needless to say, Sam's kids were none too pleased about the arrangement. The life estate meant that the A-frame wouldn't revert to them until I either died or moved out. Neither of which was in my plans for the foreseeable future. At first, they tried legal means to squeeze me out, but Sam's will was airtight. His son Joel, who was divorced and lived in Vail with his mother, would try to monetize me out of the place from time to time, but I always held firm. Sam's daughter, Lydia, lived in the east with her husband and children, and wasn't nearly as concerned about getting rid of me, because if I outlived her and Joel, the house would go to her kids at my death. After losing a few legal go-rounds, Joel stepped out of the picture and my residence was secured. For the time being.

The only other house on my street is a Pan-Abode. The mail-order log cabin was put together in the sixties around the same time Sam built the A-frame. Like Sam, Stan and Gwyn Greene were long-time locals and the last of their kind. They'd opened a restaurant back when town was really hip. The Bella Montagna was popular with locals as well as tourists, 'tourons' in local lingo. It had one of the best bars around, not to mention a damn good eggplant parm. But the restaurant got put to rest in the early noughties when their landlord ratcheted their rent to Manhattan levels, breaking the hearts of locals and tourists alike when it closed. The space now boasted yet another unneeded art gallery and, where once stood a lively venue that employed dozens of people and entertained hundreds more, a sole woman occupied a lonely desk sitting amongst overpriced and misunderstood paintings.

The Greenes kept to themselves, and I didn't see them much aside from Stan running his plow up and down the street and shoveling his walk when the snow got really deep. This afternoon happened to be one of those occasions, and Stan was shoveling as I drew near his house. He was always curious about ski conditions, though neither he nor Gwyn skied anymore, and sometimes I would stop to update him. But being in no mood for small talk, I gave him a quick wave and drove past.

I parked in front of the house and unloaded the car while Floyd ran straight for the woods to attend to his business. After racking my skis on the deck, I went inside, leaving the door ajar for Floyd. I crunched my jacket and pack onto the crowded hooks in the entry and was putting away the groceries from before when the phone rang.

There's no cell service where I live, so a landline is essential to stay connected to the outside world. I'd kept Sam's phone after he died, an ancient rotary-style with a cord that pooled on the kitchen floor. I supposed I could have gotten a newer model, but it was hard to find mustard yellow anymore and the color had grown on me.

"Pronto!" A greeting picked up from an Italian ski patroller.

"Oh good, there you are." I didn't have to ask who it was. The voice was more familiar to me than anyone else's. Judy was the first person I met in Aspen and was one of my two dearest friends. Make that one dearest friend. "I'm surprised to find you home. The lifts are still running."

"Day off," I replied. I wanted to tell Judy about the mitten, but Dan's admonition to keep it under wraps stopped me. "If you didn't think I'd be home, why are you calling?"

"I was going to leave a message on your answering machine since your cell is full. You have to remember to erase every once in a while. I'm calling to remind you about our party tomorrow night." *Party tomorrow night?* I searched my memory banks. "You haven't forgotten about it, have you?"

Actually, I had forgotten. I'm not much of a party girl though Judy was forever inviting me to parties with people I didn't know and didn't care to. I usually managed to beg off, but when Judy called to invite me last week, she wasn't buying any of my ready-made excuses. Gene had an author friend who was working on a book with a woman ski patroller as the protagonist. He was going to be at the party and wanted to meet me. Judy had begged me until I'd given in, and that was only after she had guaranteed me it wasn't a set-up.

"He just wants the female perspective of the job," she'd said.

Now I was sorry for going against my own wishes. The last thing in the world I wanted to do was go to a party, especially after all that had happened today. I thought of Dan's admonition again and decided it didn't apply here. If the discovery of a dead friend's hand didn't merit an excuse to pass on a party, I don't know what would.

"Listen," I said, "if you're near a chair, you better sit down. I've got some pretty gruesome news. But first you have to promise you won't tell anyone. Not even Gene."

"I've already forgotten."

"When I took Floyd up to Gulch Creek for avy training today, he found a mitten with a hand in it."

The intake of air came across the line clearly. "That's so creepy," she gasped.

"It gets creepier." Sorry, Dan. "The hand is Evie's."

Instead of another gasp, she responded in a dismissive manner she had taken on since marrying Gene. "That's ridiculous. We all know Evie went missing up Independence Pass. Not Gulch Creek. Why would you think it was Evie's hand?"

"Actually I don't *think* it's Evie's hand. I *know* it's Evie's hand," I clarified. "There was a Claddagh ring on the ring finger. Dan broke about a half dozen rules to check it for me which is why this has to stay secret. And she didn't go 'missing.' She vanished."

"Un-friggin' believable." I could picture Judy standing in the window of her Red Mountain manse, watching end-of-the-day skiers come down the Ridge of Bell, the same route the three of us had taken so many times, before that side of the friendship cracked. "I'm sorry, Greta. I know how close you were. How are you doing with all this?"

"How am I doing? Freaked out to put it mildly. I mean, we've all known she was dead, but I figured she'd had an accident or froze to death. Now who knows what happened?"

"It had to be an animal," said Judy, defaulting to the same conclusion I had.

"Dan's not ruling out an animal attack. But he says he's got to treat it as a criminal event until we know otherwise. There's a recovery team up there looking for any other remains right now. I tried to help, but they chased me away."

"What else could it be?" she asked.

"I don't have an answer to that. But, I'm thinking whatever happened to her happened up Independence. The question is how did that hand get carried to Gulch Creek?" I paused and then put into words something I'd been thinking about since leaving Dan. "I'm wondering if the rest of her could be up Independence."

"Hard to believe we're talking about a dead body in the present tense." Then Judy said something that really p'ed me off. "This isn't going to stop you from coming tomorrow night, is it?"

I wanted to throw the phone out the open door. In fact I might have actually done it if it hadn't belonged to Sam. "I can't believe you just asked that. Haven't you been listening? I find a piece of Evie in the middle of nowhere, and you're worried about your party?"

"Greta, we've known Evie was dead for weeks. We just hadn't found her body yet. Now we have. Part of it anyway. And I'm sorry if I upset you, but it's not like anything's changed. There's been a lot of time to face that she's gone." There was a long silence and then: "You coming tomorrow is very important to Gene. Which makes it important to me."

Of course, it was important to her if it was important to Gene. That's how things worked with her now. That's where all her beautiful things came from, the clothes, the jewelry, the furs. Things I didn't care about. I tried to tamp down my anger by reminding myself what a good friend Judy had been to me. We'd stuck together through thick and thin. Evie floated away from Judy after she married Gene, flat out accusing her of marrying for money among other things. I didn't let our friendship go.

I got a grip on my emotions and relented. "Fine. I'll be there."

"I appreciate that. And Greta?" She paused for emphasis. "Will you wear something nice?"

My thoughts roiled like a snow squall where it's impossible to see through to the other side, and I had to work hard to not tell her to stuff the damn party 'you know where.' But I couldn't forget that I owed my life in Aspen to her, and it was a debt I could never overpay.

"Don't worry, I won't embarrass you," I acquiesced.

SIX
Greta

Mom died just before the Millenium. I dropped out of college to take care of her when she got sick and nursed her until the ravages of breast cancer took her three years later. As tragic as her death was, it relieved me of my caregiver duties, and I was finally free to start my life.

My twin and I sold the little house we'd grown up in and split what was left after paying off the mortgage. Toby followed his dream and joined the Army Rangers. As for me? Any ideas about what to do with my life had been dulled by the years of caring for my mother. I hadn't had a life since she got sick and not much of a life before that. One thing I knew for sure was I wanted to get out of Milwaukee with its long, dull, grey winters, but to where? To do what? I signed a month-to-month lease in a crummy apartment complex and took a job waitressing, waiting for inspiration to come to me.

And one miserable January night it did. I was waiting on a four-top and one couple was raving about the fabulous vacation they had just taken. They couldn't stop talking about this phenomenal ski town where it snowed at night and the sun came out nearly every day, even in the dead of winter. They spoke of the charm of the valley and the surrounding mountains. Of the restaurants and the lack of crime and how many people there were from exotic places and how nice the locals were. One of the women called it the true Camelot.

Wherever this was, it sounded like the perfect place to kick-start a new life. Or actually start life altogether. This town was calling to me. While my mother didn't have a lot of money to spare, she'd surprise us sometimes, like the time she signed Toby and me up for the school ski trip to Northern Michigan. I'd fallen in love with skiing then. And though I never had another chance to ski after she got sick, I'd look at ski magazines and dream of conquering the slopes. I summoned up the nerve to ask them the name of this fabulous ski town. Why, Aspen, Colorado, came the reply.

In one fell swoop, I found my raison d'être. My plans were made before they paid the check. I'd use my inheritance to rent an apartment in Aspen or maybe even a cute little house. I'd waitress at first and meet exciting people and live the life of a ski bum until whatever came next. The college degree could come later. I turned in my apron at the end of my shift and went home to pack.

Three days later I pulled into Aspen with all my earthly goods crammed into the back of my Toyota and my half of Mom's estate in my purse. The town was even more magical than my customers had described. The hamlet was nestled in snow-covered mountains with vintage miner's shacks and Victorian houses lining the streets. Small yet vital. And the sun was out, bringing a shine to my sugarplum dream. The dull gray winter of Milwaukee was in the rear-view mirror and good riddance to it. I swore I would never go back there again.

Unfortunately, my plans were derailed before they got started. I quickly learned that in Aspen housing was in short supply and the prices were astronomical—if you could even find housing. There were no apartments advertised in the newspapers and a drive around town did not turn up a single window with a For Rent sign like you'd see in Milwaukee. I checked in at a couple of real estate agencies. The first agent gently explained that rentals were few and far between. And expensive. The second agent literally laughed at me.

The reality was that I'd chosen a place where finding a bed was nearly impossible, much less an apartment. Aspen was packed with people wanting to realize the same dream I had. My new life was deflating as quickly as it had come on, and worse, I had no idea where to go from here. I'd left my few friends back in Milwaukee, and my brother was overseas. I was rudderless and totally alone in this world.

It was then I realized I was starving. And thirsty. It was nearing five and after hunting for the elusive apartment all day,

I hadn't had anything to eat or drink. If you can say one thing about me, it's that nothing much affects my appetite. Not pain, poverty, love or worry. I can eat through them all. I found an affordable restaurant on a side street and went inside to drown my sorrows in a burger.

Little Annie's was exactly what I'd envisioned a ski town restaurant to be. The tables were set with red-and-white checked tablecloths, and the menu was heavy on chili and hamburgers. There was a long rustic bar with beer on tap and paneled walls plastered with ski photos. Though it was early for dinner, the place was already filling with smiling skiers and their families. I sat down at a booth in the window, hoping I didn't stand out as the latest loser in town.

The waitress came over and introduced herself as Judy. She was about my age and very pretty, with shiny dark hair pulled back in a ponytail and a ready smile. She filled my water glass, and I drained it in one long gulp.

"Just get into town?" she asked.

I nodded silently. I was feeling so out of place that the mute response was the best I could muster.

"Very important to stay hydrated," she said, refilling my glass.

She handed me a menu and left me to work the crowd. I was struck by how happy she looked as she glided between the tables taking orders. Unlike me waitressing in Milwaukee, which was pure torture, she obviously loved what she was doing. Or maybe it had something to do with doing it in Aspen. When I looked around the restaurant, it seemed like everyone shared in the happiness.

Judy came back to take my order, and I ordered a hamburger and a milkshake. Comfort food. After she disappeared through a swinging door into the kitchen, I took another look around the room and the hopelessness of my situation hit home. I could never have what they had. My dream was just that. A dream. My eyes welled with disappointed tears, and I fished in my purse for a Kleenex. I wiped my eyes and dug deeper into my purse for my book so I wouldn't feel so lonely. With a book, I always had a companion.

I was reading *Beloved*, the story of Sethe, a black woman who was born into a life of poverty and powerlessness. I told myself my misery was nothing compared to hers, but that did little to assuage me. My focus was on my problems, troubles that seemed insurmountable.

It was getting dark and I had nowhere to sleep. With the season in full swing, all the hotels were full which meant I would have to drive the winding road back to Glenwood Springs and hope to find a hotel room there. If there were no vacancies in Glenwood, what then? Denver was a four-hour drive and it was starting to snow. I wasn't used to driving in the mountains in a snowstorm, but that wasn't the real problem. The problem was going back to Denver meant giving up on my dream. I pulled out another Kleenex.

By the time Judy arrived with my food, the tears were streaming down my cheeks. I tried to hide them, but that was near to impossible with my soggy tissue. She put down the hamburger and shake and, without asking permission, slid her slim body into the booth beside me.

"Problem with a guy?" she asked.

"Worse," I sobbed aloud, letting it all go to this stranger. "My mom died and my brother is in Afghanistan. We sold our house, and I have no home anymore. I drove here from Milwaukee hoping to find a place and get a job and there's nowhere to live. I don't know what to do." I buried my face in my hands and sobbed harder.

She wrapped a friendly arm around me. I raised my head and looked into her bright blue eyes. I must have looked a mess, my blonde hair a bird's nest and my brown eyes puffy with tears. She studied me for a minute and drew closer. "Hey, no worries about getting a job here," she said soothingly. "That's never a problem in this town. But beds? That's the challenge. I don't suppose you have any money?"

I opened my purse and showed my thousands to a perfect stranger. Her eyes actually lit up. Seems I was the rare dreamer who landed in town with cash. Her next words were a gift from heaven. "I might have a place for you. But you have to play well with others."

Judy shared a Victorian house with around ten other people, depending on the day. The rent was usurious, even split between so many warm bodies. She told me if the owners of the house had any clue how many people were living there, they would have croaked. But they lived in West Palm since they could no longer handle the elevation, and out of sight was out of mind. As long as the rent was paid on time.

And it turned out my timing couldn't have been better, because a bed in the house had just become available.

When Judy finished her shift, she took me home with her. The Victorian was exactly what I'd envisioned, a two-story, red brick beauty with a covered front porch and leaded windows that dated back to the silver days. It looked so perfect, I could hardly believe the vision was real.

Reality came into play when we walked inside. Spread out on the living-room floor, a long-legged woman with a Gumby-like body was executing yoga poses. A pile of auburn hair in a scrunchy sat high upon her head and her pale arms were ropy with muscle. She didn't bother to look up as Judy and I walked into the room.

"Hey Evie, you've got a new roomie," Judy told the woman. She pointed me toward a brocade sofa in the window overlooking the snow-covered front yard. "There's your bed," said Judy. "You can stick your bags in the corner." A similar sofa I assumed to be Evie's looked onto the side yard and was piled high with wrinkled clothes.

"What the f . . ." Evie glared up and I saw her face for the first time. It was heart-shaped with perfect skin and a pair of deep-set hazel eyes that glared at me from beneath a widow's peak. She unfolded herself to a standing position and took a strident pose in front of me. We were eye to eye, and I met her glare with a smile, trying to look friendly and not frightened. Something told me my survival in paradise depended on her approval.

Judy introduced me. "This is Greta. Susie's moving in with Greg and Greta's going to be taking her place."

"Good riddance to that bitch," said the Gumby I now knew as Evie. I presumed she was talking about the woman whose bed in the front window would hopefully be mine. She huffed and looked me over like a horse she was considering buying, stopping shy of pulling my lips back to examine my teeth. "I hope you'll be better at paying the rent than Suzie was."

"Oh she will be," Judy piped in on my behalf, flashing a satisfied smile that told me we'd made the hurdle. "I've already vetted her. She comes with cash."

Evie gave me a final once-over and held out a firm hand. "Good. Then we're going to get along fine, my friend," she said. Without another word, she dropped back down to the floor and resumed her previous pose.

Judy smiled. "See, you'll get along fine."

SEVEN
Greta

But we didn't get along fine. In fact, at first Evie and I didn't get along at all. It was all I could stand to be around her. She was brash and abrasive and pushy. While she wasn't much of a drinker and only occasionally smoked weed, she did have one Achilles heel, and it was a biggie. In a town where casual sex is a given, she ratcheted it up a notch. If Evie wasn't a candidate for the twelve-step sex program, then no one was. My mother may have been a nymphomaniac, but Evie was my mother on steroids.

Even now, I cringe to think of the parade of guys that filed through the living room that was our shared bedroom. You couldn't believe the number of times I'd awaken to hear her wrangling with some hook-up on the other couch or under the coffee table as if there was no one else in the room. I could write a book on ways to fold a pillow over your ears.

But if I wanted to stay in Aspen, I had to suck it up until some other opportunity for housing presented itself. As much as having Evie for a roommate bugged me, I wasn't going to let it ruin my newfound life. And while housing was tight, Judy had been spot on about jobs being plentiful. I found three jobs right away, a breakfast waitress gig which left the rest of the day for skiing, making pasta in the window of an Italian restaurant three nights a week and a coveted coat-check shift at the Bugaboo Club, which the previous occupant of my sofa had given up when she moved in with Greg, whoever he was. The Bug was the trendiest club in town, and tips for one night's work could run into the three digits. I kept a polite distance from Evie in order to keep my bed, turning down her invitations to go out at night and only skiing with her in groups. I found her to be obnoxious and saw no reason for getting any closer to her than our sleeping situation necessitated.

Then something happened that changed my opinion of her big time.

Aspen was a new world to me. It was physical and social and exciting and even work was fun. We were young, and we skied hard and partied hard. The bars were filled with good-looking and friendly people, locals and tourists alike, and money was no problem despite the high rent because jobs were plentiful and paid well.

But in Aspen, I was also exposed to a kind of person way different from the people I'd known growing up. I called them the Others. Women and men, they were curious and smart and accomplished. They oozed class and money and travel and experience and education, about as far from my Midwest working-class neighborhood as you could get. I have to confess to holding them in awe at first.

Then one spring day during that first season, I rode the gondola with a guy from Boston. He was one of the Others, classy and charming, slick and super good-looking. If you don't believe in selective breeding of the wealthy, I suggest you take a look around Aspen. People there take good-looking to another level.

Anyhow, this guy from Boston was smoother than a groomed run first thing in the morning. We talked skiing the entire fifteen-minute ride to the top, and as we exited the gondola he asked me to take a few turns with him. We ended up shredding powder all day and after the last run, he asked me out for dinner.

He took me to the most expensive restaurant in town. After a three-course dinner with far too much wine, we stopped at the Jerome Bar for a nightcap. One nightcap turned into two and it would be lying if I didn't admit to being bombed. When the bar closed, he offered to walk me home and I accepted.

The Victorian was a short five-block walk from the Jerome, and it was a beautiful night with a gentle snow turning the streets into a Christmas card. He was a perfect gentleman, holding my arm steady as we navigated the slippery streets with me stumbling from time to time. When we got to my door, the lights were out and the porch was dark. I turned to say goodnight, and he surprised me by grabbing my wrist. Hard.

"What do you mean goodnight?" he hissed. "Do you think I bought you that dinner and all those drinks for nothing." The man had changed completely, a chameleon from the polite guy I'd spent the day with. Without any further conversation, he pressed his body against mine, pinning me to the wall next to the front door. I'll admit there may have been possibilities until that moment, but when he took possession of me like that, all I wanted was to escape him.

But it was too late. He was strong and before I knew it, he had locked both my wrists in one hand and was tearing at my jeans with the other. I'm no weakling, but as hard as I tried to fight, I was drunker and he was stronger. He'd gone animal, and there was no doubt in my mind that he intended to rape me. This wasn't about sex. It was about having power over me.

"No, I don't want to," I cried out, hoping to draw attention. He slapped his hand over my mouth.

"I bought you a fucking lobster dinner and a bottle of Puligny-Montrachet. Now you're going to show your appreciation."

"No," I repeated, turning my head free of his grasp. But his strength was overwhelming and his hands were everywhere all at once under my bra and yanking down my pants. He kept me pinned against the wall and I could hear his zipper come down, sense his bare dick pressing against me. My hat had fallen off and he had me by my hair, making it even more difficult to fight.

He had his pants down and was pressing himself between my legs when the light came on and the front door flew open. Onto the porch bounded Evie wearing one of Judy's Little Annie's T-shirts and a pair of Uggs.

"She said she didn't want to, dickhead. What's the matter? You deaf?"

She had startled him, but after taking one look at her narrow frame, he raised a hand to slap her away. She grabbed his hand

and, in one swift motion, twisted it behind his back. The next thing I knew the guy was on his knees and she was holding a gun in his face. I'd never seen anything like it and stood there with my jaw hanging open in drunken awe.

"I hope I'm not ruining your date?" she asked.

I shook my head stupidly.

"Just making sure you're not kinky." She let go of his arm and he backed away from her on his knees like she was a cobra, his eyes fixed on the gun. "Get the fuck out of here, Bozo. And it might be a good idea if you cut your trip short and head back to your wife. Next time I see you, I won't be so nice."

The guy turned to run, but his pants were down and the street was icy. He slipped and landed on his bare butt, stood again and pulled up his pants. Then he took off running. I don't know that I've ever seen anyone move so fast.

Evie and I went into our shared living room and there was a prolonged silence. She threw the gun on the table and said, "Don't worry it's plastic. Just a precautionary thing." Then we both broke out in hysterical laughter at the thought of him running down the street with his dick hanging out.

"He took off like the guys in *Deliverance* were after him," I laughed.

Then Evie stopped laughing and turned serious. "It's one thing when you want it and an entirely different bird when you don't."

Later, after a beer I really didn't need, I asked her where she'd learned a move like that. "You only need to get raped once," she replied. "I learned a long time ago how to protect myself."

"Once when I was fourteen, one of my mother's boyfriends tried the same thing," I admitted. "But my brother stopped him."

"Well you should learn to protect yourself better," she said. "Your brother isn't here."

My opinion of her changed, and we were fast friends from that day forward. I bought an eye mask and ear plugs, and we continued to share the living room the rest of that first winter. The next year, I won the lottery and got my own bedroom in the Victorian. Judy, Evie and I became a trio and were practically inseparable. We were three young women who shared challenging upbringings. We understood one another and we had one another to lean on.

In a backwards way, I had that Boston asshole to thank for both my friendship with Evie and my job in ski patrol. It was the second time in my life I'd come close to being raped, and I was not going to allow myself to be in a position like that ever again. The next week, I started strength training and classes in self-defense. The two combined to make me stronger and more agile, and I became a better skier. I soon moved on to teaching skiing which then became my springboard to ski patrol.

And though I would never want to relive the experience of that night, I learned, that which doesn't kill me makes me stronger.

EIGHT
Greta

I had hung up with Judy and was putting the rest of the groceries away when Floyd came running back inside. He evidently didn't see me in the kitchen, because he ran right into the living room and leapt onto the Barcalounger, curling himself into a ball of ownership. The Barca had been Sam's throne, the place where he had drawn his last breath, and like his other dinosaurs, the phone and the Wagoneer, it was sacrosanct. The chair was barely clinging to life, held together in places with the same duct tape I used on my ski boots, but I couldn't bear to part with it. It was a verboten for Floyd and he knew it.

"Hey, what do you think you're doing?" I shouted, reaching into the refrigerator for a much needed beer after the day I'd had. Busted, he skulked to the ground sheepishly and settled his muzzle on his paws, avoiding my eyes. "And you better not be getting up there when I'm not home," I added, knowing for certain the first thing he did anytime the door closed behind me was commandeer that chair.

I settled into the Barca with the beer, flicking the cap off with a practiced fingernail. I'm not much of a drinker anymore, nothing like my party days, but I needed to take the edge off. A long drink of the Heineken did the trick.

I turned on the television with the intention of watching something mindless. Sam had added a satellite dish when driving into town to watch the games at Scooter's wasn't an option anymore. Having the satellite TV still felt self-indulgent, seeing how in our Milwaukee home we never advanced past rabbit ears. Mom earned her living as a hairdresser and had to watch every penny to keep us dressed and fed and herself in booze. Why pay for television when you can get it free, was her motto. The upside of growing up with limited TV was that I turned to reading to entertain myself instead. I devoured everything from Nancy Drew to *The Brothers Karamazov* to Harry Potter. Reading can take you anywhere without spending a cent. Besides, you can only watch so many Dick Van Dyke reruns.

I scrolled through the basic channels and finding nothing of interest, I settled for the news. The lead story was about some virus that caused passengers on a cruise ship to be quarantined for weeks. "That's what you get for taking a cruise in the first place," I said out loud, lecturing the unhearing hundreds imprisoned on the ship.

As for me, my worst nightmare would be getting stuck on a ship packed with Boomers and germs. My preferred vacations involve action like rock climbing or trail running or heli-skiing or surfing. No organized tours for me. No bronzing on an island beach. And certainly never a spa unless it's one in Bali that includes yoga. The only cruise you'd ever find me on would be one taking me out to burial at sea.

But I'm a mountain girl, and my upcoming travel plans will take me as far from sea level as you can get. This spring I'm going to fulfill my dream to climb Everest, a dream inspired reading *Into Thin Air*, turning pages into the night while my mother struggled to draw breath beside me. Instead of being put off by the tragic events of the climb, it created in me a longing to some day sit on top of the world myself. I've been preparing for over a year, climbing most of the fourteeners in Colorado, and while Everest is over twice as high, 14,000 is a good start. I've already put down a deposit for a mid-May climb out of Katmandu and am counting the days. And the dollars. I'm a few thousand short of the $30,000 for a Nepali guide, but I've got a couple of months to go, and I'm counting on my coat-check shift at the Bug to come through.

I sipped at my beer and stared at Floyd asleep on the floor, his chest rising and falling in a smooth rhythm and his legs moving in some dog dream. Hindsight being twenty-twenty, I now regretted not bringing him on the initial searches for Evie after she disappeared. But his lack of discipline would have made him more hindrance than help around all those people and dogs. No matter how I tried to break him, he still had a mind of his own. Today being a good example.

Out of nowhere I had an epiphany about why Floyd chose to bypass my buried things in Gulch Creek and went for Evie's mitten instead. The entire time I'd been out in the meadow alone, Floyd had been in the back of the Goner with his nose buried in Evie's sleeping bag. It would have been rife with her scent, and that scent would have been in the forefront of his dog memory.

I flicked off the TV and stared into space, replaying Dan's words. *Until we know what has happened here, we have to consider it a criminal event.*

I didn't want her death to be a criminal event. That implied the unthinkable. My reflexes twitched with inspiration. If the rest of Evie was up Independence being picked apart by animals, Floyd and I were going to find her. They wouldn't let us help in the search up Gulch Creek, but they couldn't stop us from searching where she had vanished in the first place. I was going to put Floyd's nose to work where it hadn't been used before. If Evie was up there, he would find her.

I checked my watch. It was four o'clock and true sunset wasn't until after seven. If we hurried we had just enough time.

I got up and grabbed my pack from its hook. Floyd opened a lazy eye and watched me from his position on the rug. I stared back down at him.

"Yeah, I'm tired too, but we're on a mission here. Vas-y!"

NINE
Judy

The view from her walk-in closet was exquisite, the white puzzle maze of Aspen Mountain framed in floor-to-ceiling windows with the former mining town puddled at its base. A picture postcard. Judy stood in front of the window thinking about what Greta had just told her. She wished she could feel something other than shock, but she'd cut her emotional ties to Evie a long time ago when it came to choosing between their friendship and Gene. Evie had said horrible things about Gene, accused her of marrying him for the wrong reasons. Which was only partially true, but still. The truth hurt.

She turned back to what she'd been doing before calling Greta, searching out the perfect ensemble for the party. Though her mood had changed, she intended to finish making a selection. She'd bought something fabulous at one of the couture places in town, an outrageously expensive sheath of gold silk that accentuated her thin waist. But she was having second thoughts about it, as she always did after buying something that cost nearly as much as her father made in a year.

Tomorrow's party was important for them, the guest of honor being one of Gene's clients, Humphrey Gibbons, the CEO of Regal Oil. Humphrey had bought both his first and second Aspen home through Gene's company. With the price of oil finally creeping back up after cratering for years, Texans were feeling rich again which translated to more referrals from Humphrey for Gene, which translated to a good thing for Judy. Gene's business had been lean for some time in the aftermath of the recession. Not that Judy really needed any more spending money. In her wildest dreams, she had never thought she would have a portion of what she now possessed, but she sure was glad those dreams had been realized. At a price, but what in this life came without a price.

She stopped thumbing through her wardrobe and thought back to the macabre news that Greta had just delivered. While Judy had tried to be cavalier about it, there was no getting around that finding someone's hand was terribly disturbing. She couldn't begin to imagine how much more traumatic it must have been for Greta to learn it was Evie's. Even Judy remembered how much Evie had cherished that Claddagh ring. The whole thing was horrifying and what made it worse was where the hand was discovered. She and Gene had gone up that way in the summer years ago, before they were married, and made love in the grass. Gotten bitten by all kinds of bugs.

She pressed her face against the window. The cold glass felt good against her cheek. The sun was slipping behind the hump of Shadow Mountain, casting the town into the grey. She tipped her head west and imagined she could see the Victorian where the three of them lived together all those years ago. The house was gone now, torn down and replaced by something bigger. Gene had been the broker. He told the buyers the house was supposed to be preserved, but they should just tear it down and plead ignorance afterwards. The location was amazing and they could well afford the fines.

She smiled internally as she recalled the naive excitement of those early years. They skied hard and played hard and were willing to do anything to make ends meet. It didn't matter what: wait tables, clean houses, run errands for the rich. They were young and living in paradise, and she had to admit it was the sweetest time of her life.

She heard a noise behind her and turned to see Gene standing in the doorway. He was wearing his ski clothes, his thick gray hair flattened from his helmet. He was nearly twenty years older than she, and he wore his age in the manner of the very rich. He hadn't been born into money, but wealth became him like a second skin. Just like her. She was very comfortable being rich. She knew she'd been lucky to not only marry a good-looking man, but one with financial benefits. Then again, she never would have considered marrying anyone who didn't bring money to the table. Not after spending her entire youth being the one without.

The one absolute of their marriage was that it was childless and would remain so. Gene had been insistent about that. He already had three daughters and a son from his two previous marriages, and he had made it unequivocally clear that he was finished with offspring. His vasectomy left no possibility of a 'whoops' that might have brought her the financial security of a child. The thought of a childless marriage hadn't particularly bothered her at first. Falling into the pot of gold was good enough. She was overjoyed to see her life of having less than everyone else in the rear-view mirror.

But as the end of her reproductive time drew near, she could sometimes feel her body scream. Which worked out well for Gene because nature's last surge left her always primed for sex. And with Gene as a husband, she had to be. The man couldn't get enough.

His sixtieth birthday was coming up, a little over a week away on the Ides of March. With the help of her assistant, Cecily, she'd been working on a surprise party for weeks. It was going to be a Roman-themed food orgy at the Bugaboo, complete with togas and laurel wreath crowns for the guests. What better way to celebrate the decadence of being hugely wealthy in an already wealthy town. But for now, the surprise party was on the back burner. She had to get through tomorrow's party first.

The lopsided smile he gave her told her that one après ski drink had turned into several and she had a good idea of what would come next. He walked over to her and tipped her head up with a long-fingered hand. A wisp of dark hair escaped from the clip at the back of her head, and he brushed it aside. Even without make-up, she was beautiful, her skin a brushed amber, her blue eyes rimmed in black lashes under an equally dark brow, looks inherited less from her Irish descent father than her Jewish mother. And while having a Jewish mother made her technically Jewish, her father insisted she be raised Catholic, and he made her go to mass every Sunday though he never went to church himself.

Her father was a truck driver and a drinker with a loud mouth, his blue collar job a source of great embarrassment to her. Since they lived in Seattle, most of her peers were the offspring of Microsoft millionaires. Even more embarrassing, her mother worked as a grocery store clerk. What Jewish woman works in a grocery store anyhow? The very day she graduated high school Judy left home and headed to Aspen. She never looked back. She hadn't spoken with her parents in years and wondered what they would think if they could see her now.

"Good ski day?" she asked by habit, stepping back slightly to rebuff his advance.

"Acceptable. Snow was nice, but visibility was crap. Roman collared me at the base and dragged me into the Nell for a drink. Actually a couple of drinks. Of course, he wanted to tell me all about his new book."

Before she had a chance to say anything more, his hand went to her butt and he pulled her closer possessively, kissing her in a manner that left no guess as to what he expected next. Usually, she'd comply and fulfill her part of the deal, but thoughts about Evie were weighing on her more heavily than she would have wished. Certainly more than the former friend merited. As his kisses grew more intense, she could smell the booze on his breath.

"Wait," she said, twisting away. "Something terrible happened today. Greta found a piece of Evie."

This time it was Gene who backed away. His mouth fell open in a mute gasp followed by a 'huh' on a barely whispered puff of air. Judy remembered how Gene had put in so many hours with the other volunteers during the search for Evie, covering every accessible part of the pass, coming home at dark nearly frozen himself.

"A piece? What's that supposed to mean?" His words were more command than question.

"It was her hand. Greta found a mitten with her hand inside."

"What?"

"I know, it's totally freakish. The thought of it makes me sick. She's not sure if it was an animal . . . or something else."

"Where did this happen?" he demanded.

"Up Gulch Creek," Judy replied. She lowered herself onto an upholstered bench in the closet and crossed her arms. Behind her, the city lights were coming alive in anticipation of dusk. "She went up Gulch Creek to do some avalanche training with Floyd, and he came back with a mitten in his mouth. With a hand inside."

"What makes her think it's Evie's hand?"

"She and the sheriff checked it out. There was a Claddagh ring on the ring finger. It's a secret. No one's supposed to know yet," she added quickly.

And then from nowhere, she felt her stomach buckle and was overcome with nausea. She ran into the bathroom and knelt on the cold marble in front of the toilet, staring into the water as she emptied the remains of her lunch into the bowl. She was at the sink splashing water on her face when her husband's image appeared behind her in the mirror. He was ghost grey.

"Are you all right?" he asked her.

"Yeah. I guess the news about Evie really shook me up."

"It is pretty sickening," he said. "And I know you used to be good friends."

He turned and left. She was drying her face when he reappeared a moment later. "Greta's still coming tomorrow night, isn't she?"

At that moment, she hated his reflection in the mirror. She couldn't count how many times she'd invited Greta to parties at his request and how many times she'd bowed out. He knew how much Greta hated parties. But because she was angry with him, she decided to torment him. Instead of telling him she had gotten Greta to commit to the dinner, she said, "Greta's not sure she's coming now."

"What? I promised Roman she'd be here."

She looked at him over her image in the mirror and said calmly, "I'll give her a call after dinner and try to convince her."

"That's better," he said, smacking her on the ass, back to his old self. He was on his way out of the bathroom, any thought of sex clearly having left his mind, when he stopped abruptly and turned back to her.

"How the hell do you suppose that hand got to Gulch Creek from Independence Pass?"

She didn't know if it was her imagination, but she thought she heard anger in his voice.

TEN

Greta

It's three miles up Highway 82 from my street to the Winter Gate. The gate closes the road over Independence Pass to all motorized traffic from November until the spring thaw. Drivers going to Denver in the winter have to take the long way round. And it's a good thing. The road is narrow and treacherous enough during the dry season. Leaving it open through winter would invite a mountainside littered with cars. The day the traffic is cut off, the pass takes on a new life as a paradise for winter sports enthusiasts, especially cross-country skiers. And that's exactly what Evie had been doing the day she went missing.

The drive up to the Winter Gate was solitary. There were no more houses along the road and we didn't see any other cars along the way. I parked the Goner in the empty lot and got out. Floyd jumped out behind me, startling a winter white weasel with a hard-sought mouse dangling from her mouth. Upon seeing Floyd, the weasel dropped her prize who took full advantage of the sudden release and scurried into a snowbank. The weasel gave me a spiteful glare and disappeared into the snowbank in search of her lost dinner.

I felt kind of bad that Floyd ruined the weasel's day, but then again, he'd improved the mouse's day immensely. It was the cycle of nature in play in the mountains, predator versus prey. I tried not to wonder if this might have been the case with Evie. Had she been prey and if so, who had been the predator?

I walked to the back of the car and opened the hatch. Evie's sleeping bag was still in the back, and I held it to Floyd's nose a long second before strapping it onto my pack. I clipped into my skis and locked the car, stowing the keys in their usual place inside the rear bumper. We locals hide our keys in one of two places, over the rear tire or inside the rear bumper. We generally don't carry them with us, because that presents the opportunity to lose them. This way we always know they'll be with the car when we come back. I've never been quite sure who we're hiding the keys from. Tourists, I guess, since there's virtually no car theft in Aspen.

Sometimes I wonder why I just don't leave the keys in the ignition. I mean who would steal a 1980 Jeep Wagoneer? Then again it might be worth it for the parts. My mechanic tells me parts are becoming increasingly difficult to find and that I better put some funds aside for when they price out. But for now the only funds I'm putting aside are for Everest.

I started the uphill climb with Floyd fast on my heels. Skiing uphill through deep snow is much harder work than skiing through the meadow was, and though this climb would usually be a nothing for me, the day's events had left me more drained than I realized. The afternoon was waning, and we had a lot of territory to cover before true dark. My eyes went skyward where a violet sky was filling with heavy clouds, deadening the light. The ever-changing mountain weather was tipping its hand. I started wondering if we should turn back and rejected the thought just as quickly. Searching with Floyd was the right thing to do. I ignored nature's warning and continued the uphill trek.

The night before Evie went missing, I was in the loft reading *King Lear* for my Shakespeare class. I've pined for a college degree ever since dropping out of school to take care of Mom, so I'm working on an associate degree at the local community college. Since my work schedule only allows for one class a semester, it's going to take a while. But this class has really turned me on to Shakespeare. To think of what that dude came up with some 400 years ago; how he was so dialed into the duplicitous nature of man and the family dynamic. If you think about it, we humans are pretty much the same as we were during Shakespeare's time, the only differences being electricity and healthcare.

I was so absorbed in reading about Lear's ingrate daughters that I didn't even hear her car pull up. But Floyd did, and he started barking, followed by a mad scramble down the ladder. There are so many wild animals around my house that he's always barking at something, so I didn't think much of it at first. But when someone started banging at my door, I nearly jumped out of my skin. As a woman living alone at the end of a deserted street, an unannounced visitor can be unnerving. I tiptoed down the ladder and peeked out the blinds next to the door.

My fears were put to rest when I saw Evie standing on my deck, clutching a sleeping bag and a duffel bag. Even in the dim porch light, I could see her shoulders heaving and knew she was crying. This was alarming because Evie never cried. She was a stoic who held the cards of her personal life close to her chest. I'd watched her go through crises like losing jobs and boyfriends without shedding a tear. Her skin was so thick, I seriously wondered whether she'd cried when her parents died.

It had taken Evie a long time to open up to me about her family, and if I thought my childhood was difficult, hers made mine look like a cakewalk. My mother was a binge drinker, and my brother and I never knew quite who she was going to bring home. We called her the nympho-dipso behind her back. But Mom always kept a roof over our heads and we always had plenty of healthy food to eat. We went to normal schools and made normal friends. And despite her shortcomings, we never doubted that our mother loved us. We had that security.

Evie's life was quite different. Her parents were hippies straight from the playbook, down to the Volkswagen van and panhandling on street corners. They never got married, that was too confining, but they were married to their bohemian lifestyle. They lived from hand to mouth, traveling the west with their only child in tow, seldom staying anywhere long enough for her to make friends or go to a regular school. Sometimes they would leave her alone in the van for a day or longer, and come back stoned, acting as if it was normal to leave a twelve-year-old on her own like that. When she reached high school age, they parked outside Boulder long enough for her to finish her senior year. When she somehow managed to graduate, her parents told her they were hitting the road again. It was then she told them she was done. She was of legal age and there was nothing they could do to make her go. They headed to southern California and she hitched a ride to Aspen. Four months later her parents were dead after a semi jackknifed on a mountain pass and crushed the tin can bus into a pancake.

She confided in me that all she'd ever wanted growing up was a home and dinner every night. Learning about her upbringing kind of explained why she was always moving from one man to another. She was like that VW van, always in motion, never parked for long, much less permanently.

But that all changed when she met Buzz.

I opened the door, and she fell into my arms crying. I'd never seen her like this; her tears flowing like the summer monsoon and her nose covered with snot. I walked her to the couch, and when we sat down, she buried her face in my shoulder and cried even harder. She tried to speak, but she was sobbing so hard she couldn't catch her breath. Finally, the tears slowed enough that she was able to spit out a few words.

"He threw me out."

"Who threw you out?"

"Buzz." A heart-wrenching sob. "Buzz threw me out."

The very thought of Buzz throwing Evie out defied imagination. Buzz was crazy about Evie and it showed in everything he did, the way he watched her cross a room, the way he smiled whenever she showed up, the way he always put her first.

If you think a good man is hard to find, just try it in a ski town. Most of the single guys around here are hot and sexy and they make you think you're their world until you find out you aren't. They can't be pinned down. Ski bums aren't guys in search of a family. They're sailors in search of another port.

But Buzz was the anomaly. He was righteous. He wanted to be tied down to Evie from the day he met her doing trail work at Maroon Lake. He was crazy about her, and she was crazy enough about him to swear off her indiscriminate ways. Before Buzz, Evie was more like a guy. Not into commitment. But she changed after they got together. She said she would never be with any other man again. She loved Buzz and was totally loyal to him. And Buzz was as loyal to Evie as Floyd was to me. Though he was totally buff and one of the best skiers on patrol, a therapist would say Buzz was in touch with his feminine side, like the Hawkeye character in the MASH reruns my mother watched from her sickbed.

They were an ideal couple, individuals in their own right, but totally supportive of one other. They moved in sync and everything one of them did enhanced the other. They shared a love of mountaineering and skiing and were experts at both. They donated time to environmental causes. They knew every flower and bird, every hidden trail, the genus of every tree. Hiking with either of them was like hiking with a naturalist encyclopedia. I couldn't imagine what could cause Buzz to throw Evie out.

But before I could ask, Evie filled in that blank.

"Buzz accused me of cheating on him. He found a pair of boxers in our bed," she sobbed. "Red ones."

My first thought was what a gut punch this had to be to Buzz, and I almost hated Evie for it. Sometimes it's beyond comprehension what human beings can do to each other when it comes to matters of romantic love. I've been there before and can still resurrect the pain of learning someone you thought was there for you actually isn't. It's a feeling of abandonment like trying to climb glass. And though Evie was one of my dearest friends, my early time spent with her left me well aware of her weakness. Maybe she hadn't been domesticated after all.

And if that was the case, I couldn't blame Buzz for throwing her out. He didn't deserve this. I wanted to say, Really Evie, if you're going to cheat on an amazing guy like Buzz, wouldn't you'd be smart enough not to do it in your own bed? Or at the very least change the sheets. But she was my friend, so I didn't say that to her. But I thought it.

"I know what you're thinking," she said, reading my mind.

"But I didn't cheat on him. I love Buzz more than anything. He's the world to me. I have no idea how those boxers got in our bed. You have to believe me."

"I'm trying," I said honestly. "Tell me what happened."

She started talking in words periodically choked off by fits of crying. "Buzz came home from his shift at Downtown Pizza and we were getting ready for bed as usual. I went into the bathroom to brush my teeth and when I came out he was holding up these red boxers. I go 'what are those?' and he started shouting at me. He's never yelled at me before. He said when he pulled down the sheets they were crumpled at the foot of the bed. I'll never forget the hurt look on his face. It tore me apart. And then he stopped shouting and just said, 'Get out.'

"I swear I never saw those boxers before in my life and I don't know how they got into our bed. You have to believe me, Greta."

And I believed her. My faith in humankind was restored. At least as far as Evie went. It was like dropping into a forty-five-degree chute and landing on my feet.

But that didn't answer the unanswered question. "Where do you think they came from? Could you have picked them up at the laundromat?" I offered.

"Our place has a washer and dryer." Evie went mute for a three count of thought and then her face changed like she'd found a solution. "You got anything to drink?"

We talked for hours about the old days, avoiding the crisis at hand. We finished off a six pack of beer before moving onto the bottle of vodka I kept around for emergencies. Thank the lord it was only three-quarters full. When the bottle was almost empty, I asked her what she planned to do.

"I don't know," she said draining the last of the vodka from her glass. She was slurring her words, as was I, and her head sank forward in transit to unconsciousness. She jerked herself awake and wobbled off into the bathroom. When she came out, she unrolled her sleeping bag on the sofa and announced, "I've decided what I'm going to do. I'm going home tomorrow after work to beg him to believe me. If I have to confess to something I didn't do, I'll do it. I'll tell him I made a mistake. All I want is for him to take me back."

Her mind settled, she snuggled into the sleeping bag and was asleep within seconds. I made sure she was still breathing before taking on the perilous climb to the loft and flopping into bed fully clothed. For the first time ever, Floyd didn't follow me up to the loft. He slept next to Evie as if he sensed she needed a friend.

When I came downstairs the next morning with a head the size of a medicine ball, Evie was gone. Her job at the day care center called for an early start. I stared at last night's detritus on my kitchen counter, the empty beer cans and the depleted vodka bottle, and my head ached even worse. If she felt anything like I did, I wondered how she was going to make it through her day with all those screaming kids. It was going to be rough enough for me, and all I had to do was ski.

She'd left a note on the counter:

> THANKS FOR LETTING ME CRASH. I'M GOING BACK HOME AFTER WORK. IF HE LOVES ME HE'S GOT TO BELIEVE ME. THANKS FOR EVERYTHING, E.

Then I noticed her sleeping bag on the ground near the front door and wondered if she'd left it in case Buzz didn't take her back. I threw it into the back of the Goner on my way to work in hopes that wouldn't be the case. When I got home that evening and Evie's car wasn't there, I figured they'd patched it up.

It wasn't until a red-eyed Buzz showed up at my door hours later, wanting to talk to her, that either one of us realized she was missing. We drove up to the Winter Gate and found her SUV in the lot with the keys atop the driver's rear tire. Her phone was on the front seat, a devastating blow since it ruled out any help from GPS in locating her. We spent over an hour searching for her, calling her name until we were hoarse. But we were no match for a raging blizzard. We needed help.

Mountain Rescue was called in. The search was futile in the dark, not to mention in a blinding storm. Usually such a late search has to wait until the next day and this one only happened because Evie was so well known and loved. The search was called off at midnight, but the team was back at first light, this time joined by dozens of locals.

For days the volunteers looked for her, Buzz harder than anyone, out at dawn before work, back after his shift on the mountain until sunset. I knew he was carrying tremendous guilt about their fight. Even after the search was called off and all hope was gone, he still continued looking.

But it was all to no end. Evie had vanished.

ELEVEN
Marynell

Marynell Hennings sat in her bay window, peeking from behind the lace curtains as the sheriff pulled up in front of her house. Her long-time home felt like a doll's house now, squeezed between monsters on either side, the brick edifice to the left built on the bones of a miner's shack like hers, the glass-and-metal fishbowl to the right sprung from the teardown of a mid-sixties chalet. The owners of the fishbowl were called on the carpet over the unpermitted teardown of the historic property, but they played stupid, paid the fine, and built the contemporary monstrosity anyway. There was a time when people couldn't have gotten away with that, but money and lawyers seemed to rule everything these days.

Clive's blue pickup sat in front of the house, as it had for nearly half a century, on two strips of gray concrete laid as a driveway during the fifties. The truck was nearly rusted through much to the chagrin of the fishbowl neighbors who wanted it to go away. It was seldom driven anymore, if at all, but Marynell wanted to keep it, and there was no room for it in the barn on the alley. That's where her chickens lived.

Driveways weren't even in the imagination when the house was built during the silver boom of the 1880s. Or cars for that matter. There hadn't been indoor plumbing or electricity back then either, but time and technology had remedied that. Despite those upgrades the exterior of Marynell's house remained much the same as it was during those mining days except for a mustard paint job and a few new roofs. The house had been vacant when she and Clive picked it up for a few hundred bucks after moving into the valley when their life in Alaska didn't pan out. At the time, the miner's shack was so rundown that when the wind blew the wallpaper in the parlor would rattle.

But they made the house habitable, and after that, they'd bought a small ski lodge a few blocks away for not much more than they'd paid for the house. The Deep Powder Lodge was incarnated, a bed and breakfast for skiers, and they settled into a life as lodge keepers.

That sixty years didn't seem so long ago, but property values told her otherwise. The neighborhood once considered the most tired part of town was now the poshest. Posh. A realtor's word, not her own. The little shack she and her husband had picked up with the last of their savings was now worth around ten million dollars for the land alone. Realtors were always buddying up to her like hyenas on a carcass. One told her she and her husband had gone from Queens to Manhattan without packing a bag. Which didn't matter to Marynell. She wouldn't want a house in a jungle like Manhattan if they gave it to her.

The sheriff got out of the vehicle and hitched up his pants. That belly of his got closer to the ground every time she saw him, a far cry from the lean young guy Clive hired to chop wood at the lodge forty-some years ago. She watched him straighten his cowboy hat, pull his jacket down over the swollen midsection before ambling up the walk. Even with her hearing going bad, she could hear the styrofoam crunch of his boots on the front stoop.

"It's open," she called out, letting the curtain slip back into place.

"Howdy, Marynell," Dan greeted her as he let himself in and bent to remove his boots so as to not track snow into the house. The parlor, as Marynell liked to call it, was tidy and spotless, a stark contrast to the worn exterior of the house. The furnishings spoke of earlier time with two love seats upholstered in a green and pink floral pattern that matched the wallpaper. A low walnut coffee table with a crystal ashtray, now used as a candy dish, sat between the two love seats. Against the far wall, a carved bookcase held a mélange of photos telling the story of a life as well as a town: family photos of a mother, father and daughter with the girl growing over the years, skiers dressed in ever-changing styles, staff from the Deep Powder Lodge, vintage photos of miners on Durant Street back when it was the red-light district.

Always mindful to be polite, Marynell stood to greet her visitor. She was a deceivingly fragile-looking woman with a face that always looked ready to smile and a long silver braid that fell over her small dowager's hump. A length of plastic tubing looped around her ears and rested just below her nostrils, connected to a portable oxygen unit that let out a low pish every couple of seconds. Oxygen was a nuisance to be dealt with when you were eighty-nine years old and lived at 8,000 feet. Nothing more.

She smiled at Dan with yellowed teeth, her light-blue eyes as close to sparkling as they could be set deep among her wrinkles.

"Well, how do, Sheriff? It's nice to see you."

"And back at you, Marynell. Lookin' good," he added.

"And you too. Can I offer you something to drink?"

"No thanks, Marynell."

His response went unheeded as she was already headed toward the kitchen at the rear of the house, the length of plastic tubing trailing behind her. "Now you just make yourself at home. I won't be but a minute."

The door closed behind her, and Dan settled onto the second love seat and looked out the window, his mind occupied with the teams he sent up Gulch Creek. The found mitten was as serious as it gets, and he wondered what the odds were of them finding the body that belonged to it. That was the protocol. You had to conduct searches when there was any possibility of finding a living human, no matter how remote the chance, though this one was way the other side of remote as far as he was concerned.

He wished he could be out there looking with the teams, but his bulk put him long past those days. Which made him glad to have somebody like Jim Roark taking charge of the search. Jim was the guy who usually handled the routine evidence, the pictures and prints, but because he wanted Jim out in the field right away, he'd asked Elsa Blanding to step in.

Elsa was the county coroner and ME (they were one and

the same), and she had shown up at his office right away, always happy to handle anything that smacked of gore. Tall and blonde with big boobs, she had a body that would have turned Liberace straight. She was a real 'hottie,' just like Greta, although if he ever used that word with either one of them he'd be lucky to escape with his balls. Dan had a hard time imagining Elsa's slender hands cutting into the bowels of a human being, but that's what she did, and far as he could tell, she enjoyed it.

While Dan watched, Elsa took multiple pictures of the mitten before taking it off the hand. And there was the Claddagh ring encircling the right ring finger clear as day. The hand looked remarkably good for having been left in the cold for possibly a month, but what did he know about tissue. Elsa wanted to take the hand back to her lab for further examination and he was OK with that. It sure wasn't doing anyone any good sitting in the freezer at his end. After bidding Elsa and the hand adieu, he'd set off to get the unpleasant visit to Marynell out of the way.

The kitchen door swung open and Marynell emerged carrying a tray that belied her petite size. It held a teapot with two cups, a small plate with sugar and lemons, and another plate piled high with chocolate chip cookies. Dan started getting up to help, but she sat him back down with a stern look.

"I may not be able to breathe, but I can still lift and carry. My muscles are just fine," she chided. "Where are you when the walk needs shoveling after a storm?"

She placed the tray on the table between them and noticed Dan eyeballing the cookies. "Just baked up this batch for the seniors over at the senior center. But don't worry. You won't be taking the food out of their mouths. I made plenty."

A visit to Marynell always shot Dan's diet to hell for the day. Those homemade cookies were just too good to pass up. And true to form, he helped himself to a couple and then a third. They were warm as if they just came out of the oven and he wondered if she'd really baked them for the seniors or for him after he'd called to tell her he was stopping over for a visit.

Marynell smiled, the pleasure of an artist seeing her creation enjoyed. "Now please tell me this visit is social and not official."

Dan gulped, his large hand hesitating over yet another cookie. He didn't want to seem piggish, but he dove in for it anyway. Something to steel him for going up against Marynell.

"You know I'm always happy to see you, Marynell, but as a matter of fact, I'm not here for purely social reasons. Though I truly wish I were. You see, there've been some complaints from your neighbors."

The fourth cookie disappeared into his large mouth as quickly as the first three had.

She leaned forward with her hands clasped on her chest in mock ignorance. "Now who would that be? I know it's not the author. We get on just fine. So it's gotta be the newbies. They've already told me they want the truck gone, and I've already told them it's staying put. That truck's been there for God knows how many years and it's going to stay there as long as the bottoms of my feet still touch ground. Is there something else bothering them?"

Dan had known Marynell a long time, since he'd worked for her and Clive at the Deep Powder Lodge, his first job in town. The pay was for shit, but they gave him housing in the basement of the lodge along with some of the other staff. It had been a great year. The job was brainless, and they got to ski after they finished their work. Marynell even cooked a staff dinner every Sunday night that they ate right here in this house.

He was saddened when they retired and sold the old lodge. It was torn down soon afterwards and replaced by something far more modern. When Clive died not long after, Dan figured it was more from boredom than cigarettes. But Marynell wasn't going anywhere soon. She was a tough bird back then and there was no indication she'd softened. Knowing her, she was good to bust a hundred.

He cleared his throat with an ahem into his large hand. "Marynell, we've been getting complaints that you're keeping farm animals on your property."

Her laugh was hearty and unencumbered by hostility. "Farm

animals? Surely they're mistaken. There aren't any farm animals here. I hope you're not talking about my pet chickens."

Dan shifted uneasily in his chair. "You may call them pets, but your neighbors are calling them a nuisance. They claim they are a health hazard and noisy."

"That's ridiculous. My chickens can't be any noisier than those yappy little dogs of hers." The mischievous eyes flashed towards the house next door and then turned skyward. "Do you believe this crap, Clive? They buy the shack next door, tear it down and block out my sunlight with their monstrosity. Now they're suddenly the lords of the manor, and I'm the serf. And they want to evict my chickens." She looked back at the sheriff, her blue eyes firm with resolve. "I have no intention of eating store-bought eggs because some yahoos think they're living in the Hollywood Hills."

Things were going the way Dan had feared they would. "There's also been a complaint about the smell," he ventured, knowing full well what her response would be.

"Smell? I can't imagine what smell they're talking about. They bothered by a little chicken shit?" The expletive rolled off her ancient tongue on the back of a wry smile. "You and I both know the truth is they want to get rid of me. And I don't care how much money they offer, I'm not leaving. Clive and I raised our daughter here." She paused and her eyes traveled upwards again. "This place is too filled with memories. The only way I'm leaving here is tits up."

"I get it Marynell. You don't have to go, but the chickens have to. They did their homework. This part of town is not zoned rural. They'll take you to court."

"Then I guess I'll be contacting my lawyer." She picked up the tray and offered him another cookie. He started to wave it off but reached out his hand instead. Was that four or five?

The cookie count totaled six by the time Dan climbed back into his vehicle. He was starting to feel kind of sorry for the Californians. Marynell might be old, but she was not one to be pushed around. Then again, she had no idea what she was up against with these people and their bottomless pockets. The town he had known for forty years had basically evaporated, morphing from miner's shacks and Victorians into glass palaces. Most of the long-time locals who had protected it from the unwelcome changes had either died off or cashed out for lower elevations. He hoped Marynell would be able to keep her chickens, but he doubted it. Not when going up against the kind of money and arrogance these people had.

He laughed aloud at his next thought. It was going to be a game of chicken between them and her.

In spite of having eaten all those cookies, his circadian clock was telling him it was time for dinner. He got back into his sheriff's vehicle and headed for the Hick House. Hell, he'd already blown his diet for the day. Why not do some ribs with biscuits and gravy?

TWELVE
Greta

Floyd and I made good time our first couple of miles up the pass, staying alongside a rock face to our left and avoiding the drop off to the right. It was still snowing, the clouds dumping harder than ever. I tried putting myself into Evie's head on this route a month ago, desperately sad over the loss of Buzz. For a fraction of a fraction of a second, it crossed my mind that maybe the breakup with Buzz had caused Evie to do something stupid. Then I shot that thought down quicker than it came on. Evie was never one to give up.

Judy had coldly pointed out: 'We've known Evie's dead for weeks.' That was a reality still hard to accept. If I was to make a list of people least likely to get lost in a storm, Evie would be in the number one spot. She was prepared for every eventuality from bivouacking in sub-zero temperatures to administering CPR. Her pack was a survivalist's general store with everything you could ever need from toothpicks to flashlights to epi pens. I used to tease her that if there was a nuclear war, she'd outlive the cockroaches. I'd been wrong on that count. Cockroaches were still here and Evie wasn't.

The snow started coming down even harder, and it occurred to me that maybe this might be a good time to turn around. Traveling any farther meant flirting with dusk on the way down. Any sane person would have turned back, but I had moved beyond sanity. I was a woman on a mission. If Evie's handless body was up here, I was going to find it.

We came around a bend and passed a huge rock that had fallen onto the road. Rock fall is a phenomenon that comes with living in the Rockies, and in a perfect world rocks fall before you get there or after you leave. In an imperfect world they don't. So if that Volkswagen-size rock doesn't hit you,

you're OK. If it does—well then I guess you won't have much to worry about either way. It occurred to me that maybe that was what happened to Evie. That she was hit by a rock and knocked from the road.

I pressed myself to ski faster to beat the clock. My pace was torturous, slicing my skis through the snow and pushing my poles. The snow was now coming down so seriously that it was getting hard to make out Floyd just yards ahead of me. But I wanted to get to Weller Lake, Evie's usual turnaround point, before turning around myself.

When we still hadn't reached the lake fifteen minutes later, the folly of starting out so late came home to roost. While spring days were getting longer, they weren't long enough yet. The light was getting grayer and it wouldn't be long before it started getting dark. I was tired, and even Floyd seemed to have lost his earlier vigor. I decided I was being careless and that it was time to turn around.

I put the sleeping bag to Floyd's nose one last time, just for the hell of it. This time his head jolted upwards, just as it had this morning in Gulch Creek. As he measured the air with his nose, he started making crazy circles, a dog chasing his tail. He stopped circling and ran to the side of the road. Then to my absolute horror, he leapt off the edge.

My heart was banging like a six-year-old with a new drum set. I skied to where he'd gone over and looked down. In the dimming light, I could make out his dark figure at the bottom of the bluff. He was digging furiously, a canine snowblower with snow flying all around him. I inched forward to get a better look at what he was after when suddenly there was no longer a road beneath me. I'd been standing on a cornice that had given way, and now I was racing my stomach to the bottom of the bluff. I landed face first and the world exploded into a cloud of white.

I woke to Floyd tugging my shoulder. I have no idea how long I'd been out. It could have been seconds, it could have been minutes. I'd lost one of my skis, but the other was still attached to my boot, pointing straight down into the snow, making it impossible to move. I managed to reach back far enough to release the binding of the trapped ski, so I could get my foot out. I used my hands to give my body a quick inventory. Nothing was broken—which was a miracle. However, any gratitude over divine intervention evaporated when I looked up the bluff. The road might as well have been the top of El Capitan.

I cursed myself for my stupid decision to come up the pass alone in a winter storm. I knew better than that. But hubris had won out and here I was. I cursed myself further for ignoring the golden rule of mountaineering. Always tell someone your plans.

I managed to wiggle to a stand for all it was worth. I was in snow up to my thighs. I tried moving towards the bluff, but walking in the deep snow was like walking in quicksand. You don't move unless you want to sink. I tried to focus. My mind traveled back to the Milwaukee winters of my childhood, when Toby and I would play in the backyard of our little house after a snowstorm. The snow drifts were taller than either of us, but we were fearless and climbed through those drifts, laughing and out of breath when we got back to the safety of the house. Have no fear, I told myself. Survival takes patience and strong will, and a deep dig for strength. Panic is to be avoided at all costs. I put myself back in Milwaukee. This was not a challenge, it was a game.

My poles were still strapped around my wrists, and I recalled a trick we use in patrol to get up in deep powder. I took off both poles and crossed them on the surface of the snow, creating a platform. I swam onto the platform and little by little, I was able to use my feet to push me forward. My progress was glacial, but at least I was moving. After a long fifteen minutes, I stood at the bottom of El Capitan, looking up.

I tried to keep my head about me. It was nearing dark and I was at the bottom of a cliff, miles away from the Winter Gate and the Wagoneer. I figured the road to be about thirty feet up or the equivalent of a three-story building. It was a fairly steep climb, but there was an upside to that. Steep aspects didn't hold much snow. I tried taking a step up the bluff, but my foot slid backwards. I tried again with the same result.

Now I'm no math whiz, but it only takes simple arithmetic to know one minus one equals zero. And that was exactly the progress I was making. Zero. If things continued along these lines, they would not end nicely. It wasn't as if someone would come strolling by in the night and find me. I had to get out of there or I'd most likely be frozen by morning. I thought about Floyd's furious digging and wondered if Evie's body was nearby. If so, would they find us together next spring?

I was determined for that to not happen.

Floyd was dancing around me nervously, his webbed paws helping to keep him atop the surface. He would race up the hill to demonstrate how easy it was and then come running back to me. Seeing his success on four legs got me to thinking and I wondered if four legs could work for me. I got down on all fours and tried crawling. But this was even harder, the snow giving way so that I slid down farther than before.

I ordered myself to dig deep for a solution, figuratively, not literally. I recalled a story I'd heard on public radio last fall about a Frenchman who had slipped into a crevasse in the Alps and climbed out by crab walking.

Using your hands and feet to propel you from your backside is a highly unnatural movement, unless you're a crab. But I had nothing to lose, and hopefully my body wouldn't punch through the snow so much if my back was resting on it. With no other options it was worth giving it a go.

It didn't take long to realize that if I was on my back, my pack couldn't come with me. I dumped it in the snow, leaving Evie's sleeping bag and everything I needed for survival behind. I turned my back to the bluff and planted my hands firmly against the incline and then planted my feet, digging my boots in with my knees bent. Then I straightened my legs and found I'd moved up the hill. A little. I repeated the process and moved farther. The crab walk was working. But the poles that had helped me earlier were now slopping around, more hindrance than help, so I threw them into the snow beside my discarded pack. See you next summer, I thought.

As I inched up slowly, Floyd stayed beside me. He seemed perplexed as to why I was playing this game. With his webbed paws and four legs, he was far more capable of climbing than I was, but it didn't matter. I was moving.

I was three-quarters of the way to the top when I heard a distant hum. My first thought was it was my imagination, but the noise drew nearer and I realized it was a snowmobile. My head felt light with glee. Someone had seen my car in the lot and sent out an alarm. They were looking for me.

I tried moving faster to intercept the snowmobile before it could pass. My shoulders hurt and my legs ached, but still I kept working harder. As the noise drew nearer, I knew I wouldn't make it to the top in time, so I started to scream—a futile effort considering the eardrum-shattering noise of a snowmobile's engine. I screamed anyway and kept screaming until the snowmobile passed above me and the sound of the engine faded in the distance. I felt shattered until it occurred to me that sooner or later the driver would come back down the road. And I needed to be standing on it when he did.

I started moving faster. I had nearly made the top when I heard the snowmobile returning. It wasn't moving as quickly as it had before. It kept moving forward and idling which meant it was searching for something, hopefully me. Determined not to miss him again, I decided to push it.

Big mistake there. Instead of securing each hand and foot, I tried scrambling. One foot slipped and the next thing I knew, I was heading back downhill feet first. I flipped myself over and dug in the toes of my boots and my gloved hands. Somehow I managed to stop sliding before falling all the way back down. I could hear the snowmobile idling up above.

I started screaming first at the snowmobile, then at Floyd. "Go boy, up, go stop it," I ordered, but my loyal dog stayed rooted at my side. My insides went hollow as I heard the vehicle start up again and the driver throttle down the hill. Hope dissolved as the sound faded out, and I returned to the slow uphill crawl.

THIRTEEN
Greta

I have no idea how long it took me to finally make it up top. That part of memory is buried somewhere to never be revisited. I flopped onto the road and lay in the snow exhausted. Floyd stood at my side, glad that this particular game was over. I was shivering and weak with hunger and thirst, but at least I was out of the gulley. I thought longingly of the mini Snickers and water bottles stashed in my pack, the pack that was gathering snow at the bottom of the bluff. Food and water were going to have to wait for home.

I pulled myself to my feet and looked around for Floyd. He had returned to the edge of what was left of the cornice. I ordered him to come, and he stared at me like a child told to put away his favorite toy. He shook his head no, and as I watched in frozen terror, he inched over to the edge and disappeared from sight . . . again.

I stood there for a long thirty seconds, not knowing if Floyd was playing a game or if he had hurtled to his death. I wanted to go back to look for him, but self-survival had kicked in, and I couldn't afford the time. I was already tempting hypothermia and needed to get moving before confusion set in. The only option was to turn my back on Floyd and get my ass downhill to the Goner and safety. Hopefully, he would show up along the way.

Everest, I told myself. Think of Everest. I walked into the whiteout. In open space, I wouldn't have stood a chance, but having the mountain to my right kept me focused. Breaking trail in the heavy snow on foot was hard work, much harder than on skis, but there was no alternative. It was what it was. Primal instinct kept me moving, my heart sickened at the loss of Floyd. But there was no time to think about such things. I had to get to the car.

I'd made about a half mile when I heard a noise behind me. I turned around to see Floyd coming up fast, dragging something in his mouth. My relief was overwhelming. Even more overwhelming, it looked like my backpack he was dragging. The pack meant supplies.

"Good boy," I praised him, rewarding him with a good chuck under the jaws. He stood back wagging his tail with his mouth open and his tongue hanging out. Down to my last bit of energy, I unzipped the compartment where my Snickers stash lived and was hit with a stunned disappointment to see a first aid kit, some maps and a compass. It was then I realized the pack wasn't mine. I didn't have to unzip any more compartments to know whose pack it was. It was Evie's. It was identical to mine except there was a Greenpeace sticker on the side of hers.

I wondered how she'd been separated from her pack. Maybe she had gone over the edge of the road like me and taken off her pack in order to climb up as I had. Only she hadn't made it. Was her body down there, buried too deep for even Floyd to reach? There were so many questions, but one thing was for sure, those answers would have to wait for another day.

Delirious with exhaustion, I slipped the pack over my shoulders and continued the downhill hike, so compromised by the cold I didn't think to look for sustenance in any of the other pockets.

Another couple of hours passed before we finally came around the bend on the last approach to the Winter Gate. The car and safety were within reach. I was shivering with cold and hunger, and was ready to cry with relief. But suddenly Floyd screeched to a halt behind me, refusing to move forward. I commanded him to heel. He followed me hesitantly for several yards and then stopped dead in his tracks again. His head swayed to and fro as he sought something through the falling white. He turned his bloodhound eyes on me for counsel.

"Vas-y" I repeated, urging him on before I collapsed. And then Floyd started growling just as he had with the cadaver dog. My first thought was there was a wild animal in the vicinity, and my heart quickened. The last thing we needed was to be surprised by some rogue bear or, even worse, a moose. I grabbed his collar to keep him with me, re-energized by the knowledge the car was within reach.

My legs were rubber jello and the dark was opaque when the barely visible shape of the Winter Gate came into view. I was flooded with a huge sense of relief, thankful my keys were on my rear bumper and not in my backpack at the bottom of the bluff.

And then Floyd started barking again. I could make out a large dark figure moving ahead of us in the snow. I shushed Floyd and slowed our pace, my eyes glued ahead of us. Then there was the sound of an engine followed by the lights of a car coming to life. Seconds later the dim red glow of taillights disappeared into the white. I couldn't figure out why anyone would be up the pass in this weather and at this time of night.

When we reached the parking lot, I did figure out one thing. Leaving the keys inside the rear bumper wasn't such a great idea. Those lights that had receded into the distance were mine and someone had just stolen the Wagoneer.

FOURTEEN
Greta

Those last three miles to my house were a struggle every step of the way. I was so exhausted it was a fight to maintain consciousness. Once I stumbled and fell into a snowbank and thought maybe I could just rest here for a while. But Floyd barked and tugged at my parka and wouldn't let up until I was back on my feet. I started walking again, shocked at how easy it would have been to just sleep there and never wake up.

It was a miracle that I kept moving. My feet were frozen blocks blindly obeying the command of my legs. My clothes were drenched with cooling sweat that was causing me to shiver convulsively. My thoughts shifted to the Everest climbers who suffered such severe frostbite they lost fingers and noses. This was nothing, I told myself. This was preparation for Everest.

The snow let up and the visibility improved. Soon I saw a highway lamp and my spirits lifted. Home was within blocks and this ordeal was coming to an end. It had taken me over two hours to walk three miles.

I turned onto my street putting one plodding foot in front of the other. Floyd walked ever watchful beside me. I could see the Greenes' house, the lit windows assuring in their hominess. Smoke was drifting from the chimney and perfuming the air with the pine scent of burning logs. I contemplated stopping there but decided to keep going since I was so close to home. I was on Everest with only a few more steps to the top of the world. Only a few more steps. Then the world spun into black.

Someone was slapping my face. Hard. I peeled my eyes open from the warmth of my dream and saw Gwyn Greene hovering over me, her small eyes buried in her weathered face. Stan stood behind her holding a flashlight on me, his intense dark eyes staring from an equally weathered face. An old German Shepard sat rigidly obedient at Stan's side, clearly undisturbed by Floyd franticly weaving around me.

"There you are," she said.

I pulled myself to a sitting position and looked around, trying to figure out where 'there' was. Stan's flashlight illuminated the space around us, but everything outside the beam was darkness. Upon seeing me sitting, Floyd ducked the beam of light and ran up to lick my face.

"There she is," Gwyn repeated. I couldn't tell if she was talking to me, her husband or Floyd. "Are you all right?"

I checked out my environs. Evidently, I wasn't quite all right. Two people and a dog were checking me out. The windows of a house glowed behind them. "What happened?" I asked.

"Looks like you fainted. Good thing that dog of yours is persistent. He wouldn't stop scratching at our door until one of us answered. Then he kept barking until we got our coats and boots on and followed him. We found you here in the street.

"You know if you had laid here all night you probably would have froze to death. Let's get you inside."

Even in my addled state I understood what nearly 'froze to death' meant. For sure I was frozen, just not to death yet. I was also hungry and thirsty and tired beyond comprehension. But it was the cold that was the worst, my feet past any sensation. My body shivered uncontrollably at my circulatory system's failed attempts to warm me. The Greenes helped me to my feet, and I stood in the street, dazed and confused, trying to piece together what had happened. And then I remembered it all, falling in the gully, the snowmobile passing by, the long walk down, my car being stolen. Suddenly all discomfort took a back seat. I needed to get home to report the car theft.

"I'm OK now. Really. Thanks for the help," I said. My frozen lips made it difficult to speak. I took a wobbly step and nearly fell back to the ground. Gwyn grabbed me by the arm and held tight.

"No, you don't," she said. "You're coming inside until you

get warm and have something to eat. What the hell are you doing out in weather like this anyhow?"

"Looking for Elvis?" I said. They exchanged glances behind my back and I couldn't say I blame them. It seems stupid to me now, but at the time it felt clever. "I mean Evie."

"See . . . you're dopey from hypothermia. Now, no nonsense. You're coming inside."

Deciding maybe that wasn't such a bad idea after all, I limped to the Pan-Abode with one of them propping me up on either side while Floyd ran nervous circles around us all. The Shepherd shuffled behind. The moment we set foot in the house, Floyd bee-lined into the kitchen and a second later the messy sound of a tongue lapping was heard as he drained the Shepherd's water bowl.

It was the first time I'd ever been in the Greenes' house despite living on the same street as them for ten years. The main room spoke of earlier times in the world of skiing, the walls covered with vintage ski posters that probably weren't vintage when they were first hung. A pair of wooden skis with bear trap bindings hung over the entrance to the kitchen and old strappy snowshoes hung in the hall. The room smelled mildly of cedar, the solid logs of the mail-order cabin still holding their scent sixty years later. A roaring fire in the stone fireplace called out to me.

Stan pressed me into a deep chair in front of the fire while Gwyn warmed up a bowl of bean soup in the kitchen. I consumed the soup in practically one bite the way my dog does, though he was in the kitchen noisily consuming what Gwyn had put into the Shepherd's bowl for him. As I started to warm and the energy from the food reached my brain, rational thought kicked in.

I told them about how Floyd had found Evie's hand in Gulch Creek earlier in the day and how I had taken him up Independence to see if we could find any more of her. Gwyn stared at me for a long time, her face fixed in disbelief. "Greta, it's been over a month since she went missing. Going up there alone was really dangerous. The snow is really deep. No matter what happened to Evie, finding her is gonna have to wait for spring."

"But the hand . . ."

"Could'a been anything that took that hand. Lots of wild things roaming around out there," said Stan.

"And then there's one other thing," I told them. "Someone stole my car."

"That's strange," said Stan. "I could've sworn I heard your car coming down the street a couple of hours ago. Fact I heard a couple of cars."

I would have asked him more, but my feet were beginning to thaw and as the blood returned to them, the pain was thousands of needles piercing my flesh. My boots were already off, but now I took off my socks to rub my feet. They were white as a salt lick, but thankfully there was no telltale black of frostbite. Knowing I had dodged the worst made the pain a little more tolerable. But only a little. Having survived, all I wanted now was to be in my house where I could scream as loud as I wanted while my feet thawed out the rest of the way.

"Thanks so much for your help," I said, grimacing through a fresh spike of pain in my big toe. I started to put a wet sock back on and a fresh stab of pain made me cry aloud. Fire and ice. "I really need to get home."

"No way," said Gwyn. "You're staying here in front of the fire."

It was hard work convincing them that I would be fine on my own, even though my feet were hurting so badly I wondered if I'd even be able to walk on them. But my desire to be in my own space to lick my wounds, not in the house of strangers, kind as they were, overrode everything.

Stan finally agreed that I could go home if I let him drive me.

"Drive me? That's crazy. It's only a couple hundred yards."

"No arguing. I won't sleep until I see you go through your door,' he said. He went out to the garage and a few minutes later his Jeep's headlights lit up the driveway. I grabbed Evie's backpack and climbed into the front seat while Floyd jumped into the back. I rubbed my feet in the warm dry socks and slippers Gwyn had given me. The pain was so excruciating I wondered if frostbite might have been less painful.

"I'm sorry to have interrupted your quiet night," I told Stan as he backed onto the snowy street.

"That's what neighbors are for, Greta. You know sometimes I worry about you being up here all by yourself."

"Oh, I'm fine, I've got protection," I said, insinuating that I had a weapon on the premises. Which was sort of true if you counted the old Smith & Wesson that lived behind a blanket in Sam's former closet. I think guns only bring trouble, but living alone on a dead-end street in the middle of nowhere without cell service, I've never tipped my hand that I'm pretty much defenseless. In fact, I kept a pair of Sam's size twelve boots and a dog bowl outside the front door as a deterrent.

As the Jeep drove slowly down the snow-covered street, the road bent and my A-frame came into sight. A sense of unreality surged through me like a bad chord on a piano. The Goner was parked in its usual place out front.

FIFTEEN
Greta

I got my key from under the planter on the porch and let myself inside, giving Stan a quick wave before I closed the door. After hanging Evie's pack and my soggy parka on the entry hooks, I cranked up the furnace from its default temperature of fifty-eight to a balmy sixty-five. Then I threw some logs into the Franklin for good measure. Within minutes a roaring fire was radiating heat throughout the room. I dialed the thermostat back to fifty-eight and threw another log on the fire. Propane is expensive. When you live in the forest dead wood is yours for the taking.

I peeled off my soggy clothes and stood in front of the fire, rotating like a pig on a spit until the heat had baked the chill from my body. My feet were still throbbing as blood found its way to the smallest capillaries, but the pain was nothing like before, aside from an occasional poker hot stab to remind me of the abuse they'd suffered.

I put on my flannel pajamas and robe and settled into the Barca, my brush with death an unpleasant memory now that I was safe and warm. I assume the same principle applies to women after giving birth. In fact, I felt exhilarated. Having teased the Grim Reaper and evaded him brought on a sensation of immortality. The way I see it, we flirt with death every day. We just don't recognize the times he's given us a pass. If he really has us in his sights, there's no beating him.

I wished he'd given Evie a pass. She'd always been so careful, and he found her anyway. I went and got her pack and sat down with it in front of the fire. We'd bought the packs at an outfitter's show in Denver last autumn, and then gorged ourselves on Indian food afterwards. I unzipped the top compartment and my eyes filled with tears upon seeing the wool sweater I'd bought her at the resale shop for Christmas. I took it out and rubbed it against my face.

I opened the rest of the compartments and turned the pack upside down. The contents tumbled to the floor. I sorted through them and started an inventory. There were extra gloves and thermal hand and foot warmers. Spare socks. A foil blanket for emergency warmth. A first aid kit, extra water, a compass, a sewing kit for buttons or stitches depending, safety pins, Tylenol, matches and the nub of a candle, a down vest. An extra hat. A small flashlight. A pair of rubber shoes for summer water crossings. A treasure trove of nut-filled baggies and enough M&M gorp to keep a small scout crew alive for weeks. Two melting bottles of frozen water. I couldn't believe I hadn't thought to check for sustenance back on the pass. Shows what hypothermia can do.

I looked into the largest compartment and found an ancient postcard stuck to the bottom. I peeled it off slowly, careful not to tear it. The postcard was addressed to Evie, care of her grandmother in Ohio. It must have been sent the time they had dumped her there one winter. The postmark was smeared, but the fourteen-cent stamp gave away its age. The photo on the front was an image of Main Street Telluride. On the flipside was a blurry message. *Dear Evie, Will be back for you soon. Mom and Dad.* I thought about her waiting for them to return, and my heart ached that such a small memory meant so much that she carried it with her always.

I put everything back into the pack to be delivered to Dan in the morning. Except for the sweater. I kept it for myself. Something to remember her by.

Gwyn's bean soup had barely dented the hole in my stomach, so I microwaved myself a macaroni and cheese dinner and was scraping the last shredded bits of macaroni from the aluminum tray when the phone rang. My eyes went to the oven clock. It was midnight.

There's no caller ID on the mustard dinosaur. It hadn't been invented when Sam bought it, but he'd shared his number with enough women over the years that from time to time the phone rings at some odd hour, and it's an old fling looking for a little nostalgia. I try to let them down easy when informing them of Sam's death.

I picked up and gave a cautious hello.

"Oh my God, you're all right," said Judy in a frantic voice. "I've been worried sick. I've been trying to reach you for hours. Don't you listen to your messages?"

For the first time since setting foot back in my house, I looked at the old-fashioned answering machine. The red light was blinking and the missed calls numbered fourteen.

"When I saw your car in town, I got worried."

"You saw my car in town? Are you sure it was mine?"

"Greta, there's no mistaking the Goner. It was parked in a tow zone by the way."

"When was this?"

"Somewhere around nine. I ran into town to get some two percent and there it was."

"What the . . .?"

I gave her a condensed version of my near-death experience ending with my car being stolen and the long walk home. She didn't seem overly concerned. After all I was talking to her which meant I was fine. She didn't seem to realize how bad it had been or didn't really want to think about it. Either way that was Judy.

"Are you going to report the car?"

"Yeah. I was just getting around to it." It was only then I thought of the snowmobile up the pass and wondered if it had anything to do with my car. "Maybe it was some local kids pulling a prank."

"Some prank. I'd hate for you to end up like Evie." There was a respectful silence before she shifted gears. "I hope you're still coming tomorrow night."

I was justifiably enraged. "Did you call to see if I was all right or to see if I was coming to your party?"

"A combination of both," she confessed. "When I didn't hear from you, I wanted to make sure you were all right. That's most important of all. But you sounded so hesitant about the party when I talked to you earlier, that I wanted to double check."

"You're kidding, right. With everything that's happened today I can't believe you're still yanking my chain about tomorrow night."

"Greta, I know finding Evie's hand was traumatic, but it just proves she's dead. You've got to accept that. Do you think sitting at home staring at walls will bring her back?"

"You know how much I hate dinner parties." Her persistence about this damn dinner party was growing annoying. To be honest, I didn't hate all dinner parties. Just hers. They were filled with lots of people who Gene wanted as clients, self-aggrandizing bores with more dinero than any one human had use for. I preferred the company of lowly locals such as myself. Like Evie was. Like Judy used to be.

Judy switched tactics from begging to sales. "Yes, I know you hate dinner parties. But like I told you before, Roman Judge is coming and he's writing some book with a ski patroller in it. And Gene really wants you here."

And there you had it. Gene was the one behind the push. I felt kind of sorry for her in that regard, but at the same time I understood it. While all three of us had been needy back in the days of the Victorian, Judy had been the neediest. Her feelings of inadequacy ran far deeper than either Evie's or mine. Marrying Gene helped her overcome a lot of it, but it was never enough.

"You trying to take me off Triscuits and Jarlsberg?" I sprung back.

"You'll get a good meal."

"Remind me the time again," I said, too worn out to fight.

"Seven thirty," she gushed. "And remember . . . wear something nice."

After hanging up, I called 911 to report the theft and subsequent return of my car. The dispatcher took the information and a minute later the phone rang again. It was Sheriff's Deputy Roark, the guy who had been so rude to me this morning. At first, I thought he might be calling to update me on the search. Instead, he told me he had just talked to dispatch and wanted me to know he was the one who had brought my car home.

"I was in town and saw the tow truck getting ready to put

your car on the hook. I was feeling kind of bad about this morning with the dogs and all, so I had the driver stop. I found your keys on the rear tire and drove it to your place. The deputy on duty followed me and gave me a ride back. I figured you'd rather take a taxi home from town than have to go all the way to Rifle to get the car out of the pound. It's not a good idea to park in tow zones. You know we're serious about keeping the roads clear in this kind of weather."

"Yeah, well, I have no idea how the car ended up in town."

"Come again."

"I wasn't in town tonight. My car was stolen from the lot at the Winter Gate."

There was a long pause and then: "What was it doing at the Winter Gate?"

"I took Floyd up there to have another look for Evie."

Another pause. I was glad I couldn't see his face. "Didn't Dan tell you to stay out of this?"

"Dan told me to stay away from Gulch Creek. And, by the way, what's going on up there?" I asked,

"Not that I have to report to you, Greta, but we put in a full day until the snow made us stop." Then, clearly not wanting to take the argument any farther, he ended the conversation curtly. "If you want to come in tomorrow, we'll fill out some paperwork on the car."

By the time I climbed into the loft it was one in the morning. Floyd settled into his usual spot at the foot of the bed and fell into exhausted sleep. Cozy and warm, I pulled my duvet up to my chin and waited for sleep to come. Though I've had experiences that would keep a narcoleptic awake, falling asleep has never been a problem for me. I can switch off my mind the moment my head hits the pillow.

But that night I was getting a taste of what Ambien addicts go through. Though I was completely exhausted, sleep was evading me. Something deep in my brain was keeping me awake. I stared out the skylight over my bed into the black night, replaying the longest fucking day ever in the history of the planet. Then it dawned on me exactly what was keeping me awake. Evie's pack. There was something missing. In my mind, I laid everything back out on the rug, looking for what it could be. But try as I might, I couldn't find it.

But I was finally finding sleep. Or rather sleep was finding me. I started counting backwards from a hundred and by the time I reached eighty-seven I was down for the count.

SIXTEEN
Greta

Day two

I woke at first light despite getting to sleep so late. The sky was the bluebird color of Paul Newman's eyes, my mother's favorite actor. I think part of her attraction to him was they both had the same color eyes. But while Newman's eyes had a transparency that made them warm and inviting, my mother's eyes were cold and closed, opaque instead of transparent.

The blue sky meant it would be a busy day on the mountain. Sun combined with fresh snow makes for awesome conditions, drawing out fair-weather skiers as well as the hardcore. Blue sky could also mean cold. I checked the thermometer outside my window. It read a blazing two degrees Fahrenheit. With the memory of yesterday's frozen travail still lingering, I pulled on an extra layer of long underwear and climbed down from the loft.

The fire in the Franklin had long since burned out and the floor beneath my bare feet was painfully cold. A thin layer of ice in the toilet dissolved into steam as I peed. Standing in front of the sink brushing my teeth, I questioned for the umpteenth time in my life the origin of the dark eyes staring back from my mirror. They were so different from those of my mother, so dark they were almost black, the polar opposite of her aqua blues. And while my blonde hair most likely came from her Swedish gene pool, its uncontrollable frizz and my olive skin most likely didn't.

My entire life I'd wondered about my father, and at one time I almost signed up for one of those ancestry deals. But after thinking it through, I decided it might be better to stay in the dark. In my childhood dreams, I was the daughter of an African king or an Italian racing car driver or a Moroccan sheik. How demoralizing would it be to learn I was the issue of a third generation Cheesehead who worked in one of the local breweries? Why waste good Everest money on something that could be a bubble buster.

After dressing and grabbing some chow, I picked up Evie's pack and went out to the Goner with Floyd in tow. I couldn't find the keys at first because Roark left them on the rear tire instead of their usual place inside the rear bumper. Despite everything that had happened yesterday, one thing hadn't changed. Today was Floyd's day to certify as a K9 avalanche dog, and I was determined to stay on point.

The car turned over painfully slowly, the battery protesting the sub-zero temperatures before finally kicking into gear. I smelled a trip to Howard for a new battery, an expensive thought. Stan had plowed the road earlier and the flattened snow squeaked beneath my tires as I drove down the street. Stan was in front of the Pan-Abode, shoveling his walk with the old Shepherd watching intently. I stopped and rolled down the passenger's window. He walked over to the car, his breath trailing clouds of steam behind him.

"All good today?" he asked.

"I'm top," I replied. "Thanks so much for your help last night."

"It wasn't anything," he replied. "But I tell you, I'd give that dog of yours an extra dog biscuit today. If not for him, I'm not sure we'd be having this conversation right now."

"Don't let him hear you. It'll go to his head."

I rolled up the window and drove off. The state had done the plowing on 82, so the road into town was clear. The lifts didn't start for a couple of hours, so things were quiet in town as if every turtle had pulled in his head during the storm.

I parked the Goner where I always did, at a condominium building in town. The parking spot was a true luxury, gifted to me by a grateful condo owner who I performed CPR on a few years ago after his heart seized up on the Silver Queen gondola. He came out on the upside after a medivac to Denver and a few stents. With one of the most valued things in Aspen being parking, I got the best end of that deal, especially since it was only three blocks to the mountain. People on Red Mountain would sell their first grandchild for a parking spot in town. Twins if it was anywhere near the gondola.

I leashed Floyd to keep surprises to a minimum and walked across town to the sheriff's office with Evie's backpack. I hoped Dan wouldn't be pissed at me for not calling him directly about my car being stolen the night before. I tied Floyd to the bike rack outside the glass doors and went inside. The cop at the desk didn't know me, so he called Dan to clear me coming in. The buzzer sounded and I headed down the hall, reminiscing about the days when a person could just walk into the sheriff's office without talking to anybody. Dan was at his desk working on a pastry. An open Paradise Bakery box gave testimony to how well his diet was going.

"Trying to break a record?" I asked.

He dragged a napkin across his bushy moustache and smiled. "Man's gotta take some enjoyment in this life. You won't go out with me, so this is a last resort. And if you had to deal with Marynell Hennings' new neighbors you'd be joining me in trans fat delight."

"I eat. Just not entire boxes of pastries. What's up with the neighbors?"

"They want her to get rid of the chickens. I didn't tell you yesterday because . . . well, because."

Ignoring his veiled reference to Evie's hand, I stayed on topic. "Get rid of her chickens? I think she's had those chickens since the end of the silver boom."

"Yeah, well, these newbies are pulling a power play. Saying the neighborhood isn't zoned rural. Claiming the birds are unsanitary."

"Well, I wish them luck going up against Marynell. She's one iron bronze maiden," I said, something I knew first-hand. The year the Victorian was sold and we needed a place to live, Evie, Judy and I worked a season as maids at the Deep Powder Lodge in exchange for housing and a few hundred bucks a month. Working for Marynell was no nonsense. Make beds, vacuum rooms, clean toilets. We were free to ski as soon as we'd finished our work, but if you happened to 'accidentally' skip a few rooms on a powder day, there was hell to pay.

Dan ran a hand along his moustache, tamping the wiry hair down. "But that's not why you're here, is it? If you want to know what happened up Gulch Creek yesterday, it was a dead end. Too much snow. They're heading back up today."

"That's not why I'm here."

I dropped Evie's backpack on the desk in front of him. He stared at it without picking it up, paying special attention to the Greenpeace sticker on the side. "Don't tell me you're bringing me more body parts."

"That's not my pack. It's Evie's. My pack is somewhere up Independence in about five feet of snow."

His look went ultra serious. Enough to make him put down the last pastry. "Tell me about this."

"Well, since you wouldn't let me help up Gulch Creek, I decided to do a little more exploring up the pass. Floyd and I went up towards Weller Lake, and Floyd found the pack down an embankment. We would have searched more, but it was getting dark and I was more interested in getting home." I left out the part about falling down the embankment and the aftermath. It wouldn't have been worth the discussion.

"Greta, you went up to Weller after you left here? Alone in a full out snowstorm? Have you lost your mind?" His look was one of true concern. "You could've ended up as dead as Evie."

"Don't I know," I said and meant it.

"That's some dog you've got."

"Yep. Probably should have named him Buck," I said in all seriousness. Dan gave me a blank look. "*Call of the Wild*. Jack London. Alpha dog. Didn't you read growing up?"

"Tried not to. Too busy playing lacrosse." He raised a single eyebrow at me and unzipped the top of the pack. "I'm assuming you've already been through this."

"You assume right. I thought it was mine at first," I lied. Well, it was a partial truth. "We bought the packs together in Denver."

"I'll pass the info on to Detective Roark. I don't know how

long they'll be out there today. You know there's another storm blowing in, so they'll probably have to quit early."

"If they don't come up with anything maybe they want to go back to the Weller Lake area."

"We gotta concentrate on Gulch first. That's where the hand was found and that's the possible crime scene."

"Don't call it the crime scene yet. We still haven't ruled out a wild animal." I turned to leave and stopped in my tracks. "Oh, I almost forgot, there's one other thing. Someone stole my car at the Winter Gate last night. Roark found it in town and brought it back to my house."

"Well that's a head scratcher," said Dan. "How'd you get home?"

"Walked."

"You walked home from the Winter Gate?" he asked, incredulous. "You're lucky you didn't freeze."

"It was a little cold, I have to admit."

"Why do you suppose someone would steal your car and then leave it in town?"

I walked to the door, and turned around with my hand on the knob. "If you find the answer to that question, I'd love for you to share it with me."

SEVENTEEN
Judy

Judy sat at the kitchen nook drinking a cappuccino and staring at Aspen Mountain, the top half glowing in the sun, the lower slopes still somber in morning shadow. Dark clouds in the distance threatened snow later in the day, but for now it was sunny atop both Aspen and in her kitchen on Red Mountain.

"Morning, babe," Gene greeted her, coming out from the master bedroom down the hall. She grimaced as he kissed the back of her head through the nest of shiny black hair. Though she was a pro at concealing her irritation, sometimes his air of ownership rankled her, even if the gesture was meant to be affectionate. He was dressed for skiing in khaki-colored ski pants and a red jacket, and his thick waves of silver hair were damp from a comb. He sat down next to her and peered into her empty cup.

"Another cappuccino?" he offered.

"I was actually going to offer to make you one."

"No, I'm picking up Roman. We're grabbing breakfast at the Nell." He gave his watch a quick glance and slid from the booth to his feet. "In fact, I've got to get going. You know how impatient he can be."

"I don't know why you cater to that man like that," she said, sliding from the booth and walking over to the Italian espresso machine that occupied the better part of the long counter. She scooped fresh coffee into the filter. "Maybe you should have married Roman instead of me. You sure spend enough time with him. Personally, I think he's a little weird."

"He's a writer. All writers are weird." He came around behind her and pulled her back against him. Taking ownership again. "Besides he'd never do what you did for me this morning."

"Actually he probably would. At least one part of it." She pushed a button on the machine and steam sputtered from a spout.

"I love it when you talk dirty." He gave her a slap on the bottom and headed down the back stairs to the garage. She poured hot milk into her coffee and carried the foam-covered mug back to the table. She sat and sipped the cappuccino with satisfaction, not wanting to admit she was always a little relieved when he was gone.

She opened the smooth leather folder that held her daily planner. It was her bible, and she would be lost without it. It held her calendar as well as her list of TTDs and all the plans for Gene's sixtieth next week. She and Cecily had been working on the surprise for the last month, and thus far they had been successful in keeping it a secret. Gene lived to be in the limelight and would be overjoyed at the surprise party. Which was the desired goal. The happier he was, the easier her life was.

But the birthday plans had to be pushed to the back burner until tomorrow. First she had to get through tonight's party in honor of the oil baron who had bought his Starwood mansion through Gene. He used to send Gene referrals, but the referrals had tapered off in the last year, much to Gene's dismay. Good wife that she was, it was her job to polish the friendship and make it shine. She could never forget, the better Gene did, the better she did.

She ran a manicured nail down the checklist. Flowers, place settings, the menu, wine, the music. She swore it never stopped. Sometimes running Gene's life was worse than having a job. Actually it was a job.

And then there was the Palm Beach house. Owning two houses sounded so sexy, but in truth it was nothing but a lot of work. Instead of dealing with the furnace, it was air conditioning. Chlorine instead of snowmelt. She'd so rather stay in at the Breakers where everything was taken care of, including her, instead of her taking care of everything. She would just be caught up with the details of managing the Aspen house, coordinating the maintenance staff, housekeepers, the cook, etc. before it started all over again. Judy didn't even know why they paid a chef. They ate out most of the time, and the chef was just another personality to deal with. But Gene kept Jeffrey on for appearances, something Judy really didn't understand. Why did you need to show off for friends who already knew you had a bucket of dough? She thanked God all the staff was part time and didn't live with them. Except for the house manager. Paul was another thing entirely.

Sometimes she wanted to scream. Actually not sometimes. Oftimes. Though it was mental work and not physical work, she was tired of it just the same. Especially when she didn't need to work. Her mother had needed to work. Judy didn't.

She was tired of the help and the commitments and the other house. Though she had to admit she didn't mind the private jet. That almost made it all worth it. When she was on the jet she just sat back and let the purser take care of her. It seemed to be the only time nothing was asked of her. It wasn't like she could fly the plane herself.

When had being rich gone from being fun to grueling? There were women who thrived on it and others who didn't. The ones who thrived on it kept up their appearances, their clothes, their skin, working out with personal trainers to keep their bodies perfect. Ten thousand a week for maintenance wasn't uncommon for an Aspen wife or girlfriend. Their men paid the overhead with a smile because the better their women looked, the better it made them look.

She had come a long way from Bellevue, Washington and being the only blue collar kid among all those spawn of Microsoft millionaires. A long way from a truck driver father and a mother who worked retail. The Microsoft kids had birthday parties with real circuses and imitation racecars and had sailboats anchored in Lake Washington. They took vacations in places like South Africa and the Galapagos and the Canary Islands. A big trip for her family had been Disneyland. At the time she finished high school, she had only been on a plane twice.

The thing that hurt the worst was wearing knock-offs of the real labels the other girls wore.

To this day, she cringed with embarrassment at the memory

of two high school friends coming to study at their little ranch home where she shared a room with her two sisters, because her brother had to have his own room. The girls were kind, but she knew they were laughing behind her back. They had boats and cars and second homes in Sun Valley. She had a bicycle.

Judy finally had the material things she pined for her entire life. But now that she had those things, she wondered why she felt so ambivalent about them. Of course, she didn't mind everything, just some of it. She wished there was some way to take a vacation from her dream life. What is it they say about getting what you ask for?

Her mind turned back to the party and she looked at her watch. Where was Cecily, anyway? She didn't think she could survive without her personal assistant. Cecily had been Gene's secretary at one time, but he turned her over to help Judy keep organized after they got married. Cecily knew exactly how to do things in a way that suited Gene which in turn suited Judy. She had an unparalleled knack for details such as which wines Gene liked with what food and what size clothing his grown children and grandchildren wore. She kept lists of their preferences which made things easier when she did the shopping for their Christmas gifts.

Judy thought of how dreadful the holidays would have been without Cecily's help. The house had been filled with visitors, the guest suites taken by Gene's kids and siblings, the two bunk rooms filled with their children. It had been true chaos. Even in this huge house, she had felt like a stranger with no space to call her own. On top of it, the guests had to be fed and entertained and shuttled to skiing and balloon rides and parties.

And then there were the parties they hosted during the frenetic two weeks. Judy had to be a gracious hostess, something that used to be fun, but it too had turned into a labor. She had tired of holding conversations with people she didn't really know and skiing boring intermediate runs with people who didn't know a ski from a ski pole. Having to tolerate children who refused $800 a day private lessons so they could be with the adults. Picking them up and putting their ski gear back on.

Looking at the holidays in the rear-view mirror, she wondered if she could ever love Christmas again.

By the time New Year rolled around she'd been so worn out, she didn't even feel like going to the party on top of the mountain. All she wanted was to be alone and sip a quiet glass of wine in front of the fireplace.

But she did go, and that's when she had seen Paul for the first time in years. He was working the party and she managed to slip off with him and have a quiet toast. It felt good to be with someone who came from the same coarse background, someone she didn't have to make pretenses around. Seeing him made her feel so good, she suggested he apply for the recently vacated house manager job at the Red Mountain house.

A footstep behind her caught her attention and she turned around, fully expecting to see her assistant. But it was Paul. He had applied for the house manager job after all, and to Judy's delight, Gene had hired him. Part of the compensation included an ADU on the premises, accessory dwelling unit in Aspen lingo, which also served to make him available when needed.

He'd been downstairs in the media room working on the sound system. He wore denims and a blue work shirt and a duck-billed hat advertising one of the local restaurants. A triangle of blond hair sprouted under his lower lip and emerald-rimmed blue eyes glowed from between light yellow lashes. An earring dangled from his left earlobe.

"Is Gene still here?" he asked, taking in the room in a quick glance. "I figured out what's wrong with the sound system."

"No. He's gone skiing. But I'm sure he'll be happy to learn that when he gets home. He was going ballistic watching the Avalanche game with no sound last night."

Paul took off his hat, revealing a fresh buzz cut. He walked over and sat down in the booth beside her, his hand sliding between her legs. "How about you? Will you be happy when he gets home?"

She reacted as if he'd just put a hot iron between her shoulder blades, turning her head from side to side to check out the room. "Are you crazy? Cecily will be here any minute."

"That's all right," he said, moving his hand up her leg into that special spot. "I'm watching the entry on my phone."

His hand moved even further and she purred. He pushed her down flat on the upholstered cushion and climbed on top of her. She could feel he'd gotten hard just sitting next to her and it really turned her on. She'd already gone one round with her husband this morning, but this was one she was going to enjoy. She hiked up her skirt and pulled her panties aside. "Be quick," she said. His jeans came down and he slid into her right there in the booth.

EIGHTEEN
Greta

I freed Floyd from bored misery on the sidewalk, and we headed towards Aspen Mountain, looming massive in the early-morning shadow. The sidewalks were empty except for early skiers grabbing breakfast, and the streets sported rarely seen empty parking places. We walked past the brick façades of mining-era buildings that once housed local stores and restaurants, that now housed real estate offices, banks and upscale boutiques way beyond my pay grade. A purse in one of the windows carried a price tag of $5,000. Who in hell pays 5,000 bucks for a purse anyhow? I wouldn't if I could, that was for sure. I had a far better use for that kind of money, like sitting on top of the world.

As if there wasn't enough on my mind, I couldn't believe what Dan had just told me about Marynell's chickens. It was a travesty that her neighbors were trying to make her get rid of them. The way things were heading these days, the neighbors would probably win. That's what was going wrong with Aspen. People with buckets of dough were coming in and changing a place that the townspeople had fought hard to keep authentic, which was what attracted the outsiders in the first place. And a lot of the newcomers didn't even ski. I mean, why else live here?

Most of the old restaurants, like the Greenes', had closed because their rents had spiraled to ridiculous levels. The restaurants taking their place were fueled by big city interests and outside the financial reach of most locals. Developers were erasing the last semblances of the old town with homes that needed eleven people to service or staff them, and the service people had to drive from as far as one hundred miles, turning the morning drive to town into an urban nightmare.

Stores that used to sell local products or reasonably priced clothes had been replaced by high-end chains with products that sported logos to either advertise or impress, or art galleries where one sale paid a year's expenses so they could afford to sit empty most of the time.

I imagine it's an age-old problem with beautiful places. Everyone wants to be there, and opportunists will always wring out the money beauty draws. I'd only been in the valley twenty years, so I was a newbie myself, but I'd become possessive of this world and the people who wanted to save what was left of it. When I worked for Marynell at the Powder, the town was filled with small lodges, and her street had been lined with miners' shacks. Most of those homes were ghosts now, either gone altogether or moved to the front of the lot to make way for monster additions in back. Or torn down without permission in those 'whoops' with fines that were readily paid.

Dan was right when he said dealing with Marynell was going to be tough. Though she was getting up there in years, she still had the constitution of a mule. Strong and stubborn. You didn't dodge grizzlies in Alaska without growing a thick skin. She was probably tougher today than when we worked for her. A smile came to my face thinking of the sound of Marynell's booming voice every morning at the Powder, welcoming guests at the top of her lungs or urging us to vacuum, vacuum, vacuum.

She'd been a true taskmaster and woe be to the maid who skipped cleaning a toilet in a hurry to hit the slopes. No prima donnas were allowed. Though it wasn't as bad as it sounds. We'd drag ourselves out of bed after a late night out and clean the rooms quickly, so we could get out on the slopes. And when we were suffering hangovers, what better place to be than in rooms with beds and toilets at our disposal.

After the work was finished it was time for skiing. I was already a good skier, but afternoons on Aspen Mountain with Evie really helped polish my game. Evie had spent many a winter of her childhood parked in ski area lots where her parents negotiated work for free lift tickets. She was skiing practically before she could walk, her first skis plucked out of a garbage bin in an alley. Her patient skiing with me must have been boring as hell for her, and I was always jealous watching her rip down double diamonds that would have eaten me up and spit me back then.

But the one who really helped me turn pro was Marynell. Her motto was work hard and play hard, and it was a motto that both she and Clive held to. On top of running the lodge, they worked as ski instructors, both for the extra money and for the free ski pass. It wasn't uncommon to see Marynell leading a class on the mountain after I'd finished my work at the lodge. But if I got real lucky, I'd catch her out free skiing and she'd take me under her wing. Marynell taught me how to dance on my boards. She even helped me get my first ski instructor job.

That year we worked at the Deep Powder Lodge, Marynell had been both boss and mother to Evie, Judy and me. She was getting over the loss of her own daughter, as if you ever get over something like that, and she had taken us under her wings as her little chicks. She had been our compass, a proxy mother, a stable influence, and had taught us the true joys of the valley and not the moneyed ones. She made sure we ate well and allowed for a late start on mornings with six or more inches of fresh powder. The sweetness of that year could never be recreated, and we all cried when the Powder was demolished, replaced by an all-suites boutique hotel at five times the price.

By the time Floyd and I reached the gondola, it was up and running to ferry resort staff to the top. A line of hardcore powder hounds waited for the lift to open to the public, eager to hit the powder before anyone else, hanging on to snowboards and skis while they relived last night's conquests in the clubs.

Floyd and I bypassed the line and jumped into a gondola car, settling in for the ride to the top. As we passed over the smooth corduroy of the intermediate runs and the untracked powder of the expert trails, the beauty of the white-capped mountains in the distance barely dented my consciousness. There were too many other things jockeying for space in my mind. Floyd's certification test. Evie, Everest, Marynell. The dreaded party at Judy's tonight.

My cell started vibrating, but by the time I dug it out of my pocket, it had gone to voicemail. A smile replaced my inner turmoil as I listened to the message. It was my brother calling from Afghanistan just to say hello. I always took comfort in the sound of his voice and in the knowing there was no crisis and he was still breathing.

He'd attached a picture from his wedding and the sight of him looking so happy took me to an oasis far from Evie's demise and Marynell's chickens. He was wearing his fatigues and a bow tie improvised from boot laces. His face was clean-shaven, his blond hair military short. His bride stood beside him, her dark chocolate skin a stark contrast to his pale white, her kinky black hair an even greater contrast to his yellow stubble. She was leaning into him warmly, her prosthetic leg peeking out from the pashmina wrapped around her waist as a makeshift skirt.

He'd told me he was going to marry Fenicia when he visited me last year on leave. They got together after a roadside IED upended their vehicle on the way back to camp. He emerged unscathed, but she'd lost her lower right leg. Toby had that kind of karma, like he was protected by a force field. We both did actually. We had the ability to ignore danger, and luckily danger hadn't bitten either of us . . . yet. It had tried to take a piece out of me last night, but I'd won. I moved the wedding photo to my screen saver and tucked my phone back into my parka, smiling at the only shared blood I knew of.

When the gondola slid into the terminal up top, Floyd jumped out ahead of me and headed toward patrol headquarters without looking back, his tail wagging with excitement. I grabbed my skis and followed him, glimpsing at the overhead thermometer on the way out. The needle read zero and my cold nose verified it.

The ski patrol building was fashioned after a Swiss chalet, inspired by the Europeans who came after the war to build Aspen into a winter resort. Despite its age, the wood-clad building had changed little, keeping its Alpine feel with vintage skis mounted over the entrance and messy racks of skis out front. The building was a sacred place, and we clung to it jealously, praying it would never be replaced by something more upscale like the nearby club that cost a quarter million dollars just to join. And that doesn't include lunch, though there are free boot warmers.

I stepped into the shack and was greeted by the smell of melting wax coming from the workroom where patrollers tuned their skis. The temperature inside was a furnace compared to the frigid outdoors, the wood fire in the lounge throwing off enough heat to warm the whole building.

There were a dozen patrollers milling around the fireplace or lounging in chairs sporting considerably more duct tape than the Barca. I snagged a banana muffin from the stack the breakfast crew at the cafeteria next door provided and poured myself a cup of coffee. Dogs are revered by patrol and Floyd was greeted with a lot of head rubbing and butt slapping. Basking in the attention, he ignored me to circle among the other patrollers and sniff at the patrol mascot, a black Lab named Cookie who ignored him and retreated into the workroom to escape his advances.

Neverman sat on a couch in front of the fire with his head bent over the day's paper, his long legs propped on the log table in front of him, his grey curls falling around his weathered brown face. Just banging sixty, he's been my boss since I came on patrol, and despite his age, he's one of the best skiers I've ever seen outside the racing circuit. He keeps this mountain as safe as is humanly possible, knows when to dynamite potential slides, when to open or close particular runs, when it's time to groom an over-bumped run. He has a particularly good eye for spotting a boarder caught upside down in a tree well. Once he even saved a skier who slid out of bounds and ended up hanging upside down in an open mineshaft.

By the time I came on board ten years ago, women were fairly well integrated into patrol, unlike the pioneers of the seventies and eighties who had to put up with pranks like the guys putting twenty pound rocks in their packs. Most of the guys these days are pretty down with women being on the team, but there are still some who haven't read the memo on equality. Sadly, Neverman falls into that second category. He has a bug up his ass about women on ski patrol and isn't subtle about comparing the physical abilities of women patrollers to those of our male counterparts. Though he tries to hide it, the attitude simmers beneath the surface just waiting to boil over whenever one of us screws up.

When I first came on board, he mistook my looks for weakness and worked me twice as hard, giving me all the worst duties. A known ladies' man, Neverman has steered clear of me in that regard, and I'm grateful for that. But since we have to work together, we have come to an understanding. I do my job with no complaints and he doesn't bug me too much. His dark eyes flicked upwards as I walked in and settled on me in not too subtle disapproval.

"Have you seen the news today?" he asked, waving the newspaper at me as if he was waving off the cooties. I snagged the paper from him on an upward swing. The small town headline glared at me in a big city way. 'HUMAN HAND FOUND IN GULCH CREEK WILDERNESS.' Smaller print below read: 'Ski patroller makes gruesome find while cross-country skiing with dog.'

I shook my head in frustrated disbelief. It seemed unbelievable that after Dan and I talked about keeping this quiet, it was a front page story. I would have bet anything the nugget of information slipped out at the Hick House last night. Everyone knows everyone there, and talk is the grease of companionship. For some people a martini is loudmouth soup. For Dan it's a slab of ribs. Or maybe Elsa Blanding had dropped the dime. The lady coroner was known to sip tequila when she wasn't dissecting human livers, and one could never know what might slip her lips after a shot of Patron.

Whatever. It was what it was. My eyes moved down the page looking for either my name or Evie's, and I was relieved that neither of us made the cut. The article attributed the news to confidential sources and said more information would be forthcoming. But Neverman's next words told me that while the source was confidential, it didn't take a rocket scientist to figure who the anonymous ski patroller was.

"Am I out of line assuming this was you?"

I'm not much of a liar, only lying in order to save someone's feelings like when someone asks if they looked good on that last run or if a certain pair of pants makes them look fat. I gave him a clueless shrug and said, "Could be."

His next words were exactly what I didn't want to hear. "You think that hand was Evie Kearney's?"

Neverman had known Evie—just like practically every other local in town. She'd been around a long time and had made her mark in Aspen. From leading climbs to volunteering for the forest service to teaching outdoor ed at the middle school, she'd touched just about every aspect of Aspen life. She seldom missed a fundraiser whether it was for a local kid with cancer or an uninsured waiter with a broken leg. She was a true angel, albeit a bit of a dark one.

When I looked up at least a half dozen pairs of eyes were focused on me. I shrugged again and gave an evasive answer. "I don't know. Gulch Creek sure is far from Independence."

"Could've been an animal. They cover a lot of terrain," said Neverman, unknowingly backing my theory. He pondered that for a moment, and then added in an ominous tone, "Or maybe it wasn't an animal at all. What if she'd been attacked . . ."

His sentence died in the air. All eyes turned to the doorway as Buzz walked in, his soft red beard speckled with powder. He grabbed a muffin from the tray and flopped onto the sofa next to Neverman. No one said a word.

"Someone get attacked?" he asked.

There was a rare apology in Neverman's eyes as he handed the paper over to Buzz. The blood drained from his already pale features as the possibilities sank in. He put the paper on the table and sank his head between his knees. He knew. We all knew. No one said a word. I wanted to say something comforting, but there was nothing comforting to be said.

Without a word, Buzz got up and banged out of the shack.

NINETEEN
Judy

Judy had to restrain herself from chewing her assistant out for showing up an hour late. But she was highly annoyed, nonetheless. It was unusual for the young Englishwoman to be anything other than early. Cecily was detail oriented and regimented and her punctuality reflected it. But today she came running in flushed and sweaty with the aura about her of someone who had just been making love.

Which was a ridiculous thought. Unfortunately for Cecily, God seemed to have passed her over the day he was handing out beauty. Though Cecily didn't do much to help herself. She wore her dull dishwater blonde hair in a messy scrunchie and never used any make-up despite her blotchy red complexion and the residual marks of teenage acne. The way she dressed didn't help her much either. Judy often wondered if she owned anything other than baggy jeans and flannel shirts.

For her birthday, Judy had thought about giving Cecily a day at the spa as a gift, but upon further reflection decided that her assistant's plainness was actually a good thing. After all, who wanted to compete with the help? She didn't want to risk what happened with Arnold Schwarzenegger and his housekeeper happening under her roof. Then again, Gene's vasectomy ruled out the risk of any offspring. Just the same, Judy had given her a gift certificate to Paradise Bakery instead.

"I'm terribly sorry to keep you waiting," Cecily gushed in her fancy British accent. "Traffic into town was bonkers."

As if traffic wasn't always 'bonkers' during the season. The lines of tourists and service workers coming into town brought traffic to a crawl in the morning. Judy wanted to tell Cecily that since she came from her down-valley apartment nearly every morning, she should have had that factored in by now.

But Judy bit her tongue. Never far enough away from her own humble background, she empathized with the help and understood how it felt to be on the outside looking in. While a lot of her nouveau riche acquaintances terrorized their employees, Judy was always kind to them and never talked down to anyone, no matter what she was thinking. She was grateful that people were looking in the window wanting to be her now instead of the other way around.

So she rose over her irritation with the girl and said sweetly, "I'm just glad to see you. There's still so much to do to get ready for tonight. What should we use for china? I was thinking of the white Christian Dior."

Cecily put a thoughtful finger to her lips. "I don't know. With tables full of Texans, I think the Stoneware would be more appropriate. What are we? Forty? I believe we have place settings for four dozen. And we can use your western-themed placemats and napkins and put a decorated cactus on all the tables."

Judy sighed internally. See? This was why Cecily was a treasure. English people just seemed to have a better sense of hosting and etiquette. Judy's upbringing was about as lacking in etiquette as you could get. She grew up eating off paper plates and using plastic utensils most of the time, so her mother wouldn't have to do dishes. Half of their meals were carry-out washed down with Coke. How do you learn etiquette from that?

Her assistant knew what wines to serve with what food, how to properly set a table, that charger plates were to be removed after the first course and not remain on the table for the entire meal no matter how nice they looked. These things were all alien to Judy with her low bank balance upbringing. She couldn't begin to imagine what would happen if she had to figure out all this stuff for herself. She appreciated that Cecily made her look good.

The caterers were arriving, and Cecily instructed them as to which dinnerware to use. While the staff was setting up the tables in the great room, Judy and Cecily worked on the seating. When they got to Gene's author friend, Roman Judge, Judy placed Roman's name beside Greta's on the chart.

"You're putting Greta next to the author?" Cecily asked. "I thought you always put Michelle Gorman next to him."

"Orders from the master," she said. "Gene specifically wants Greta seated next to Roman at the head table. Michelle will be pissed, but there's nothing I can do about it. Now let's see if we can find another single man to put her next to."

"Emil Rankin was just widowed last month," Cecily suggested.

"Perfect," Judy chirped. "He owns a national restaurant chain. That should make Michelle happy."

TWENTY
Greta

Despite everything going on in my complicated world, it was still Floyd's day to qualify as a proper Avalanche Working Dog. As his handler, I'd been drilling him for weeks per K9 avalanche training protocol, rewarding him with his favorite toys and praise when he did his job right, rewarding him with nothing when he didn't. Doing the job right meant finding the buried victim within thirty-five minutes, that being the accepted window of time to find an avalanche victim alive.

So far 2020 had already brought numerous avalanches to the valley, and while inbound slides at ski areas are rare, they can happen. Trained canines were critical—even on Aspen Mountain. Their role turned even more critical when renegade skiers and boarders ventured out of bounds and triggered slides that took them along. Even though they're not technically our responsibility, we'll still head out with the probes and dogs to look for them, often putting ourselves at risk. The bottom line is we are dialed in to save lives no matter how idiotic the victim is.

In today's drill, Floyd would be searching for more than smelly socks. Today his job was to find a living human buried beneath several feet of snow. Patrol kept a pit on the far side of the Sundeck restaurant to simulate avalanche conditions for training purposes, and that was where Floyd's test would take place. Everything was set to go, except for one thing. At the moment Floyd and I were tasked with finding someone to play victim.

The volunteer has to spend up to an hour in a confined space beneath two feet of snow with a tube providing the only air and light. I've done it before and, frankly, it's about as fun as an MRI, only darker and colder. I'd sweet-talked Buzz into volunteering last week, but after the way he'd banged out of the shack, I'd ruled him out. Now I was looking for another candidate.

That's when Singh had the bad timing to walk into the hut. Singh's a New Delhi native who dropped out of medical school after taking spring break in Aspen years ago. The narcotic effect of champagne powder hooked him, and much to the dismay of his parents, there's no twelve-step program for this kind of addiction. Singh had gone after skiing even harder than he had medicine. He could carve a turn like a hot knife through butter and ski bumps like a pinball wizard. When his parents complained they had wasted their money sending him to medical school, he assured them that his classes in anatomy were being put to good use. I was pretty sure Singh was gay, though we'd never had that discussion. That would have really croaked his parents seeing how he already had an arranged marriage awaiting him back in India.

You could tell he had already been skiing hard, because when he peeled off his helmet his shiny black hair glistened with sweat. He gave me his customary smile, his teeth gleaming white in his beguiling face.

"Ah, just the person I'm looking for," I said, returning his smile while trying not to appear sinister. "I need an avalanche victim for Floyd's test."

His smile withered. "Damn, I knew I should have taken another run. You know my blood is way thinner than yours. New Delhi isn't exactly an igloo."

"Yes, but think of how good you're going to feel when Floyd finds you," I said, giving him a push toward the door. "The sooner you get going the sooner it will be over."

While a none-too-happy Singh submitted to burial by a couple of the other patrollers, Floyd and I killed time in the shack so he wouldn't catch on. Everyone else had gone except for Meghan O'Malley, a fellow ski patroller, who was manning the radios. Meghan was as Irish as they came, coated with freckles from the forehead down, her head a coil of wiry red hair. A true endomorph, she could probably lift more dead weight than most of the guys. She and I share the same opinion about Neverman, that he's a misogynist. But we keep it to ourselves. Still, it's good to have someone to share with.

There was no chatter on the radio, so she came over and sat with us while Floyd and I waited to be called to the pit. I kept checking my messages the entire time, hoping for some news from Gulch Creek. Meghan rubbed Floyd's head, and he thumped his tail on the wooden floor in appreciation. She looked around to be sure we were alone and asked, "Was that you who found the hand?"

"I guess that's not much of a secret anymore," I replied.

"Well, the way Neverman is acting, you'd think you put it there. What's up with him, anyway?"

"Your guess is as good as mine. I'm beyond understanding his moods."

"That had to be traumatic," she said sympathetically. Then she asked the dreaded question. "Do *you* think it was Evie?"

Before I could answer, the door banged open and Buzz walked back into the shack. His goggles were raised onto his helmet, and his blue eyes looked paler than ever beneath his wisp of a brow. His eyelids were rimmed in red which told me he'd gone off to have a private cry. Meghan took one look at him and retreated to the radio room. He sat down beside me and stared into my eyes, not letting them go.

"That was her hand, wasn't it?" he asked softly.

I couldn't lie to him. He had already suffered enough. I answered with the slightest nod of my head.

"Are you sure?" His eyes drilled into me in a way that left me no choice but to respond.

"There was a Claddagh ring."

He lowered his head into his hands.

"There's more," I said gently. "I went back up Indy yesterday and found her pack up near Weller Lake."

"Why didn't you call me?" he asked in a voice barely a whisper.

I didn't want to let him know that Dan Nichols had instructed me not to tell him, so I stupidly said the first thing that came to mind. "I didn't know if it would be appropriate."

"You didn't know if it would be 'appropriate.'" His fingers etched quotation marks in the air and his voice grew louder. "Not appropriate to let me know you found a piece of the woman I loved more than anything in this world. The woman I've been searching for nearly every free moment since she disappeared. When would it be appropriate?"

I could hear Meghan close the door to the radio room. Even though we were alone I kept my voice low. "I wasn't sure where you guys were anymore, Buzz. She told me about the boxers. How you treated her." A well-placed punch to his gut would have drawn the same response that came over his face. He drew a deep breath before exhaling his next words. They came out half laugh, half disdain.

"You know, I knew all about Evie being a free spirit when I met her. But I thought I'd changed all that. We loved each other. Really loved each other. Can you imagine how I felt when I saw a pair of boxers in our bed? I don't even wear boxers." His eyes squeezed shut for a moment, and when he reopened them, there were tears clinging to the edge of his lashes. "You have no idea how that hurt. Maybe I should have been the one to leave. But instead I threw her out."

"You have to listen to me, Buzz. She didn't cheat. She had no idea how those boxers got there."

He started to laugh, but it turned into a sigh. "You know, she came home after work the next day and begged me to believe her. I wouldn't hear any of it. Then she started crying and said, 'OK, if you want me to say I did it, I'll say it. "I did it and I'll never do it again. Please take me back."' That's when I told her to leave and that I didn't want to see her ever again."

I thought about our conversation that last night and what she said before passing out. "I'm going home tomorrow to beg him to believe me. If I have to confess to something I didn't do, I'll do it. I'll tell him I made a mistake. I just want him to take me back."

"But she didn't cheat on you, Buzz," I said, wanting him to believe me. "She told me she had no idea where those boxers came from. She had no reason to lie to me. I believed her completely and you can too. She was just telling you what she thought you wanted to hear."

"Why are you telling me this now? So I can feel worse that she disappeared after I rejected her?" He put a hand to his face and sniffled. "Whether she cheated or not, I basically sent her to her death. At least if I knew she cheated I could hate her."

"She didn't cheat, Buzz." Not knowing what else to do I put a hand to his arm. "Come with me and watch what Floyd is capable of. If they don't find her body in the next days, I'm going to. We can go out and look together, if you want. Maybe that will give you closure."

TWENTY-ONE
Greta

By the time Buzz and I arrived at the snow pit with Floyd, Singh was already a few feet under, most likely swearing me up and down a tree and praying that Floyd's nose was as good as promised. There were other patrollers milling around, some dropping probes into the snow in search of imaginary victims, others standing to the side playing traumatized friends, all the drama for Floyd's effect. And as would be in a true avalanche, there was nothing of the buried victim's belongings to give Floyd his scent. But Floyd needed to find the victim (Singh) within eighteen minutes which was the time frame with the greatest possibility of survival. Go longer than thirty-five minutes and you're looking for a corpse.

Floyd was on his best behavior today, fixed at my side waiting to please.

"Vas-y," I said, sending him to work. OK, I may be his mother, but I gotta say, that dog of mine is something else. His outrageous nose took control, and it wasn't more than twenty seconds before he was looking to me for permission to dig, right above where Singh was freezing his ass off. When I gave him the thumbs up, he went at it, looking to me occasionally as the snow flew as if saying, Did you ever have a doubt? Singh was uncovered in record time and Floyd was rewarded with a handful of biscuits and a game of tug of war with his stretched-out fire hydrant.

When all the excitement was over, I looked around for Buzz and didn't see him anywhere. He'd slipped away while Floyd was digging. I checked my messages to see if the searchers up Gulch Creek had found anything that might give him some closure. And me as well. It was radio silence.

I took Floyd back to the patrol shack where all the patrollers made a fuss over him. I left him basking in praise while Singh and I went out to do some routine patrol work, marking hidden obstacles, checking on fallen skiers, retrieving lost skis. We hadn't had any injuries so far today, and I kept my fingers crossed it would stay that way.

Which it did. When I went back to the patrol shack at the end of the day, Floyd was lying on his back with Meghan rubbing his belly. He jumped up when he saw me.

"Wouldn't it be nice if all the alpha males responded like this," she joked.

"Don't let him fool you. This one has a mind of his own."

I smoothed his ears and he pushed his head against my hand, basking in his glory. If he were a cat he would have been purring.

Floyd and I had an uneventful ride down the gondola until we were unloading, and I spotted Dan Nichols standing in the plaza. He was in uniform with his hat set tight upon his bald head. His cheeks were rosy with cold and his nose even redder. When he saw us coming down the steps, he took off the hat and waved me over. When he started working the rim of the hat in his gloved hands, twisting it in ways it was not meant to go, I knew he had something to tell me. My heart skipped a beat.

I tucked my braids out of his reach and walked over.

"News about Evie?" I asked.

"Nothing new up Gulch Creek. But there is something I wanted to let you know."

"And that is?"

"I pulled a few strings and already got the prints back. We've verified that the hand is Evie's," he said.

"You and I knew that yesterday," I said.

"Yes, but now it's official."

"Thanks, Dan," I said, a single tear working its way out the corner of my right eye. "Anything on how it got separated from the rest of her?"

"Nope. Elsa will get back to me as soon as she knows more."

He put his hat back on his head and looked out over the

gondola plaza. He seemed to be avoiding my eyes which made me wonder if he was hiding something.

"Are you sure that's everything, Dan?"

"Now, Greta," he said, turning back to address me in an avuncular voice, "I want you to listen to me. No more putting yourself out there like you did last night. No more nosing around. I don't want to have to come looking for you somewhere tonight."

"No worries about that," I said in complete honesty. My command performance at Judy's precluded anything else. "Now if that's it, I have to get going. I have a dinner to get ready for."

TWENTY-TWO
Greta

I stood in front of the cedar closet in Sam's old room trying to decide what to wear to a party I didn't want to go to in the first place. It's not that I don't love Judy and Gene. Judy's one of my best friends which makes Gene a good friend by association. He's really not a bad guy for a real estate agent. Local done good and all. But as I've said before, I'm just not overly into their scene.

But Judy was right when she said it was better to be someplace other than staring at the walls at home tonight. Now that it had been officially confirmed the hand was Evie's, I was feeling worse than ever. Somehow, I wanted the hand to not be hers. To belong to another missing woman who wore a Claddagh ring. That come summer we'd find her whole body up Indy Pass, not a handless one. But that thought was now put to rest.

I moved myself off that maudlin subject to focus on the challenge of what to wear tonight. Ninety-nine percent of my wardrobe is better suited to sports than an evening with some of the world's most important people. Finding something 'nice,' as Judy put it, isn't easy in my closet even under optimal conditions. My most elegant tops, if you can call them that, are one black cashmere turtleneck and one low-cut black cashmere sweater, both purchased at the Thrift Shop for five dollars, and usually reserved for my shifts at the Bug.

Floyd watched with curiosity as I pulled old clothes from the recesses of the closet with increasing frustration. He had never seen me fuss over getting dressed and it had him perplexed. I unearthed a couple of silk blouses from a stint as a restaurant hostess years ago, but they were too wrinkled to even qualify as bag lady couture.

I gave up and went back to my default outfit, black slacks and one of the cashmere sweaters. It's the same outfit I wear whenever some grateful family insists on taking me to dinner for ferrying their kid with the twisted knee down the hill. The one I wear when I'm comped tickets to a charity event like Challenge Aspen or for disabled vets where I see a lot of the locals—not to mention some of the best athletes and competitors going.

The big question for tonight was turtleneck or low-cut? Doing sexy is not really my gig, but I've found a flash of cleavage really makes a difference in tips on Saturday nights. (The Friday night coat-check girl shared that little hint with me years ago.) I once ran an unscientific experiment and learned that tips run about fifty percent higher on boob nights. Everest is expensive and if a little cleavage brings me closer to the top of the world, I'm willing to compromise myself a little since Bugaboo tips go straight into my travel bucket. That travel bucket has served me well over the years, taking me to the Galapagos for diving as well as a summer ski holiday in New Zealand. The success of the low-cut sweater was so extraordinary that I'd gone so far as to invest in a push-up bra. Results? Another twenty percent.

Knowing tonight's festivities wouldn't involve gratuities, I opted for the turtleneck. I topped the sweater off with a chunky turquoise necklace that Judy had given me for Christmas the year she married Gene, when cash was no longer a problem and she could afford to be overly generous with gifts. There were matching earrings, but I never bother with earrings when my hair is loose. When it's freed from braids, my hopeless blonde mane covers my ears. I did a light make-up and stood back to look at the end result. I had to admit I looked pretty good. I'm not completely without vanity.

I said goodnight to an unhappy Floyd and headed out the door to do my duty as Judy's friend.

TWENTY-THREE
Greta

I pulled up in front of the Red Mountain manse and was startled to see Paul Glendale parking the cars. Paul's a forty-something-year-old local who migrated from Vermont in the late nineties. Like most locals, he's scrambled from job to job and place to place every season. He's tall, sexy and blond with a buzz cut and killer blue eyes. He's also an Ivy League grad who never held a serious job. Paul has a well-deserved reputation for doing two things well. He is legendary for doing laps of Highland Bowl and for doing women with the same enthusiasm, me being an unwitting conquest some time back. Or was it a mutual conquest? Either way it ended friendly. That's how things work in a ski town. It's way too small to hold grudges.

"Lookin' good, Greta," he said, holding the door of the Goner open while flashing me a killer smile equal to his killer eyes. "This beast is still running?" I flushed momentarily at the memory of borrowing the car from Sam for trysts with Paul, who was living with two other guys in a tent off the Rio Grande trail during our brief relationship. There's a lot to be said for upholstered bench seats with no hump in the middle. Front and back.

I acknowledged him with a partially forced smile. "Yep. Howard keeps breathing new life into this baby. He's always warning me that she's on her last legs, but somehow he always finds the orthopedics when needed." I handed over the keys. "Last time I saw you, you were working the bar at Shooter's. You get a promotion?"

"You might say that. I'm the house manager here. Comes with complimentary apartment. Wanna check out the views?"

"No," I said, aghast that Paul was not only employed by

Gene and Judy, but that he was living with them—sort of. In Aspen, the county code requires new construction to include an accessory dwelling unit, also known as an ADU, a rule implemented with the intention of homeowners renting the apartments to local workers. Most the units sat empty except when the owners needed household help and housing was the only way to entice them. Which clearly was the case with Paul. I'd seen Judy's ADU and let me tell you, it far exceeded the housing most locals squatted in. That was Paul. He landed on his feet in life the same way he skied.

"Judy hired you?" I was incredulous. Judy had been the one to hold my hand when Paul ghosted me those years back.

"Well, Gene actually. But I think she's happy about it," he added.

"I just hope you're toeing the line," I said.

"Would I do otherwise?"

He offered up that wry smile he'd used on me all those years ago. I turned my back to him and headed through the European-church-size doors into the entry. There I encountered yet another long-time local, this one collecting coats. Jason Click was a former bartender from the Bugaboo who got fired for hitting on clients and then turned Evangelical. He was living in the Victorian when I first moved in, but moved out a few months later when he found a job with housing. But that's how it always is in Aspen. People are moving targets and house-hopping is a local sport.

Jason was a small guy, about five four, but his athleticism more than made up for his diminutive size. He could rock his skis with the best of them and skin up Tiehack Trail in record time. A cowboy hat was perched over his receding brown hair-line, and he wore chaps over faded jeans that hung on his skinny ass. Cowboy boots went without saying.

In his pre-Jesus days, he used to be barely interesting, but since finding God he had become even less so. He was a good soul though, no pun intended, but was insufferable when it came to the religious stuff. Since his conversion, he never seemed to do anything without bowing his head in prayer first, whether it was skiing the bowl, biking the Rockies or a movie.

"Hi, Greta." His brown eyes were dull in his wind-chapped face. "Never knew you were part of this crowd."

"Me neither," I said, handing over my parka, the one that didn't have a cross on the back. I didn't own any warm gear that wasn't sports related and unless Judy wanted to spring for a Moncler, my less than stylish jacket was about as upscale as my outerwear was getting. I braced myself for conversion as Jason hung my coat, but was spared when another couple walked in behind me and handed him their coats.

Taking leave of Jason, I headed up to the party, dragging my hand along the winding banister in delay. Thirty steps later—I counted—I emerged into a great room the size of a hotel lobby. At the far end of the room, the white ghost of Aspen Mountain glowed through the floor-to-ceiling windows. Elk-antlered chandeliers provided soft light from the high-beamed ceiling and slouchy furniture grouped in seating areas added to the feel of a hotel lobby. A section of the room had been set like a restaurant with linen-draped tables and tall cactus plants. As one might have guessed, the party's theme was Texas. The servers wore suede vests and leather chaps just like Jason, only they had six-shooters strapped to their thighs. A huge Lone Star flag hung from the highest beam.

Had this scene greeted me when I first hit Aspen, chances are I'd have kept driving. But after twenty years of big money craziness, I'd developed an immunity to its excesses. Aspen is a place where people spend $100,000 on temporary kitchens and tear them out when their custom cabinetry arrives. A place where baby grand pianos are brought in by private plane and where friends of presidential candidates hold $50,000 a ticket fundraisers.

But the great equalizer is the mountains ski the same no matter how much money you have. And the wildflowers that grow along the trails are free for everyone to view. And the clear crisp air is anyone's for the breathing. Add to that no poison ivy, poison oak or poisonous snakes and you have near perfection.

I had just summited the stairs when I heard someone calling my name. I turned around to see Mike Neverman coming up behind me. He was hatless, his silver curls neatly combed close to his head. He wore a black turtleneck under a corduroy jacket, and it dawned on me that it was one of the few times I'd ever seen him in civvy gear. The frightening thought occurred to me that if I didn't know him so well, I'd probably find him attractive.

"Hey, Westerlind, what are you doing slumming it?"

"I might ask the same of you," I replied.

"You dress up pretty good," he said giving me the once-over. "I thought the only clothes you owned were ski clothes."

"And once again, I could say the same of you." We stood for an awkward moment before I asked, "How'd you merit an invite to this august occasion?"

"I fly-fish with the big oil dude in the summer." He looked around at his surroundings. "Not bad digs. Judy did well for herself."

"I think they could use a little more space," I said. And then afraid he might take me seriously, I added, "A bit over the top for my taste."

Neverman gave his head a shake that made his curls quiver. "I remember when the only lights on this mountain were from a few shacks halfway up the road. It was literally black at night," he reminisced. His voice turned somber. "The people on this mountain were far more into nature back then. Then again, nature was all we could afford." He laughed an ironic laugh and added, "I'm just thankful for my little abode. And my solitude—while it lasts."

The sincerity of his words made me dislike him a little less. Though Neverman had arrived on the scene long before me, I got what he was talking about. He was part of a core group who were the foundation of this community. He lived in a rustic cabin on the backside of the mountain that he built himself decades ago. It stood at the end of a long path with an impressive view and a pile of firewood stacked beside it year round. In the summer he got around via dirt bike; in the winter he drove his snowmobile to work. And he wasn't kidding about his solitude being threatened. Several monster homes were under construction on the backside of the mountain not far from his cabin, being built by people whose idea of solitude was moving in on someone else's.

Judy's personal assistant, Cecily, came over to give us our table assignments. She was wearing a close-fitting black dress that made me do a double take. I'd known Cecily since she started working for Judy, and I'd never seen her wear anything that didn't resemble a sack. As it turned out, she had what the guys would call an eye-popping shape. And I wasn't the only one who noticed. Neverman was giving her the elevator eye, and none too subtly, I might add. He did manage to tear his eyes away long enough to tell her his name.

Cecily ran her finger down a printed list and then handed him a card. "Mr. Neverman, you are at table one, with the hosts and the guest of honor, Humphrey Gibbons."

I guess fly-fishing with someone counts for a lot.

"Good evening, Greta," she greeted me in her polished English. "I imagine you want your table number too?"

"As long as I'm here."

She didn't need to look at the iPad. "You're also at table number one. You are seated between Roman Judge and Dr. Peter Emmanuel. Dr. Emmanuel is one of the most renowned doctors in Texas."

"Plastic surgeon?" I asked wryly.

"Organ transplants," she replied.

"Isn't that the same thing?" I joked. She handed me a printed card with my name and the number one on it as if I might have trouble remembering. I tucked it into my pants pocket as I wasn't carrying a purse. My driver's license lives in the glove box of the Goner.

"Now don't have too much fun, Greta," Neverman chided, tucking his own card into the pocket of the corduroy jacket. "You've got to work tomorrow."

"You call it work," I shot back.

I moved away from the stairs and into the party. The room echoed with the boisterous laughter and raised voices of people enjoying themselves. For the most part the guests congregated in small groups, the women beautiful, thin and fit with big blonde hair and enhanced chests. Dressed in expensive clothes and showy jewelry, they wore their beauty as if they expected great things to come from it. The men wore button-down shirts with string ties or cashmere sweaters and navy blazers. There was no shortage of cowboy boots, including several pairs of ostrich ones that cost as much as a used car, something I learned during a brief stint in retail one summer.

Left to wander by myself, it didn't take more than twenty seconds to confirm that I didn't know any of the other guests aside from Neverman. Which suited me just fine. It saved me from having to make small talk. Although the term small talk is an oxymoron at any Aspen party. There's nothing small about the conversations of people who own G5s or Argentine ranches or yachts with landing pads for their helicopters. These are people who invite friends to their private islands and bid on Impressionist art at auctions. Who hold parties with rock stars performing for their guests. Who have room-sized wine cellars in their homes stocked with the best of French and Italian wines. We would not have a lot in common.

I did see a couple of women who were regulars at the Bug, and they came up to talk. One of them said she was trying to place how she knew me, and I told her she probably recognized me from the coat check. After which an uneasy silence ensued before they made excuses and politely dismissed themselves. I wondered if either of them planned on climbing Everest in May.

In spite of all the noise and chatter, Judy had been right about one thing. This was better than being home staring at the walls thinking about Evie. But not by much. I grabbed a Pellegrino off a passing tray and drifted down the hall into Gene's library.

The library was one room in the house where I felt comfortable, a softly lit cubby with floor-to-ceiling bookshelves, a formidable desk and a pair of leather love seats. The shelves housed an impressive collection of books that Gene must have had vetted since I never saw him read anything more complex than Vince Flynn. I've heard that people here hire professionals to put together the library of a well-read person. That is in the houses that have a library. Most of the big ones opt for theaters instead.

I set my glass down on the cocktail table and perused the shelves. The books were alphabetically arranged by author, and I took down a copy of *Dubliners* right next to a collection of Roman Judge books. I settled into one of the love seats and was paging through the book when I sensed the presence of another human. I looked up and saw a virtual giant of a man standing in the doorway. He was handsome in a quirky kind of way with a thick body and neck, and coarse black hair shaved military short on the sides. His nose was slightly oversized in his square face, and a flattening beneath the bridge hinted of some past altercation.

He smiled humbly, revealing a reasonable gap between his two front teeth. "I'm sorry. Am I disturbing you?" he asked in a melodious voice that reminded me of a famous singer I couldn't place.

"Not at all," I said, feeling awkward but oddly grateful for his company. Maybe it was the voice. "Just hiding out until it's time to eat."

"You're not lonely in here all by yourself?"

"Not really. I live alone and thrive on it. Don't tell anyone, but I'm hiding."

His hearty laugh matched his voice, the type of laugh that made you want to join in. "A woman as pretty as you shouldn't have to be all alone at a party."

I looked at him and said, "Guess I'm not alone anymore."

He laughed again and stuck out a paw of a hand. "Winks Denmark." And then as if to qualify his name, he squeezed one gray eye shut and reopened it.

I didn't return the gesture, but I accepted his hand and gave it a brief shake. "Greta Westerlind. Are you a friend of Gene's or a customer?"

"None of the above," he replied. "I'm staying with one of the guests, so I tagged along. I guess that makes me a party crasher. Looking around that room, I'm guessing there are probably more oilmen here than Cowboy Stadium during the playoffs."

"Are you military?" I asked.

"What makes you say that?"

"The haircut. My brother is styling the same do. He's Army. Special forces Afghanistan."

"Your brother is a brave man," he said.

"Yes, he is. Not a day passes that I don't worry about him. What branch are you?"

"Air Force," he said, adding, "was. Then again I guess you never leave."

He tipped his dark head towards the other love seat looking for permission to sit. "Do you mind? I'm not much into the social scene either."

"Suit yourself." I got up to reshelve the book and sat back down. My mouth had gone suddenly dry, so I took a long drink of the water, suddenly wishing I had something stronger. "So who are you visiting?"

"I'm not actually visiting anyone. I'm the hired help." He noticed the mystified look on my face and added, "I'm in the transport business. I'm a private pilot."

"Not a bad segue from the Air Force."

"It pays the bills. The guy I fly for is a big shot in the medical field. He's got a place up in Starwood and a ranch in Argentina. Does well enough to own his own Gulfstream."

"G5?" I asked.

"How did you know?"

"Lucky guess. You must like flying that piece of equipment."

"It's a good plane for tough landings like Sardy. In fact, barely made it in yesterday morning before the storm. We were the last plane to land before they closed the airport."

"You do anything exciting in the Air Force?" I asked lamely, feeling stupid the moment the words left my mouth.

"You mean other than fly in the Navy Seals who killed Bin Laden? Course that was a Black Hawk helicopter, and the army was making an exception in my case."

"Ha ha," I replied.

With imperfect timing, Judy waltzed into the room at that very moment. She was elegant in a tight-fitting gold sheath and her blue eyes were shiny above her glowing cheeks. A bucket-sized margarita teetered in her right hand.

"There you are! I've been looking for you everywhere," she proclaimed, giving my companion a smile and dismissive nod upon realizing she didn't recognize him as one of the invited guests. "Sorry, but she's in demand," she said, grabbing me by the arm without bothering to introduce herself. She pulled me to my feet.

Winks stood and picked up my glass. He handed it to me saying, "Here, you might want this for courage." I took it from him and smiled coyly. Then he reached into his breast pocket and took out a business card. "In case you ever want an aerial tour." I slipped it into my back pocket alongside my table assignment.

"Come on," said Judy, dragging me towards the door.

I shrugged a goodbye to Winks Denmark who raised both hands towards the ceiling in a gesture of acceptance. It was then I noticed the gold band on the ring finger of his left hand. I don't know why I hadn't noticed it before, but a streak of disappointment ran over me just the same.

TWENTY-FOUR
Greta

Once we were in the hall, Judy gave me the once-over and nodded her approval. "Good job, girl. The necklace is a nice touch."

"Glad you like it. You gave it to me." We walked back into the great room where a cowboy was offering gargantuan margaritas. Waving off the drink, I drained the Pellegrino and put the empty glass on the tray. "You must have dressed Cecily as well. She's almost attractive."

"Just some black dress I didn't need anymore." She surveyed the room to see if anything was amiss and, satisfied that all was in place, she looped her arm through mine. "C'mon. Let's find Gene. He really wants you to meet Roman."

We weaved our way through the party, Judy gracing her guests with a smile here and there as she dragged me along. We finally landed in an alcove with a surprised looking elk head mounted above the gas fireplace. Gene was locked in deep conversation with a man who could have been his doppelganger. The two men looked like brothers. They were both tall with rigid postures, full heads of silver hair and tanned faces that come from spending an abundant amount of time outdoors. Gene saw me and smiled the white celebrity smile that the north of fifty crowd seems to be wearing these days. No yellow teeth in this room.

"Greta, I want you to meet Roman Judge," he said, adding, "the world famous author."

"Working on it," the author said with false modesty. He took both my hands in his and squeezed them in a way just a bit too familiar. "I've heard so much about you, it's nice to finally meet you in person."

"When I told Roman about you being on the ski patrol, he

insisted on meeting you," Gene added. "He's working on a book with a woman patroller in it and he wants information from the source."

"I feel like we've met before, but I don't think I've seen you on the mountain," the author said, still holding onto my hands.

"Maybe the Bugaboo?" I asked, trying to pry my hands from his.

"You're a member there?"

"Coat check."

"Perhaps," he said. He released my hands just as I was getting ready to yank them back. "But your night job isn't important. I'd really rather talk about your day job if you don't mind. I find the physics of it intriguing. I mean, it's hard for me to envision a woman your size bringing a two-hundred-pound man down the hill in a toboggan. And with your looks I'll bet there are guys who fake injuries just to meet you."

He laughed at his own joke, but I didn't. Though it's not something I trade in, I know I'm attractive. This gift, or curse, depending on how you look at things, has been brought to my attention so many times in my life it's boring. I've never used my looks to advance myself and resent the way my appearance works against me when it comes to people taking me seriously.

"You'd be surprised what good-looking women can do," I countered. "I can hike and ski the Highlands Bowl three times in a day and bike up Indy Pass in two hours. I can bench press ninety-five pounds and deadlift twice my body weight. I regularly set off charges on avalanche-prone slopes. If you were on a plane that was going down, you'd definitely want me seated at the emergency exit.

"And I had to work twice as hard as any man to get on ski patrol," I added.

Roman was quiet for a minute and then raised his hands above his head to clap. "Bravo," he said. "That's just the kind of spirit my character needs."

"Greta is also quite a reader," Judy piped in, steering the topic in a different direction. She knew how much pandering bugged me. She turned her eyes back to the room outside the alcove as any proper hostess would. She'd delivered me to Gene's friend, and it was time to get back to her guests. When she saw a couple of new arrivals breech the top of the stairs, she grabbed Gene and peeled him off. "Look, it's Linda and Wally. Let's go and say hello."

They disappeared into the crowd leaving me alone with the author. "And you're a reader too," he said. "What do you like to read?

"A little bit of everything. Dickens to Danielle Steel. Depends on my mood." Truth is when I'm not skiing, I'm happiest in the Barca with a fire blazing and a book in hand taking me to a new destination. I pivoted and asked him impishly, "So what do you write? Romance novels?"

"I'm not that talented," he laughed. "No, I write horror. Steven King kind of stuff. My latest is *Blowhard*. Have you read it?"

I had seen the book on the stack of bestsellers at the local bookstore, but hadn't picked it up. I shy away from horror. I'm sure it serves a purpose in the literary world, but it's not for me. I equate my reading with eating. Sometimes I'm in the mood for fast food, sometimes gourmet. I'm just never in the mood for organs.

"My TBR pile is stacked high, but I'm thinking about getting a copy," I lied to be polite.

He might have made my skin crawl a bit, but I wasn't heathen enough to insult the man. "I'm not much into horror. I get enough of it at work."

"Let me get a copy over to you. You might change your mind," he offered.

"That's all right. I'll buy my own. Just give me a big tip at the Bug next time."

He laughed. "May I ask what you're reading now? I always like to know what readers are reading."

"I'm currently up to my eyeballs in *Macbeth*. For my Shakespeare class."

"And you say you're not into horror? The lady doth protest too much methinks. Lady Macbeth is quite the horror. She's also one of my favorite characters."

"Then you must enjoy difficult women."

He gave me a wry smile and started to answer when we were interrupted by a rail-thin woman, her ears corked with diamonds large enough to throw her off balance. She walked up and tapped him on the arm. You could tell she was used to getting her way. Without even acknowledging that we were in conversation, she commanded, "Roman, you simply have to meet Jonathan Rauch. He's running for a senate seat in Texas and he swears he's a huge fan."

Roman gestured towards me and said, "Sherrie, as you may have noticed I am engaged in conversation with this fascinating young woman, so the senator will just have to wait."

Her face fell, but she quickly recovered it. "OK, but after dinner then, love. We don't want to wait until your book tour comes to Dallas."

"Actually," I chimed in, "I was just about to visit the powder room, so he's all yours."

The woman took his arm. "Well isn't that just fine. We won't have to wait for the book tour after all."

"I'll see you at the table," said Roman as the earrings led him away.

I gave him a polite smile.

TWENTY-FIVE
Greta

I killed time in the downstairs powder room sitting on a closed toilet seat reading W.H. Auden poems from a collection of quick reads on the shelf behind the toilet. The sound of a clanging dinner bell penetrated the silence. Figuring I couldn't put it off any longer, I headed back to the party. I ran into Jason Click coming down the stairs as I was going up, an iron triangle and rod in his hands.

"They're waiting for you up there, Greta. Judy made me keep ringing until my arm was ready to fall off," he said pointedly. Then he added, "I didn't get a chance to tell you this when you came in, but when I heard you were going to be here tonight, I brought you something. I'll give it to you when you leave."

"Well that's mysterious."

"Nothing mysterious about it. Just a book." He started back down the stairs but not before adding, "Praise the Lord."

Please not a Bible, I thought. I continued up the stairs and, as intended, was the last to arrive at the table. This was not a ploy for attention. It was in hopes of keeping conversation to a minimum. No one seemed to notice my tardiness except Roman who stood to pull out my chair in a 'chivalry's not dead' gesture. And Judy—who gave me the evil eye for coming to the table late.

All eyes were fixed on the guest of honor, Humphrey Gibbons, who was holding court in a loud Texas twang. The oil baron was a larger than life sort of guy with a big round face and a bald head that made it impossible to know what color his hair had once been. It wasn't until I noticed his lashless eyes and lack of brow that I realized he had alopecia. The only color on his face was a pair of large tortoiseshell glasses that made his already small eyes seem smaller.

I was taking my seat when the guest of honor stopped speaking. I guess he had taken notice of my arrival after all. Then it dawned on me that the entire table had gone quiet and all eyes were now on me.

"And who have we here?" he asked in a slow Southern drawl.

Gene responded on my behalf. "This is our ski patroller, Greta Westerlind." I squirmed uncomfortably. There's nothing that bothers me more than being the center of attention. Gene took advantage of the break in conversation to introduce me around the table. Seated next to Gibbons was his wife, Mary, a small, dark and timid woman who was an anomaly in a room full of loquacious blondes. Her hello was so frail, it almost made me feel sorry for her. To the other side of Gibbons sat two couples from Dallas. The first couple included the woman with the massive diamond earrings and her husband, who was wearing a cowboy hat. The second couple were friends of theirs looking to buy a place in Aspen. Something simple, the wife said. No more than six bedrooms. I forgot their names as quickly as Gene said them.

Next to the six-bedroom woman sat Neverman, *Oh we already know each other*. Roman was seated to my right and to my left was an elegant-looking man in his mid-forties with the profile of a Roman coin and a thick wave of swept-back black hair. He was introduced as Dr. Peter Emmanuel, the doctor Cecily had referred to when handing out table numbers. The oil baron was quick to sing his praise. "This man is a miracle worker," he said. "He flies around the world saving lives."

The surgeon raised a hand in a gesture indicating 'enough.' "Thank you, but please. I do not deserve praise for doing my job," he said in heavily accented English.

"Nonsense," Gibbons countered. "This man found a liver for my son when it was said to be impossible. He saved my boy's life. I owe him a depth of gratitude." He raised his glass and everyone else at the table followed suit, raising theirs. I raised my water. "To Dr. Emmanuel," he said.

Glasses clinked, people drank, and Humphrey Gibbons took back the dais without missing a beat. He picked up where he'd left off in a diatribe against renewable energy, informing those present about the inefficiencies and unreliability of the new green technologies. I wanted to ask Mr. Gibbons if he recognized how thin the snow cover was this year despite the recent snow. Or if he noticed how we get a massive dump and then go fifteen days without a single snowflake. Or if he heard about the wildfires plaguing us or how the average temperature was getting higher every year.

In deference to Judy and Gene, I kept my mouth zipped and my opinion to myself. Until the oil baron turned to me out of the blue and said in his best down home voice, "Now you look like a sensible young lady. What do you think about all this natural energy nonsense?"

While I hadn't intended to make any waves, I wasn't about to sell out. "It's my understanding that switching to solar energy may actually allow us to continue skiing here in the future without having to move the base village up a thousand feet. If we're not already too late."

There was a stunned silence and then Gibbons turned away from me and went back to his condemnation of natural energy as if I hadn't spoken a word. I began wondering how long dinner was going to last and if it would be considered rude to leave before dessert.

"Loudmouth soup," Roman whispered from his side. "Man loves to hear himself speak."

"Well it wouldn't be so bad if he wasn't shirking off the end of our world as we know it," I said.

"Yes, but what you were saying means the end of the world as he knows it."

Gibbons's voice turned to white noise as I informed Roman of the risks we ran if we didn't do something about climate change. Natural disasters like wildfires, droughts, heatwaves. He tolerated me for a minute before changing the subject back to what he was really interested in. My job. Flashing me the same white-toothed smile as Gene, he said, "I hope you don't mind that I asked to be seated next to you. You know my latest book has a female ski patroller in it, and I'm hoping you can share some of your experiences first-hand. But can I ask you something first?"

"Fire away."

"How is it you became a ski patroller and not a supermodel?"

Unable to tell if he was baiting me or not, I rose to the occasion. "Because supermodels can't risk skiing. One good face plant and it's over." He marinated that for a minute and then laughed aloud.

The time had come for a drink. I looked around for the server and caught the eye of the pilot sitting at the table behind us. As you may have guessed, he gave me a wink. I did not wink back, but I did get a margarita. I took a good slug. And then another.

"Gene tells me you were a ski instructor before joining the patrol," Roman pushed, trying to keep the conversation alive. "What made you quit teaching?"

"Well I wasn't exactly the best ski instructor," I admitted, the margarita doing its job and turning me into a kinder, gentler person. It wasn't Roman's fault that Judy and Gene had forced me to come to the dinner. "I could teach the mechanics of skiing, but I had a problem understanding fear. The psychology of it. Which can be a problem with adult beginners. I just didn't get what could be so terrifying about a green run."

"How about being on two sticks that have a mind of their own," he said. "That's how I felt when I took my first ski class. I remember being scared to death. Would have hung up the skis then and there if my wife and I hadn't invested in a house here. Now I'm good with the double blacks. Don't look great, but I get down 'em."

"Your wife's not here tonight?"

"My wife's not here any night. She left me some time ago."

"Oh. I'm sorry to hear that."

Beginning to feel even friendlier, I turned to the doctor on my left. "I think I met your pilot earlier," I said, wondering if that was a slur I heard in my voice.

"Winks? Great guy. And an extraordinary pilot. Don't know what I'd do without him. He's my go-to guy." He picked up his wine glass, and I couldn't help but notice his hands. They were as elegant as the rest of him with long smooth fingers and buffed nails. The hands of a surgeon. Dr. Emmanuel's hands were smoother than those of anyone I hung out with, male or female.

Conversation was interrupted as salads were served. The Dallas woman asked Dr. Emmanuel a question, and he turned away to answer her, leaving me staring at his shoulder. With no other option except to stare at my plate, I turned back to the author.

Thankfully, he didn't say anything more about being a supermodel, or even ski patrol for that matter. He asked me how I ended up in Aspen and I gave him the condensed version of pulling into town with a few thousand bucks and Judy saving my ass. About my days as a maid at the Deep Powder Lodge. About Sam leaving me the A-frame.

"And how is it that you've never married?" he asked.

"Just hasn't happened," I replied to one of my least favorite and most frequently asked questions on the planet. "I love skiing more than just about anything, and I haven't found a guy who feels the same. One worth marrying anyhow. Maybe family and marriage aren't in the cards for me. My immediate goal is climbing Everest in May."

"Everest. Very impressive," he said. "And after that?"

"Getting my degree."

"And that's where Lady Macbeth comes in?"

"Exactly. Shakespeare has really opened my eyes to the essence of true writing, comedy as well as tragedy. I completely understand why the guy's reaped all the praise he has. He's truly mapped out humankind, our shortcomings and foibles as well as our admirable traits—the latter in short supply as compared to the former."

"Your favorite play?" he asked.

"*Midsummer's Night Dream.*"

"Mine's *Taming of the Shrew*," he said. We both laughed.

Though I was teed up to dislike the man, it was truly enjoyable to be in a conversation that didn't revolve around money, sports or weather. I found myself taking a liking to him, thinking if he wasn't so much older, I could go for him. But if I ever do find that someone, he'll have to be able to do laps of the bowl with me twenty years from now. Not sitting in a wheelchair with a blanket on his lap.

Roman's gaze shifted to my now empty glass. "Would you like another?" he asked.

"I'd better hold off," I said. "I'm driving."

His next words set me straight in my chair. "I understand you're the one who found the hand up Gulch Creek. That had to be terribly disconcerting."

Maybe not as disconcerting as him knowing about it. The fact that I was involved had not been made public, not even in the paper. I cursed Judy silently for sharing that knowledge with her husband, but I should have expected no less. They were married after all. But Gene sharing it with Roman was an entirely different thing. Did he think his friend could use it in a book?

"Disconcerting is a mild way of putting it," I responded.

"Any thoughts on where it might have come from?"

"Probably some unfortunate hiker had an animal encounter," I replied, playing dumb.

"Or maybe it was cut off?" He must have read the horrified look on my face, because he added, "I told you I write horror. I'm always going to the dark side."

"You know what?" I said. "I will take another drink."

The drink arrived and I should have known something wasn't quite right when I started sharing my childhood woes with him.

TWENTY-SIX
Greta

Day three

I awakened in Sam's old bed wrapped in the blankets like a cocoon. My head felt like the receiving end of a bowling pin and my mouth was the Gobi Desert. The good news: I was alone. The bad news: I was naked. The last thing I remembered from the night before was taking my first sip of that second margarita. Well, I remember a little more. Somewhere in there was a vague recollection of giving that ass wipe Gibbons a piece of my mind and then jumping up to dance with Neverman. Dancing with Neverman? "What the hell?" I said aloud to no one.

The bedroom door was shut and Floyd was whining and scratching from the other side. "Coming," I called out in a rattle that at an earlier time would be my own voice. I unwrapped myself and tried to stand, but the headache pulled me back down. Oh man, I hadn't felt like this since . . . well . . . since that night I sat up with Evie drinking vodka. Upon further consideration, that was bad but this was annihilation. I couldn't recall feeling this bad any time in the past five years. Make that ten. Make that ever.

Floyd's scratching grew more impatient. I tried standing again, but the thought of being upright turned my stomach. I got down on my hands and knees and crawled to the door. I opened it and Floyd treated me to a reproach-filled look before running for the front door. Poor guy really wanted out.

Shifting my focus to his needs, I pulled myself to my feet and stumbled across the room to where he sat whining. When I opened the door, the blast of arctic air that smacked me in the face brought me closer to this world. The Goner parked in front of the house made me wonder how it had gotten there. I sure hoped I hadn't driven it. I had no recollection of coming home, much less getting undressed. Those shades were all the way down.

Floyd ran into the yard and gave me the evil eye while he conducted his business. The landline started to ring, and I left the doorway to stumble into the kitchen, nearly tripping over the cord on my way. I stared at the phone wondering if I really wanted to pick it up and decided to let the call go to the machine. A moment later my voice echoed through the room. *It's Greta. I'm either on the hill or on my way to Everest. Leave a message and I'll get back to you.*

The prolonged beep was followed by Judy's voice. "Greta, it's me. Call when you get this. I want to make sure you're OK. You were pretty drunk last night." *You think?* Shaking off the dread of knowledge, I called her back, hoping she could offer some insight as to why I woke up naked.

"Well you sure fell off a cliff last night." Her words were both ominous and teasing, filled with unanswered riddles.

A spark of anger flared. She had guilted me into going to a party that I didn't want to go to in the first place, and now I was down the rabbit hole. Judy iced the anger cake by adding, "Do you remember going home?"

Back when Judy, Evie and I used to bar hop together, we had a joke about the five most dreaded words after a night of drinking. *Do you remember what you . . .* You could fill in the blank with a number of verbs: did, said, ate, sang. And if you changed what to who . . . well, that opened entirely different avenues.

"As a matter of fact, I do not, but I imagine you already figured that out."

"Yeah. I've never seen you that drunk, Greta. Roman said you only had two margaritas that he knew of. I mean they were strong, but for you to go off the deep end like that was weird. Are you taking some medication that doesn't mix with tequila?"

"No. But my head sure thinks it had a lot more than two drinks. It feels more like I downed a bottle of mezcal and ate the worm. So give it to me straight. What do I have to suffer over?"

"Let's just say you were loquacious. And you sure weren't subtle about your politics. Luckily Roman managed to shut you up before you started a civil war." Her tone lightened. "It was pretty funny actually. Telling a bunch of Texans that they better cash in their stock since the end of oil was in sight. You should have seen the looks on their faces. Oh and you danced with Neverman."

"I was hoping that was a hallucination." Images of my arms draped around the neck of my nemesis punched through the veil of the night before. Then I remembered the pilot watching me from the next table. The thought of making an ass out of myself in front of him made me feel even worse. I skipped to the next unknown. "How did I get home? I can't imagine I drove, but my car is here."

"Roman drove you in his car and Paul followed him in the Goner. We figured you might need your car in the morning. If you lived." This time she laughed aloud.

It was time to end this conversation. "Hey, I'm on the gondola and almost up top."

"You liar. You're at home on your landline."

"Oh right. Look, I gotta go. I'm gonna barf." That was no lie.

When Floyd came back inside, he found me in the bathroom with my head hanging over the toilet. He nudged me and walked into the kitchen where he stood sulking beside his empty bowl. I got up and duly gave him food and fresh water. For the first time since peeling my eyes open, I checked the time. It was nearly ten o'clock. I was way late for work. I contemplated calling in sick and decided against it. I needed fresh air, but even more pressing, I needed to face Neverman before the unknown grew too large.

I dressed for work and was almost out the door when it dawned on me that it was March the tenth. Sam's anniversary. Five years ago today, I came home to find his unmoving figure in the Barcalounger. A wave of melancholy passed through me over the loss of his kind and gentle friendship. I hoped they had mountains where he was and that the runs were steep and the snow was deep.

TWENTY-SEVEN
Judy

Judy surveyed the scene of the crime. Everything was back in place as if there had never been a party. The dining tables were gone, the bar taken down, the Lone Star flag folded and put away for another time. She thought about what an ass Greta had made of herself. Frankly she didn't understand it. It was really out of character for her. Maybe stress over Evie had driven her to the edge, but still the show she put on had been mortifying. It was a good thing Humphrey had taken her insults in his stride, actually finding some of them funny. Like when she said anyone taking a cruise deserved to be quarantined.

Gene was already up and gone, skiing with Roman again. She'd love to be a fly on the wall for their conversation today, wondering if Roman had gotten any worthwhile material from Greta before she went over the edge. He certainly got some material about ski patrollers behaving badly.

With the cleaning crews gone, she had the place to herself though she was expecting Cecily at any moment. Having flawlessly pulled off the Texas dinner, it was time for them to go back to finalizing Gene's surprise party. She couldn't believe the party was in only five days. Time was melting away faster than the spring snow.

She was drinking a cappuccino and looking at her calendar when the doorbell rang. She scurried down the stairs wondering who it could be. Cecily had the entry code and usually let herself in. When she opened the door, she was surprised to see Jason Click standing on the front porch in his ski gear. His brown eyes met hers before shifting over her shoulder into the entry hall where he'd been taking coats the night before.

"Sorry if I'm buggin' you," he said, "but I left something in the closet last night. Hope you don't mind if I grab it. It'll just take a minute."

"No, of course not, Jason. Come in."

He disappeared into the walk-in and came out carrying a bag. "I brought a copy of Roman's first book for Greta. I was gonna give it to Greta last night, but it didn't seem like a good idea towards the end."

"No, I'd say Greta was a little under the weather last night," Judy conceded, wanting him on his way out now that he'd found what he came for. He'd been a weird roommate in the Victorian and an even weirder co-worker at the Bugaboo. His oddness had always made her skin crawl, and it had gotten worse since he found religion. He held his ground like he was waiting for her to say something else. Then he took the book out of the bag and held it out to her, giving her no other option than to take it from him. The cover art was an empty twin bed in a spare log cabin. The title was in bold black letters: ***THE ONLY WAY OUT***. She remembered seeing it in Gene's library once. "I didn't know you were a fan of Roman's."

"I guess I have to be since I live in his ADU," he said with a smarmy smile. "Have you read it?"

"No, I haven't," she replied.

"You really should. It's his first, but it's his best." He took the book back and tucked it under his arm. He started out the door and then stopped on the threshold as if he couldn't decide whether to leave or stay. She was closing the door on him in her mind when he gave her that strange smile and said, "Remember Jesus saves."

She walked back up the stairs thinking of calling the caterer to request Jason not work her parties in the future. She went into the kitchen to wait for Cecily. The girl was late again. It was so unlike her, and she wondered what in hell was keeping her this time.

If she'd looked out the window, she would have seen her assistant had already arrived and was in the driveway talking to Jason Click.

TWENTY-EIGHT
Greta

Bolstered by ibuprofen and two cups of coffee, I closed the door on Floyd and headed to work. He was disappointed, but I had no patience for him today. My parting words to him were that I'd be home soon enough. The good thing about being late is it makes for a shortened day.

It had snowed during the night, not that I would have noticed, but I had to shovel off the Goner. I drove into town with the window down, hoping the fresh air would clear out some of the residue from the previous night. I parked in my regular spot and hustled over to the gondola, cringing at the line of skiers spilling into the plaza.

Ski patrollers typically board through the private lesson lane and get their own gondola car. But with the fresh snow there was a plethora of moneyed people in the private lessons lane, and at a thousand bucks a day it's a common courtesy for patrollers to share a gondola car with them. Most of the privates love riding with a patroller and usually pepper us with questions the entire way up. Feeling less than conversant, much less courteous, I got in the regular line and climbed into a gondola with five snowboarders, fairly certain they would have no interest in me. The gamble paid off. They had far more important things to talk about. I was invisible as far as they were concerned.

"Dude, d'you see Joser stomp that backie on S one yesterday?"

"It was crazy, dude. I thought he was going to bite it, but he pressured through it. Totally chill."

"Yah, he was like totally grinding it out. It was super gnarly."

"Gnarly? Dude, you're talkin' like my grandmother."

They burst into laughter and segued into the evening's plans which included firing off a spliff before heading to Belly Up to meet some hotties. I pressed my helmet against the frosted window and dialed them out for the rest of the ride as I pulled into myself to reconstruct the evening.

I started with turning my car over to Paul in the driveway. Then dodging conversation with Jason in the entry. Neverman coming up behind me on the stairs. Meeting Winks in the library. Talking books with Roman beneath the giant elk head. Roman next to me at the table when I ordered my first margarita. Trying to rationally explain global warming to Humphrey Gibbons. Ordering my second margarita. That's when things started to blur. I remembered telling Roman Judge how awful my mother had been, and there was a vague recollection of telling the Texan off, but OMG had I really danced with Neverman? According to Judy, Roman had driven me home followed by Paul driving the Goner. I imagine they would have made sure I got inside all right, before Roman took Paul back to his ADU at Judy's.

None of that explained why I had woken up naked. I never sleep in the nude. Not in a house where at night the thermostat is set just north of the temperature in Milwaukee on a mild winter day. Don't need to waste propane while sleeping. My flannel pajamas live under my pillow in the loft, which is where they were this morning.

Another mystery was why did I sleep in Sam's room? Had Roman and Paul decided I was too drunk to climb up to the loft and put me in Sam's room. That would answer why I slept there, but it didn't answer why I was naked. Common sense told me I would have crawled under the covers with my clothes on, but common sense was in short supply last night. The only explanation was the inexplicable actions of a drunken mind.

I thought of my mother and how she'd often black out when drinking. It wasn't unusual for her to come home with some conquest from the bar down the street and not remember bringing him home until she walked in the kitchen and saw us sharing breakfast with the stranger the next morning. But more often than not the suitors were gone before she woke up, the unlocked front door the only clue that someone else had been in the house.

But there was this one guy named Matthew I could tell she really cared about. He drove a Mercedes and wore expensive clothes and a gold watch. She'd put on make-up and dress extra special when he was coming over to take her out to dinner. They'd been together for about a month when they stumbled into the house late one night after the bars closed. There was a lot of noise before they went into her bedroom, and then things quickly went quiet. Evidently Mom had passed out. So Matthew took it upon himself to try his luck with her thirteen-year-old daughter in the room next door.

I awoke with a man in my bed, pressing what felt like a piece of wood to my backside. I remember being terrified and oddly enough embarrassed at the same time, because I had my period and was wearing a Kotex. When I tried to scream, he covered my mouth with his hand. He was pulling my panties down and I was fighting him as much as I could being half his size and weight. Things might have gotten really bad if I hadn't somehow managed to reach out and knock the lamp off the nightstand.

Within seconds the overhead light came on, and there was Toby, standing in the doorway with a butcher knife in his hand. Even at thirteen, he was unusually strong. He pulled Matthew off me and wielded the knife at him, threatening to cut off his balls. That guy hightailed it out of our house, never to be seen again.

My mother slept through the whole ordeal and looked mystified when she came out to breakfast the next morning and he was gone. Later, when she saw the broken lamp in my bedroom, she didn't ask any questions. But there were no more strange men after that.

In my early Aspen days, I'd been in full party mode, free of most responsibility in this life and feeling my oats. On occasion I'd wake up with one of the latest additions to the ski tuner or bartender community in paradise. Then one day it dawned on me I was becoming my mother. That's when I straightened out my act and put a stop to that kind of behavior. There was no way I was going to become my mother.

Now after last night, I wasn't so sure.

The gondola slid into the terminal and the boarders piled off ahead of me, in full argument over which run to shred first. My phone was vibrating, and when I saw it was my brother, I answered quickly before the call could go to voicemail. The very sound of his voice was the soothing balm I needed at the moment.

"Twice in two days. I'm starting to feel honored. What time is it there anyhow?"

"Let's just say it's time for bed. The reason I'm calling again is I had this super strange dream about you last night. You were on your deck and no matter what you did, you couldn't get into your house and you were going to freeze to death. It was so real I wanted to check in to make sure you're OK."

They talk about mothers bolting upright from sleep when their sons are killed in far off lands. Or people experiencing a sense of danger and moving out of harm's way before a ceiling caves in. Are there psychic connections between siblings in this world? I couldn't answer that. What I did know was that my brother had dialed into my distress and was calling from halfway round the world.

"Yeah, I'm OK except I have the mother of all hangovers. Oh, and I found my best friend's hand in the wilderness and then my car was stolen while I was searching for the rest of her. Otherwise everything is great." I opted to leave out the part about waking up naked. He was quiet long enough that I feared the line had gone dead. But then his voice came back on again, calm reliable Toby, my true North.

"Your best friend's hand? Man, Grets, it's sounding more dangerous there than it is here. Are you sure you're safe?"

"Of course I'm safe. I'm in Aspen. What could possibly happen to me here?"

"Let's just say I have a bad feeling. I'm catching your stress over the line. You sure someone isn't gaslighting you?" There was a rumbling in the background and then a bunch of screaming voices. "Listen I gotta go. I'll reach out in the next couple of days. You take care of yourself, promise me."

"Me take care of myself? What about you?" Our call was cut off before he could answer. "Aren't you the one in a war zone?" I said to dead air.

TWENTY-NINE
Greta

When I walked into the shack, fellow patroller Rob Winter was manning the radio and munching on a slab of pizza poached from the Sundeck. Remnants of cheese clung to his dark beard like melting snow. Rob was the type who was eating when he wasn't skiing, though his slim frame belied it. He smiled at me and kept talking to the patroller on the radio between bites. There didn't seem to be anyone else in the hut and a window of normal opened in my turbulent being. That is until Neverman's head popped up from behind the beat-up sofa. He was obviously pissed at me, his grey curls shaking as he made a gun with his pointer finger and thumb, his middle finger on the trigger.

"You missed our meeting this morning," he said coldly. The way he was glaring at me was something I would usually write off, but the hangover was making me paranoid so it carried weight. The image of me draped around his neck flashed uncomfortably. Normal had morphed back into abnormal. "What in hell happened to you last night anyhow?"

"I keep asking myself the same question."

"No shit," he said, his eyes fixed on me laser-like. "An act like that could give patrol a bad name."

I worked hard to hold his glare without shriveling to the ground. He appeared ready to say more, but thought better of it. The crackle of a radio call emanated from the front followed by Winter's voice. Neverman looked around to make sure no one was in earshot and said, "You don't remember, do you?"

"You mean dancing with you?" I went for the defensive. "Sorry if that offended you."

"No, I mean later." The words whipsawed me, and my brain shifted into overdrive searching for the missing memory. The image of waking up in Sam's room naked this morning flashed through my brain, and I killed it just as quickly. No way.

The thump of ski boots behind me saved me from the rest of the conversation.

"If it isn't the missing link." I turned to see Singh in the doorway, his head barely clearing the door frame. His goggles were pulled up on his helmet and his black eyes shone along with his smile. I told him once that I thought he was the most cheerful man in Aspen and he retorted that his smile was a reflection of his happiness at being a ski patroller in Aspen instead of a cardiologist in Delhi.

But friend that he was, upon taking a closer look at me, the ever-present smile dissolved. "What happened to you?" he asked, his words echoing Neverman's, albeit kinder and gentler.

"I'd rather not discuss it," I said. Leaving Neverman's question unanswered, I turned tail and shrank from the room.

The spring sun was blinding despite my dark-lensed goggles, sharpening the edges of every tree and object, intensifying an already excruciating headache. The insulation of cloud cover, or better yet a snowstorm, would have been far preferable. Unfiltered sun at 11,000 feet can make a hangover problematic. Add in an ample dose of shame and it is torture.

I skied down the Ridge toward the mid-mountain chair, keeping my eyes open for any needy skiers. As my skis cut through the billions of featherlike crystals, my headache started to lift and my spirits improved. I was one with the mountain, locked in an embrace only a skier can understand. No amount of psychiatry could ever equal the therapy of a few powder runs to help lift demons.

I stopped at the convergence of Spar and Copper, where Neverman had assigned me to police reckless riders merging into the tight area. For the next two hours, I flagged skiers traveling at the speed of sound around the SLOW sign, reminding them this was the easiest way down and they had to respect other skiers. Telling them if they didn't slow down I was going to pull their passes. It's a tiresome job, and believe me, you don't make any friends. By the time Meghan showed up to relieve me, I was more than ready to turn over the policing job to her.

The rest of the day was uneventful, aside from popping an injured skier's dislocated shoulder back into place. By the time I hit the base at the end of the day, my headache had eased to tolerable. But while my physical well-being had improved, my psyche was worse.

I decided to pay Marynell a visit. Of course, she would have read about the hand in the local paper, but it still wasn't public knowledge that the hand was Evie's. I wanted to be the one to tell her before it was. But more than anything, I needed to see her for me.

THIRTY
Greta

I parked behind Clive's beat-up old pickup with its two flat tires, half buried in snow. Not that the flat tires made any difference. Marynell hadn't driven that truck in years. In fact, that truck hadn't moved since Clive died and it barely moved before then. But that truck had something to say. It froze a moment in the history of a mining town becoming a ski town. It paid tribute to the characters that once made it up.

The words 'come in' echoed from inside before I had a chance to knock. Not that anyone ever needed to knock on Marynell's door. It was never locked. Her home was always open to visitors as it had been when we worked at the Powder and forever before that and since. Working at the Powder had been more than a job and a place to live. It had been a godsend. Marynell helped me make life in Aspen work, but more important she gave me the best advice I've ever had. *If you want something hard enough, Greta, you'll find a way. But you need tunnel vision.*

"I was beginning the think you sold your house and moved away without saying goodbye," she chided me as I slipped off my snow-covered boots inside the closet-sized entrance. She was seated in her usual spot on the flowered love seat in the window of the room she called her salon. Her hands were busy with a half-embroidered pillow in her lap.

"As much as Sam's kids would love it, I'm not going anywhere," I responded. "Like you, I'm here for the duration." I slapped my hands together to warm them and sat down on the facing love seat. "I've been meaning to stop over, but I've been super busy with work and my night classes and my shift at the Bug. It seems there's no free time."

My nose went to the air—which was laced with the smell of chocolate chip cookies. "What's with the cookies? You expecting somebody?"

"No, they're for the seniors at the center. Sheriff stuck his big head in day before yesterday and ate so many I had to bake a whole new batch."

There was no sense in pointing out to Marynell that she was more senior than most of the seniors in the senior center. That concept of being old would have been alien to her. As if reading my thoughts, she put her embroidery aside and disappeared into the kitchen, trailing a long oxygen cord behind her. I sat listening to the rhythmic pish of the machine, wondering how to broach the bad news I'd come to share.

She emerged from the kitchen a minute later carrying a tray of cookies and milk that she put down on the coffee table. I took a cookie and felt myself relax as the chocolate melted on my tongue. I was just washing it down with big gulp of milk when she surprised me by saying, "I see you and your dog found something up Gulch Creek."

The milk nearly came out my nose. "The paper didn't name anyone. How did you know it was me?"

"I didn't. But I do now."

I put the glass down on the table. "Well it was more Floyd than me. But whoever gets credit, it pretty much freaked me out."

"I can imagine. Clive and I found some bones, oh about twenty years ago, in a gulley just past Snowmass Lake. Turned out to be the remains of some hiker who'd gone missing maybe ten years before. The poor guy must've slipped and fell, hit his head and that was it. The animals pretty much cleaned him off, but there were still a few rags hanging onto the body and a decrepit backpack beside it.

"Finding those remains stuck with me for a long time, especially being the way Clive and I loved getting way out there in the wilderness. But the more I thought about it the more I thought, what a great way to go. Sure beats being killed in a car wreck or mugged in some big city." She was quiet for a moment. "Or inch by inch with cancer like your mother."

"Don't I know."

"I like to think Cappie went fast." She didn't belabor her daughter's death but went straight into another question. "So are you going to tell me who that hand belonged to?"

Our eyes met straight on. The squinting blue lights in her weathered face weren't going to let me get off easy. She knew, and she knew I knew. I answered with a simple nod that said, *Yes. Evie.*

Anguish waved over her face and disappeared just as fast. "I figured as much. I suppose I shouldn't ask how you know it's hers, but I'll ask anyway."

I told her about breaking rank and file with Dan to check it out. She seemed angry that Dan hadn't told her when he visited, but I explained he could get in a lot of trouble if anyone knew what we'd done. "I mean, we've pretty much known she's dead. Finding the hand just verified it."

Marynell's eyes drifted off in memory. "It figures she'd be wearing that ring to the end. I remember how she never took it off. She told me how it was a treasure from her grandmother and how her grandmother was a far better mother to her than her own. Poor thing. Itinerant child of the road."

"We were all itinerants in our own way. You were a better mother to all of us than any of our own."

Marynell picked up a linen square from her tray and dabbed at a tear forming in the corner of her right eye. "I don't have to tell you having you girls working at the lodge that winter was the best thing that could have happened to me. Three motherless girls and one daughterless mother. Quite the combo. Clive's silences would have killed me. You girls kept me going with all your noise and rowdiness. And you brought him back too. He hadn't smiled for a year before you came to work for us."

When we first started working for Marynell and Clive, we'd heard they'd lost a daughter. But we didn't know how, and we didn't want to ask. But we wanted to find an answer to the long silences. So one afternoon Evie and I went to the library to scroll through the archives of the local papers. She was the one who stumbled on the headline dated five years earlier. LOCAL GIRL DIES ON EVEREST.

Despite her dabbing at it, the tear escaped Marynell's right eye just the same and traveled along her silver hairline. "This takes me back to losing Cappie. But you know, people like Cappie and Evie take risks to feel alive. It just beats them sometimes. Evie never should have gone out alone in a storm like that."

Silence ensued as each of us retreated into her own sadness at the loss of Evie with Marynell's memories of her daughter still raw as well. A sharp rap on the door brought a welcome interruption. Marynell pulled back the lace curtain on the picture window to see who it was.

"Oh drat, it's my miserable neighbor," she said, giving me a sideways glance. "You know they're trying to make me get rid of the chickens. I wonder what's got his nose out of joint now. Answer it, will you?" She pushed the cookies aside on the table.

Glad for some distraction, I opened the door to see a guy wearing a cowboy hat, the hat looking as out of place on his head as if he was going to a costume party. His jeans had an ironed crease down the front and a discus-sized watch met the sleeve of his shearling jacket. His face registered confusion upon seeing me.

"I'm looking for Marynell," he said bypassing any sort of introduction. He appeared to have an agenda I didn't figure into. Yet.

"Marynell, you have a visitor." I stepped aside and the man walked into the entry like he owned it, his snow-covered boots parked in the middle of the hook rug.

"What can I do for you, Hayden?" she asked, returning to her embroidery without making any effort to further greet him.

"Look," he said in barely contained anger, speaking to her as if he was addressing an employee. "It's enough looking at one rusted piece of garbage in your driveway every day, but now you're adding another piece of shit to the collection? This is simply not permissible. We've invested a great deal of money in our house and we're not going to let you ruin our property values."

It took me a minute to realize the added piece of shit he

was talking about was the Goner. I admit my car had seen better times, but she was vintage and didn't deserve his insults. I was ready to give it to him myself, but Marynell took the lead.

"Look, Hayden, if you would like to come in for a chocolate chip cookie and some civilized conversation then you are more than welcome. But otherwise I would appreciate if you would take your skinny privileged ass off my property. I will park whatever and whomever I want in my own driveway."

"I'm sorry, sir," I interjected. "I'm with the city building department and that second vehicle in the driveway you are referring to is mine. We're just making a deal here for me to rent that driveway space from her. You know how tough parking has gotten in town." I put out my hand. "Gretchen Westerlind by the way. And your name is . . .?"

He ignored my feigned peace offering and looked more frustrated than when he'd first come in. Having decided to roll over on the vehicle argument for the time being, he leveled a final vicious comment at Marynell.

"And you know those chickens have to go? They are unsanitary, a real health hazard." The words came out part information and part a question he already had the answer to. He turned on a booted heel and stomped out the door. I was closing the door on his skinny privileged ass but I didn't get it closed quickly enough, because I could hear him talking to himself as he went down the walkway. "White trash," he said none too quietly.

"What in hell was that all about?" I asked.

"That was a miserable person trying to share his misery with the rest of the world instead of realizing what a beautiful place he's found." Then she laughed aloud, adding, "He's crazy if he thinks my chickens are going anywhere. Hah! He'd do better panning for gold in his back yard."

"Can he make you get rid of your chickens? You had those chickens long before they moved in. I can still taste those fresh scrambled eggs from staff breakfasts."

"They're saying we're not zoned rural. And like you just heard, he's been after Clive's truck too. Truth is, I was getting ready to have it towed off before they moved in, but now I'm just going to let it rust there. Might just take the tires off and put it on blocks while I'm at it. They come here and because they have money they think they own the town. That kind of money is destructive."

She stopped as she collected her thoughts and then continued in a melancholy voice. "Used to be you were close with your neighbors here. Now all these arrivers want to make us feel like we're the ones who don't belong. Thinking they can change what don't suit them. Well, if they think they're going to drive me out they've got another thing coming. I've said it before and I'll say it again, the only way I'm leaving this house is tits up."

"You tell 'em Marynell." I looked at my watch. It was nearly five. "I better get going. I've got to get home before Floyd tears the house up."

I grabbed a last cookie and was putting my coat on when a white Range Rover pulled up in front of the house on the other side of Marynell from the asswipe who had just paid us a visit. The house was built on the bones of a miner's shack like Marynell's, but with a two-story addition rising behind it.

Pulling the sheers aside, I could see a pair of silver heads talking in the front seat. The cookie stuck to the roof of my mouth when I realized that one of the white heads was Gene and the other was Roman Judge. If I were to make a list of people I currently wanted to avoid, Roman would top it.

I let the curtain fall back into place and scrunched myself as small as I could next to the window. Roman got out of the car and the Range Rover drove away. I pulled the curtain back ever so slightly and watched him start up the walk. Then he noticed my car and stopped. He put a gloved finger to his lips and hesitated, as if he was thinking of coming over to Marynell's. Then to my relief, he continued up the walk to his house.

"When did Roman Judge move next door?" I asked.

"The writer? He's been here for years. Nice enough guy. He had a pretty wife, but she left him a while ago. He keeps to himself and never bothers me. Much better neighbor than that one on the other side."

Once he let himself inside, I felt safe to leave. I was halfway out the door when I heard Marynell call me back.

"You still thinking of climbing her?"

"Everest? More than ever. But I still need to come up with some more cash. It's going to be tight."

"Well don't look to me for help. I don't need to tell you I'm against it," she said in a firm voice. She turned back to her embroidery as I closed the door behind me.

THIRTY-ONE
Dan

Dan Nichols picked up one last rib, thought better of it, and put it back on his plate. He flagged the waitress for his check and replayed the call he just received from Elsa Blanding. Things like that didn't happen here. Sure, there was Ted Bundy all those years back, but that was a one-off. Violent deaths here came from falling off peaks or being struck by lightning or getting buried in an avalanche. Never anything like this.

He paid his tab and pushed the chair back. It squeaked as he stood and unburdened it. What Elsa had told him seemed beyond belief, but there again, there were many things in this world that seemed beyond belief. Now that he knew, he felt duty-bound to deliver the information to Greta. Why did he feel like all he was doing these past few days was delivering bad news?

His thoughts drifted back to the first time he met Evie Kearney all those years back in the Jerome Bar. She was trouble then and Judy was too. When Greta landed in town all hell broke loose. He called them the class of 2000, female millennials testing the waters of a new life in a ski town, wild in the bars, seeing just how far they could push things. They were a pack that men drooled over, one of them better-looking than the next. Blonde, brunette, redhead, when those three walked into a bar, heads didn't turn, they swiveled. Given the opportunity he would have been happy to date any one of the three at the time, but it was Greta who tugged at his lonely heart.

Freshly divorced from a bad choice marriage, he'd met Greta when he pulled her over for speeding and it had been a coup de foudre, the term remembered from French class in the east long before. He'd given her a pass on the ticket and wrangled himself a date instead. He hadn't been excited about a date like that since prep school when he was really ruled by his hormones.

He'd taken her to the most expensive restaurant in town, which he'd immediately realized was a waste of money. It was clear she had no interest in a four-course French meal. He'd learned a lot about her at that meal though. She was open and honest, her life as transparent as her hair was blonde. She made no secret about being raised by a single mother who never told Greta who her father was, if she even knew. Evie and Judy carried baggage themselves, but the thing that set them apart was that Greta was comfortable in her skin—unlike Evie, tormented by her Bedouin past, and Judy, trying to cover up her blue collar roots.

Dan prided himself on analyzing people. In fact, his job was part psychologist. Years of dealing with people had taught him patience and an empathy he never would have achieved in the financial world, had he opted to stay. He never regretted turning his back on an entitled life and world to make Aspen his home, back when Aspen wasn't quite as entitled, back when there was only one stoplight and most of the alleys were unpaved. The town had a raw spirit and prankishness and character that had been beaten down by growing rules and regulations in recent years. Hell, he used to give drunk drivers a pass, telling them to walk home. Ignoring petty drugs and sometimes even drug dealers. None of that would fly now, that was for certain.

Greta had the spirit of the early ski bums. She was a purist, there for true love of the sport. As he had been before he blew out his knees and had to leave that aspect of life behind. He'd been puppy love crazy for her.

It didn't take long for him to learn the chemistry wasn't shared. He liked to blame their age difference, but that wasn't the reason. She just told him straight out she didn't have the jones for him. And that was that. So they'd become close friends, the next best thing he supposed. Not really. It's like second place is really first loser. His heart still picked up an extra beat every time he saw her.

He got his hat from the coat rack and set it on his head.

He usually liked any excuse to pay Greta a call, but not this time. He walked out and climbed into his sheriff's vehicle, shaking his head as he pulled from the curb, hoping Evie was at peace.

THIRTY-TWO
Greta

I took a quick detour to the post office on the way home. The USPS doesn't make deliveries up the pass and it's just as well. The post office was a great place to see other locals and catch up on the news. Sort of enforced socializing. It's an Aspen tradition that even carries over to the gazillionaires in the mansions on Red Mountain and Starwood who can't get mail delivery either. Of course that doesn't stop the convoy of Fedex and UPS trucks winding their way up the road to make deliveries.

I hadn't picked up my mail in a week, so my box was pretty full, most of it junk mail and solicitations from real estate agents. But there was one item that was clearly no solicitation—a manila envelope with a Vail postmark. I tore the envelope open and saw yet another legal action from Sam's son attempting to get me to vacate the A-frame. My headache came back with a vengeance. What better insult to his father's memory than to challenge his express wishes on the anniversary of his death. I'd already been down this road with Joel before and my lawyer assured me that the life estate Sam set up for me was airtight. Just the same, I made a mental note to call my lawyer first thing in morning.

Barry Levin is one of the best real estate attorneys around and thank God I'd rescued one of his kids from an out-of-bounds slide a few years ago. To show his appreciation he always gave me a discount—when he charged me anything at all. Not that I wouldn't have saved his kid anyhow, even if the muttonhead did venture into Pandora's after a major storm when the avalanche danger was rated extreme. I hoped he was in one of his generous moods when I talked to him, so I wouldn't have to dip into the Everest fund over this nuisance. The fund needed every penny.

I dumped the junk mail in the trash, swept up the legal notice, and was on my way out the door when I ran into Jason Click. He was wearing ski gear, an oversize jacket and black nylon pants, and had pushed his sunglasses up on his forehead over thinning strands of hair. What were the odds of seeing him twice in twenty-four hours? I cringed to think he witnessed my behavior the night before and fully expected to get one of those 'do you remember what you?' looks from him. Instead he greeted me like he hadn't seen me in ages.

"Hey, Greta, what a coincidence. I have something for you. You're saving me a trip." He reached into his backpack and pulled out a dog-eared copy of a hardcover book. I stared at the picture of a deserted cabin with the empty twin bed. Black Letters screamed the title: ***THE ONLY WAY OUT***. The author's name screamed out as well. Roman Judge.

"I wanted to give it to you last night and never had a chance."

I remembered him telling me he had a book for me. Of course, there was no sense in asking him why he hadn't passed it along to me last night. But the very fact he was in possession of the book had me mystified, especially in light of his religiousness and all. "I wouldn't think you were a Roman Judge fan."

"I don't really have a choice. I live in his ADU. He's my landlord you know."

No, I didn't know. I took an embarrassed minute to digest that bit of information, and it felt odd to think I had just been next door to the author's house not fifteen minutes before. I wondered how Roman and Jason got on and if Roman was subject to Jason's religious rants.

"Thanks, Jason." I took the book from his outstretched hand, hoping to get away before he started lecturing me either on redemption or my behavior of the night before. But he didn't do either. He just gave me a smirky smile and said, "Hope you find it as enlightening as Jesus."

Then he walked past me into the post office.

THIRTY-THREE
Greta

I opened the door, hoping my home would be intact. Floyd hates being left alone and eight hours was stretching it. The last time he'd been left for so long, he dragged my duvet down from the loft and tore it to pieces just to show me. Not only did I have to buy a new duvet, I'm still finding feathers.

When I walked in the door, Floyd was curled up on the Barca like he owned it. He stared at me defiantly before getting down ever so slowly to make his point. He actually sashayed past me out the open door before bolting for the woods where he assumed the position. He conducted his business staring at me with the same judgmental glare he'd laid on me this morning.

I hung up my patrol jacket and put Roman's book down on the steps to the loft. I still wasn't feeling one hundred percent, so I decided to go for a hair of the dog. Just one, I figured, to take the edge off. I grabbed a beer from the fridge. The first sip tasted amazing, reminding me why the expression started in the first place. The second confirmed it, the cool amber liquid a cure for all evils. But the third sip didn't taste as good. I put the bottle down on the counter.

Floyd had not come back in and I could hear him in the road barking at something. Figuring it was an animal, I walked out front to investigate just in time to see the sheriff's vehicle come around the bend. Dan was pressed behind the wheel wearing a dour look on his face. When he pulled up in front of the A-frame, Floyd ran to greet him, his tail slashing the air like a Samurai's sword. Floyd loves men and the sheriff was one of his favorites. Dan climbed out of the car and nodded to me standing on the deck. He walked up the steps wordlessly with Floyd following him like a shadow.

"We need to talk," he said.

I led him inside and he saw my open beer sitting on the kitchen counter.

"Got another one of those?" he asked.

It surprised me that he wanted a beer, being in uniform and driving a county vehicle and all, but hell, what business was it of mine. I grabbed another beer out of the fridge and popped off the cap. He took a serious swig and went into the living room where he settled into the Barca. Floyd eyed him jealously and curled up on the rug. Aside from asking for the beer, he hadn't said another word.

I sat down on the couch and waited to hear the reason for his visit. Dan drank some more beer and rolled his eyes around the room like he was taking inventory. They brushed up the steps to my loft and then to the open door to Sam's room with its unmade bed. Though it was none of his business, I felt myself blushing.

Finally his eyes settled on me, pale blue behind the thick glasses. "I just got some bad news about Evie from Elsa Blanding, and I wanted to deliver it personally."

I stared at him wondering how bad it could be, a prescient chill running down my spine.

He took another swig of the beer and put the bottle down on the table next to the remote. His mouth pursed into the shape of a bad smile. Except it wasn't a smile at all. It was a poorly hidden attempt to delay. Then he belched.

"Sorry," he apologized pathetically. "I told you we've positively identified Evie's hand."

"You told me yesterday in the plaza."

"Remember how all along I've said this was a possible criminal event."

I leaned forward in painful anticipation.

"Elsa called me a little while ago. She's come to the determination that Evie's hand wasn't chewed off by an animal. The hand was hacked off with a knife. Evie's death is now officially a crime. A murder."

I swear the blood drained out of my ears. The room took on an otherworldly aura, every edge sharpened, honed to fine lines even in my periphery. It took a lot of resolve not to scream out. I sat still in quiet disbelief, the outside of me calm, the inside in turmoil. Evie's hand had not been chewed off by an animal. It was hacked off with a knife. In a matter of days, I had gone from losing Evie to the elements to losing her to an animal attack to losing her to murder and mutilation. Evie had taught me to defend myself. Why hadn't she done the same for herself?

"Ever since you first said criminal event, this has haunted me," I said. "But I was in denial. I didn't want to accept it. I wanted it to be anything else."

Dan patted me on the arm, doing his best to offer comfort. "You OK?"

"Best I can be," I said numbly.

He finished the beer in one last swallow and got to his feet, tossing the bottle into the recycle bin on his way to the door. "Sorry to be the one to deliver this . . ." He hesitated, searching for the word and finally found it: "update."

I watched from the deck as he got in his car and pulled away, the chill of his words still upon me. My mind was swirling with scenarios. What had she suffered in the time between her disappearance and her hand turning up in Floyd's mouth? Not one of them was pleasant. I pictured her fighting her assailant and losing her backpack in the struggle. With my animal attack theory out of the picture, one thing was fairly certain. The rest of her body wasn't up Independence. The rest of her was somewhere out by Gulch Creek.

I tried another sip of beer, but it tasted foul. I poured it down the drain and walked zombie-like into Sam's room to make the bed, wondering if a day could possibly get worse. I pulled back the sheets and realized it could. Scrunched at the foot of the bed was a pair of red boxer shorts.

THIRTY-FOUR
Marynell

Marynell cut through the snow-covered patch of yard between her miner's shack and the old barn on the alley, carrying a portable oxygen tank on her back. She slid the barn door open and was greeted by a flurry of clucking as a dozen hens rushed towards her. She wished it was because they loved her, but she knew all the fuss was in anticipation of the evening's meal. As she spread their feed, the clucking quieted, replaced by the click of hard beaks hitting the dirt floor. She emptied their stale water and freshened it from a spigot in the back. Satisfied that her chores were done, she went back out to the alley and tried to slide the door shut. But it would only close halfway and then refused to budge. She swore under her breath and went back inside for the WD40.

She was in the barn spraying the track when she heard the garage door open next door. She pictured her new neighbors: him with his tortoiseshell glasses and his ever-present shearling coat; her, blonde and at least ten years younger, wearing high heels that made her long legs even longer. Honestly, high heels in the mountains.

When she and Clive first settled in Aspen anyone wearing high heels would have been laughed out of town. Everyone owned three types of footwear back then: ski boots, hiking boots and some other. The hiking boots doubled as walking shoes and work boots, and the other didn't come into play until summer when the melt and mud season dried up. Most of the streets and alleys had been dirt then, and anyone wearing high heels would have been mired in mud after about five steps.

When the house next door sold, Marynell had looked forward to having new neighbors. She wanted to give them a chance, even if they had torn down Lilly Henkel's lovely old

Victorian and replaced it with the monstrosity that went to the lot line and blocked half her evening sun. And with all those floor-to-ceiling windows, the place reminded her of a fishbowl.

She'd always liked meeting new people, the anticipation of a new face, the twinkle of new eyes, a glimpse into another life. The day they moved in she stopped over with a fresh baked apple pie. But Hayden had started up on Clive's truck before she could even hand the pie over. He went so far as to call it an eyesore, giving her all kinds of grief about how its presence in the driveway affected their property value. Then he actually had the nerve to ask her to move it. In fact he didn't ask. He told her she would have to move it.

Marynell had been alive a long time and got along with just about everybody. But these two weren't even worth trying to get along with. Drained the friendliness from a room. Worst of all, they thought they were better than everybody else when they were the low ones. When Marynell didn't like someone, she didn't like them real hard. If Hayden had been nice, she might have been a little accommodating. But he hadn't been nice. So she dug in her heels and decided that car was going nowhere.

She crouched beside the open door waiting for her neighbors to pull out of the garage. She was in no mood to risk a confrontation over the chickens. But instead of hearing Hayden and his wife, she heard Hayden's voice and that of another man. They were speaking in hushed tones that made it difficult for her to understand them.

"How long would it take to get permits?" said the voice she recognized as Hayden's.

"We've pretty much got the downtown block sewn up," the other replied. "One holdout, but he's got a sick son with big medical bills so it shouldn't be too hard to entice him. Price just has to be right."

"And city council?"

"See, that's the problem. They're passionate about their town and they can't see the benefits of what we're offering them."

"Money as incentive do any talking?"

"There is no price with these kinds of people. Most the council members live in subsidized housing, and they're entrenched. Like I said, it's not like people back east."

"There's a way and I'm sure you'll find it," said her neighbor. "What about next door?"

"Working on it. I'll let you know. You know they're all tough, these women," said the other voice. She could hear car doors opening and shutting followed by the sound of an engine. The car backed into the alley and drove away, the garage door closing behind it. She stepped out from behind the barn, her head gliding back and forth to be certain they were gone.

"Sons of bitches," she said.

Then she gave the barn door an angry yank and it slid shut effortlessly on its track.

THIRTY-FIVE
Greta

There are three absolutes in my life.

My brother.

Ski patrol.

My coat-check shift at the Bugaboo.

I don't know how, but I'll chalk it up to stress. I had somehow forgotten today was Saturday, which was my night at the Bug. And as much as dealing with the entitled topped the list of things I didn't feel like doing tonight, there was no way I could afford to miss a shift during peak season. A missed patrol shift wasn't the end of the world, and once in a while I skipped Shakespeare class, but showing up for work at the Bug was mandatory.

It was a job just about every local woman would kill for and I didn't want anyone else to ever get their foot in the door. Hanging coats for wealthy clients who stuff fat tips into the tip jar was easy duty. Saturdays at the Bug have paid for many a vacation, not to mention my last lawsuit with Joel. The world may have been crumbling around me, but the world's tallest peak still awaited in May and every twenty counted for another step. Saturday nights at the Bug have been mine since my first year in Aspen and I've never missed a single shift. No matter how lousy I felt, how dead my friend was, how red the boxers were, I had to show.

It was only seven and my shift didn't start until nine, so I had plenty of time to get ready. I went back into the closet in Sam's room and revisited my default outfits. Black turtleneck versus the low-cut sweater. I was thinking about the turtleneck at first, but then after considering a looming lawsuit, I went for the low-cut sweater *and* the push-up bra. It was that serious.

I fixed my face and loosed my hair into a style that I knew

the male club members found attractive. Floyd gave me the stink eye for leaving him alone again, but there was nothing to be done. I had no doubt he would climb onto the Barca in revenge the moment I left. Better that than eating the sofa.

I had to push back dark thoughts the entire drive to the Bugaboo. In town, the windows of the restaurants were filled up with smiling faces and the movie theater had lines just like any other day. It didn't seem fair that everyone's lives seemed so normal when mine was a dumpster fire.

I left my car with the valet and went down to the club. Nine o'clock was early for clubbing and the Bug was dead, nothing like the madhouse it would be in hours. I checked in with the manager and settled into my cubicle behind the open Dutch door. I hoped it would be a busy night to keep my mind occupied, and that the time would pass quickly. When it's slow the time drags. Especially standing in one place for five hours. I have no idea how those guards at Buckingham Palace do it. I can ski all day and feel fine, but the morning after my shift at the Bug, I always feel like I've been hit by a truck.

Nights at the Bug can range from entertaining to ridiculous and this one was no exception. There's always a lot of designer wear, large breasts, expensive jewelry. Uncle/niece couples with the men flexing their financial muscles and the women strutting their wares. It's the uber rich and the uber beautiful. Once in a while an ordinary person makes an appearance like the local fireman who gets a discounted membership or the local dentist who trades cleaning the staff's teeth for free. But as I've mentioned, you can't beat the pay. Tips during the holiday weeks can add up to four figures. And plenty of Benjamins come my way from patrons who're drunk, super-generous or just plain hot for me. I happily accept their money, smiling as I push it into the tip jar that's bringing me ever closer to the top of the world.

Luckily it was busy and the night went quickly, not allowing for much time to brood over my troubles. I always drink a lot of water during my shift to stay hydrated, and after a few hours my tip jar wasn't the only thing overflowing. I hung a 'back in 5 minutes' sign on the door and bumped through the ass-to-elbow crowd to the ladies' room. The room was empty which was unusual, and I had just made myself comfortable in one of the stalls when the door opened and a couple of women came in.

"Isn't he just the creepiest?" I heard one say.

"Makes my skin crawl."

"Then why did you come on to him like that?"

"I didn't come on to him. I was trying to get out of a ticket."

Having finished the business at hand, I came out of the stall and saw two women, a blonde and a brunette, seated in front of a vanity doubling down on make-up. They had two martinis in front of them which I felt was a little odd.

"You bring your drinks into the john?" I asked them.

"You only need to be roofied once," said the blonde.

"Isn't that how you met your first husband?" said the brunette.

"Yep. Don't want anything like that happening again," the blonde replied, and the two broke out in ironic laughter.

I went back to the coat check and stood there pondering what I'd just heard in the ladies' room. And then the clouds lifted and the world's largest light bulb illuminated my brain. I didn't get stupidly drunk at Judy's last night.

I'd been roofied.

THIRTY-SIX
Judy

Judy lay beside Gene listening to his breathing, consistent with the occasional hiccup of a missed breath. When she was sure he was dead to the world, she slipped from the bed and tiptoed into the bathroom. She grabbed her robe from the hook and cinched it tight over her nightgown before kneeling down in front of the toilet. She vomited quickly and quietly with a discipline born of necessity. She couldn't wake Gene.

When she'd finished, she sat down at her vanity waiting for the nausea to subside. The pregnancy test was hidden in the bottom drawer of the cabinet. She'd driven forty-five miles to Glenwood to buy it after Cecily left this morning. Aspen was such a small town she couldn't risk being seen in a local drugstore. When Gene asked why she had gone down valley, she gave him some lame excuse about a nail appointment. Which was beyond lame because she always had her nails done in Aspen and she'd had the full treatment a couple of days ago. Thank God men don't pay attention to women's beauty quirks, she thought.

She opened the drawer and took out the test. She didn't need to read the instructions. She'd done them before. There had been one pink line ten years ago. She'd cried when she told the father, but like practically every guy in Aspen, he wasn't into having a kid. In fact, he wasn't even into staying with her. He'd moved on to Telluride and she'd gone down to Denver alone to have it taken care of. After that she'd been religious about birth control. Until Gene. His vasectomy made birth control redundant.

She'd never known how much she wanted a child until she married Gene and knew it was impossible. She thought that marrying him would fill that inadequate spot inside her, the embarrassed, not good enough spot that she'd grown up with around all those millionaire kids. When they first married, he had been totally generous with her, letting her buy expensive clothes to her heart's content without ever having to consider the price tag. Expensive vacations, the second home, riding on private jets had all been a dream fulfilled, a longing born from the feeling of being less. And then little by little, he started pulling back on her free rein of credit cards, questioning her expenses and, finally, putting her on a budget. Thank God she did the grocery shopping so she could pad the bill with one-hundred-dollar gift cards, something he'd never notice when he looked at the monthly statement.

She sat down on the toilet she'd just barfed in and peed into the cup. She slipped the test strip into it and took the cup over to the sink to wait. Her hand went to her face as she appreciated her reflection in the mirror. Her allowance provided for anything that made her look better. Because it made him look better.

Her heart almost jumped out of her chest when the bathroom door opened. Gene stood in the doorway wearing the bottoms of a pair of silk pajamas and his silver hair was standing up on the left side where his head had rested on the pillow.

"What are you doing?" he asked.

She opened the cabinet door and threw the cup into the waste basket, piss and all.

"What does it look like I'm doing," she said, turning on the tap.

He came up and stood behind her with that look on his face. He hiked up her robe from behind. "You look so hot," he said. "Bend over."

THIRTY-SEVEN
Greta

Last call at the Bug was one thirty and I was out the door by two. I greased the valet the usual twenty bucks and hit the road. The nights I worked the Bug, it was critical to get home and go right to sleep. That seven o'clock alarm comes around quickly.

I was under the covers by half past two, waiting for sleep to come. But for the second time in days, my brain was on overload and wouldn't shut down. Two days ago my only worry in the world, other than saving enough for Everest, was Floyd getting his certification. Since then things had changed dramatically. Discovering Evie's hand was bad enough, but knowing it had been cut off made it worse. I wondered where had she been taken and how much had she suffered. I wanted answers and was beyond irritated that Roark and his team had not only cut me out, they were working at a glacial pace. Then again I did have to allow that it was tough for them to do much up Gulch Creek with avalanche danger so high.

My next trouble was Joel's letter threatening the ownership of my A-frame. Win or lose, it was going to be expensive. Even though my attorney cuts me a break, I would still be looking at a significant expense. But it was unavoidable. Losing my house would mean adios to Aspen. It was starting to look like Everest was staring at me from the wrong end of a telescope.

Particularly disturbing was getting roofied at Judy's party and making an ass out of myself, intensified by—drum roll here—finding the red boxers in my bed. It wasn't lost on me that a pair of red boxers had precipitated all of Evie's troubles and I had to think it was more than coincidence.

But who and why? I sorted through the possibilities. Could

it have been someone on the catering staff since they were the ones making the margaritas? Jason Click and his skinny ass flashed into my mind, but I shuddered it off. Not the uber Christian he was.

The next possibility was Roman Judge. He had driven me home, but according to Judy he'd returned to her house to drop off Paul. Had he looped back afterward? Or maybe it was Paul who looped back. He was the consummate libertine and we *had* dated way back when. Did he think our earlier history gave him carte blanche to hop into my bed when I was oblivious?

And then a sewer line ruptured, and Neverman burst into my thought process. *Don't you remember?* He'd seen how messed up I was. Maybe he had taken it upon himself to show up at my house after my drunken departure from the party. Would bedding me be his way of punishing me for being on ski patrol?

I lay there wideawake listening to Floyd whimper as he chased some squirrel in his dreams. The clock ticked past three and sleep was nowhere in sight. I finally decided that maybe reading would help free my mind. There was certainly nothing left to lose.

I turned on the light. The book that Jason had given me screamed at me from the nightstand. *The Only Way Out.* I opened to the first page, hoping the book was bad enough to lull me sleep.

THIRTY-EIGHT
Greta

Day four

Instead of lulling me to sleep, Roman Judge's book did exactly the opposite. It popped my eyes wide open and they stayed that way through the early-morning hours. And not only did *The Only Way Out* keep me awake, it did so in a most disturbing way.

The storyline follows a psycho who kidnaps an adulterous wife on her afternoon jog. He then transports her to a deep woods cabin where she is kept prisoner with food and water and a makeshift toilet within reach of her handcuffed hand. He returns regularly to have his way with her—in a variety of increasingly disturbing manners—and she tries to keep her sanity while she thinks of ways to thwart him.

It was nearing six in the morning when sleep beat out the book with only a couple of chapters left to go. When I woke it was bright and Floyd was on the bed licking my face. I bolted upright realizing I was going to be late for work . . . again. If Neverman was pissed at me for being late yesterday, he was going to be super-steamed today. But then, in light of all that was happening, Neverman was the least of my worries.

I thought of Roman's creepy book and the fact that Evie's hand had been cut off. Something about it was far too coincidental. I needed to know why Jason Click had given me the book in the first place. I needed to talk to Elsa Blanding about the hand. I needed to visit Marynell to learn more about Roman Judge. And then there was the matter of the boxers.

There were so many unknowns I couldn't even think about going to work. I put in a call to Neverman and sighed with relief when it went straight to his voicemail.

"Hey, it's Greta here. Look I can't make it in today. I'm really sorry if I'm leaving you short-handed, but this has to do with Evie and can't be helped. I'll explain when I see you."

I hung up satisfied with my message. I could have just called in sick, but he would have known it was a lie. I'm never sick.

I decided to start with the boxers. And the first person on that walk of shame was Paul Glendale.

He was shoveling snow from the walkway in front of Judy and Gene's mansion when I pulled up in the Goner. He gave me a quirky smile which stayed glued to his face as I got out of the car.

"I see you've recovered from the party," he teased.

"I want you to know, I'm not amused in the least," I said in a no-nonsense tone. "I'm going to ask you something and I want an honest answer. Did you come back to my A-frame on Friday and get in my bed? Well Sam's bed, but that's a technicality."

The smile faded and his blue eyes beneath his blond brow grew angry. "C'mon now, Greta. I may be a creep, but I'm not a rapist. Now it's my turn to ask a question. What the fuck makes you even think that?"

"Someone climbed into my bed after I passed out and left a souvenir."

"Like what?"

"Like a pair of boxers."

He let out a low whistle. "I'm a brief's man myself. But what was up with you that night anyhow? I've never seen you lose it like that."

"You want the truth? I think someone roofied me at the party. I'm glad it wasn't you."

His expression morphed again, this time to amazement as the blue eyes went wide. "Roofied you? Why would you think someone roofied you?"

"You know I never get drunk like that. Well almost never anymore," I added, thinking back to my last night with Evie. "That's the only explanation I can come up with."

"Well, I can assure you it wasn't me," he declared.

While I accepted that Paul wasn't the culprit, it wasn't a total relief. This may sound weird, but I would have felt safer knowing those were Paul's boxers in my bed. At least the perpetrator wouldn't be some unknown pervert somewhere out there. Having nothing more to say to Paul, I cut our conversation short. "Is Judy home? I need to talk to her."

"The lady of the house is in the kitchen," he said. He went back to his shoveling and I headed inside, wondering how the hell he knew exactly where Judy was in that huge house.

THIRTY-NINE
Marynell

Marynell turned on the flame beneath the kettle that once had belonged to her mother and her grandmother before that. The kettle was dear to her, one of the few family relics that remained from the centuries before. She sat down at the kitchen table and, in no hurry to do anything else, waited for the water to boil.

Marynell was proud of her history in the valley. Her grandfather had settled here in the 1880s during the silver rush, coming from the east to make his fortune mining silver. After his first strike, he married her grandmother and started a family. When the US went off the silver standard and the market for silver went bust, most the miners left, but they stayed on. Coming from the Midwest with its dreary gray days and humid summers, her grandfather got spoiled by the sunny Colorado weather and swore he would never go back east. He bought some acreage down valley from the town and segued from miner to potato farmer where he made a fair enough living to keep his family going.

When Marynell was growing up in the valley, the winters were guaranteed to be harsh and snowy, summers cool and pleasant. The monsoons brought afternoon rain showers and terrific lightning storms which were a relief from the dry summer air. Hers was a tight-knit family who worked together, she and her two older brothers, rest their souls. Special events were picnics and camping in the mountains and riding horses into town.

She met Clive at a mixer at St. Mary's in Aspen. She was seventeen and he was twenty-one, a couple of years out of the army and recovering from the brutality of the Battle of the Bulge where the soldiers were so cold they stuck newspaper inside their uniforms for insulation. He went home to Texas after the war and was on his way to Alaska to try his luck mining gold when he stopped in Aspen to see a buddy from the service. It was that buddy who convinced him to come along to the mixer. Sparks flew when he met Marynell and they fell in love. But he was still determined to go to Alaska. He promised her he'd make his fortune and come back for her. She told him she wasn't afraid of any cold and would go to the ends of the earth with him. A month later, with her parent's tearful consent, the two of them were married and on the way to Alaska.

Clive's gold mining aspirations didn't work out, thank the Lord. After two sub-zero winters, grappling with grizzly bears, no indoor plumbing and endless winter nights, they decided to move back to Colorado. That's when they bought the miner's shack she still lived in today. Cappie was actually born in the house, because the day she decided to make her entrance it was snowing too hard to get to the hospital.

The ski industry was just beginning to take hold in Aspen, fueled by the tenth mountain division soldiers who had trained in the valley during the war. They came back and put lifts on the mountain that sprung out of the town, nicknamed Ajax after the defunct silver mine inside it. And the legacy of silver mining gave the resort a jumpstart. By denuding the mountain of trees to line the mine shafts, the miners had created perfect ski runs.

She and Clive borrowed money from her parents and bought a six-room bed and breakfast named the Deep Powder Lodge, only blocks away from the miner's shack. The Powder grew over the years, just as Aspen did. It was becoming the go-to place to ski. But like all the lodge owners of those early years, they had to scramble to survive, doubling as ski instructors and raising chickens for eggs to both eat and sell.

Life was difficult and rewarding, and they were just reaping the benefit of their hard work with some extra money and leisure time when Cappie was taken from them. If you ever want a reason to lay down and die, just lose a child. Both she and Clive pulled into themselves and they may have been lost forever until the three orphans, Evie and Greta and Judy, came to work for them.

Marynell swore those girls had saved her life as well as her spirit. They were needy and she was needy, and they were able to shore one another up, sharing work and wilderness and souls. And now Evie was gone. Always the best at keeping in touch, Evie had stopped to see her a couple of days before she went missing. Greta had the best intentions, but she had too many balls in the air. And Judy? Well, Judy was too busy being rich.

The kettle whistled and she poured the boiling water into the china teapot that had been given to her grandmother as a wedding present. It was one of her treasures. How it had survived that trip to Alaska and back she would never know.

When the tea had steeped long enough she got up to pour herself a cup. From the kitchen window she could see the white head of the author standing in his driveway. He was talking with Jason, the young man who lived behind the house in the ADU. That one was a strange bird, that was for sure. But he was respectful and always willing to lend a hand when she needed help with something heavy or to run an errand. There was a price to pay, however. She had to sit through his attempts to evangelize her. She finally told him she was a devout Roman Catholic just to shut him up. Which was a lie, but it worked and he stopped his preaching.

She finished her tea and pulled on her down coat and heavy boots. She drew on her oxygen backpack and headed outside, across the backyard to feed the chickens. From beneath her hat, she could see the newbies moving around in their fishbowl of a house. She thought of the conversation she'd overheard the day before. That bastard really wanted her place, really wanted her out of there. Well, there was no way anyone was taking her chickens away from her. That was about all that still remained of the good days. Nope, she had no intention of leaving this life she knew so well. Not while she was breathing anyhow.

FORTY
Greta

I climbed the winding staircase to the second floor, my hand gripping the leather-wrapped railing for all the thirty steps. I wanted some answers and I hoped Judy had them. I hit the landing and crossed the great room to the kitchen at the far end. Judy was sitting at her computer in the corner booth, just as Paul had predicted. She was surprised to see me and with good reason. I seldom skipped work.

"Greta? What are you doing here?"

"I need to talk to you. I hope that's not a problem."

"Of course not." She stopped typing and rested her hands on the table. "Sorry to be so curt, but that damn Cecily is late again. I need her help finalizing the plans for Gene's surprise party. You're coming, aren't you?"

Having little concern about Gene's birthday party, or Cecily for that matter, I took a stance in front of my dear friend with my arms folded across my chest.

"I want to talk to you about what happened to me at your party."

She turned to her computer and punched some keys. "Oh that. Don't worry about it, Greta. Everyone's a little over-served from time to time. I told you there are no hard feelings. You were actually quite amusing." Her eyes remained on the computer screen. "Damn. I wish I knew how to do this Excel spreadsheet of the guest list. Cecily's the whiz at this."

"A little over-served! I was blotto. You know me better than that and you know I don't get drunk like a freshman at his first grain alcohol party. I think someone at the party roofied me."

Her eyes left the screen and settled on me. "You've got to be kidding."

"I'm not. And I'll tell you something more, I need you to help me figure out who it was."

Her fingers eased off the keyboard and her face took on a cramped look. She leaned back in the booth and stared at me like I was a child. She really did play the grand dame well.

"Greta, look, you're understandably upset, but no one put anything in your drink. I have the most reliable caterer on the planet and we know all the staff."

"Maybe it wasn't the caterer. Maybe it was one of the guests."

Now her face took on a look of pure amazement. "Greta, I'm not admitting you were roofied, but if you were, why would anyone do that?"

"You want to know why?" I pulled the red boxers from my backpack and held them up. "Someone came into my home that night and climbed into Sam's bed with me. And left these."

"That would be rape."

"You think so? Actually, I don't think they got that far. At least as far as I could tell physically—if you know what I mean. Maybe whoever it was gave up because I was a corpse."

Her expression changed little, but she held out her hand. "Let me see those," she said. I handed her the boxers and she examined them, taking her time to read the label of the waistband. A relieved look passed over her face and she handed them back to me.

"I have no idea who these belong to."

"I would hope not."

"Then why are you showing them to me."

"Because I wanted to make sure. Evie found a pair of boxers like these in her bed the day before she disappeared. Crazy, huh?

"And there's something else you should know," I continued. "Dan Nichols stopped to see me yesterday. He told me that Evie was no victim of an animal attack. Her hand had been cut off."

"Which would mean . . ." she gasped.

"That's right. Which would mean she was murdered."

I stuffed the boxers back into my pack and left.

FORTY-ONE
Judy

Judy leaned back in the booth and breathed a sigh of relief. The revelation about Evie's hand was a real shocker and, even worse, that she had been murdered. And what about Greta? Could she have been raped? Then again, a woman would know if someone violated her. She thought how sore she still was from Gene's brutal thrusting last night.

But sick as she knew it was, every other thing in the world was secondary to her thoughts about Paul. She was trying to remember if she ever saw him wearing boxers. It would have killed her if those boxers were Paul's. She knew that Greta and Paul had a fling way back when, and she was obsessively jealous that Paul might try to renew it. He'd certainly had the perfect opportunity that night. And she'd worried about him with Evie too. He'd always been attracted to her beauty and independence and athletic prowess. But leaving his shorts in the beds of two women? He'd never be that careless.

And now she was fairly certain she was pregnant with his child. She was terrified of what would happen when Gene found out. Because of course he would find out, and she couldn't exactly plead immaculate conception. She wondered what he would do.

In her fantasy, she and Paul would take off in the middle of the night and head somewhere else to make a new start. But she knew that was a crazy dream. He had no money and neither did she. She had her jewelry but it was kept locked in the safe to which Gene had the only key. The concept of being penniless frightened her more than anything on this earth. When Gene found out who the father was, he would be livid and Paul would be homeless. She'd most likely be homeless too.

She told herself not to worry until she needed to. She might even miscarry. Abortion was totally out of the question. She'd had the one and could never have another. Still, what was to become of her? Losing Gene would mean losing all the possessions and status she'd worked so hard to gain. Maybe an abortion wasn't such a bad idea after all. But even if she did have one, she wouldn't be able to have sex for days afterwards. Which would be nearly impossible with Gene. Maybe she could fake a girls' trip out of town.

She tried distracting herself by turning back to the party plans and the guest list, but her mind was a blur. She glanced at her watch. Where was that damn Cecily anyhow?

The door leading to the downstairs mudroom opened, and she turned around to see Paul standing in the entrance, his face ruddy and flushed from shoveling. She wondered if she should tell him about the pregnancy, then rethought it. She didn't want to risk losing what they had going on. For the time being she would live in the moment.

"Got a minute?" he asked. "I need to show you something downstairs."

She followed him down the back stairs into the mudroom off the garage. There was a bench with cubbies overhead that ran the length of the room. He sat down on the bench and looked at her with a dumb smile on his face.

"What did you need to show me?" she asked.

"This." He unzipped his pants and her knees went weak with what she saw. Suddenly any soreness from the night before was forgotten.

"Quick," she said. "Cecily could show up at any minute."

She never thought she'd be grateful for her assistant's newfound lateness.

FORTY-TWO
Greta

I drove from the Red Mountain mansion feeling more rattled than ever. Something was rotten in Denmark. Thank you, *Hamlet,* January's read. Something rotten that went far deeper than Evie's dismemberment and finding a pair of boxers in my bed. There was evil in the air, and my sixth sense was telling me it was connected to Roman Judge. I've read a little Stephen King and he can be downright scary, but what I'd read of *The Only Way Out* made King's work seem like a fairytale.

Eager to learn more about Roman Judge, my next stop was the library. I signed into one of the shared computers and typed in his name. Wikipedia informed me that he was born in Seattle in 1960—married to one Elizabeth Daniels Swift in 2000. Both dates were open ended. Obviously, I knew he was among the living, but the open end on his marriage told me that for all intents and purposes, he was still married to his first wife. Who left him, according to him. Wikipedia also informed me that his first book was a huge success and he went on to become a best-selling author of twenty-five more books. I scanned the list of titles, but *The Only Way Out* wasn't cited anywhere.

Thinking about what his female characters endured in *The Only Way Out* made me wonder about his missing wife. I powered down the computer and decided to head for Marynell's to see what more I could learn about the couple. When I turned onto her street, I was surprised to see Dan's sheriff's vehicle parked in front of her house. My antennae went up. There was no reason for him to be there this time of the day.

I walked in without knocking. Dan and Marynell were sitting across from each other in the salon, an untouched plate of carrot muffins on the table between them. Dan's hat was off and his giant hands rested between his knees in surrender. He wore one of the most hopeless looks I'd ever seen on his broad face. When he saw me, the sides of his lips rose in a brief closed-mouth smile.

"Well, this is an honor. Twice in two days," said an unsmiling Marynell, her chin tipped towards me. The only sound in the room was the pish of her oxygen. My stomach sank in worry. The only time Marynell wore a dour expression was when she talked about her new neighbor or her deceased daughter. "Hope you're not here to drive another spike through my heart as well."

"I'm sorry, Marynell. Don't shoot the messenger," said Dan in a voice pleading for understanding. He stood up and pulled on his coat, fixing his hat square on his bald head. Then he turned to me. "I wanted to let her know what I heard from the county assessor before some lawyer came knocking on her door. It doesn't have anything to do with me."

"Is it the chickens?" I asked.

"Worse," she said. "The house."

"It's probably best if she tells you. Sorry to be the bearer of bad news, Marynell," said Dan. He walked out the door and pulled it shut behind him.

"What about the house?" I demanded.

"Evidently my neighbor had a survey done of the West End and discovered that part of the land my house sits on actually belongs to his parcel next door. They are going to sue for encroachment. Force me off my land."

"What?" I asked, flabbergasted.

"Isn't that convenient? Not only do they think they can get rid of the chickens and Clive's truck, now they think they can get rid of me!" There was a moment of angry silence, but when she resumed speaking she'd regained some of her usual spunk. "Ha! You know as well as I do it's not happening. I'll beat them. I'll take them to court. I don't care what it costs."

"Maybe we can get a group rate on that lawyer," I said, not entirely kidding. "I need to call my lawyer anyhow."

"Is Sam's son at it again? Why doesn't he just get a life and give up on taking yours?"

"Because that would take time and effort. The joke is, the A-frame probably isn't worth much. But it's worth the world to me." I shrugged and sat down. "It's all about the land."

Crisis made me hungry, so I grabbed a carrot muffin and took a bite. The sweet cinnamon-tinged flavor transported me back to morning meetings at the Powder when Judy, Evie and I joined the rest of the crew at the kitchen table. Sweet times gone by.

"Maybe we can get a place together," I joked. I was chewing on the muffin as I walked to the window and stared at Roman's house next door. It still held some nineteenth-century flavor despite the addition on the back. The house was dark with all the blinds pulled down. "What do you know about him?"

She took a minute to realize who I was talking about. "The writer? Don't know much. He's a polite man and pretty much just comes and goes without troubling anybody. Doesn't take issue with my chickens or anything for that matter."

"Did you know his wife?" I asked.

"Just over the fence. She was a pretty thing. Small. He seemed to really dote on her. She was the friendly one. But when I didn't see her for a while I asked after her and he told me she'd left him. I didn't push, but I could tell it hurt him. I've never seen him with another woman since."

"Do you know what happened to her?"

"I never asked. None of my business."

Right on cue, Gene's white Range Rover pulled up in front of the house with the two silver heads in the front seat like a pair of human bookends. Roman climbed out the passenger side and grabbed his skis from the rack. It was only noon, so they must have hit the mountain early. Roman gave Gene a brief wave and the Range Rover pulled away.

From behind the curtain, I saw Roman flash the same curious glance at the Goner he had the day before. This time his body language changed as if he might come pay us a visit, but then thought otherwise. He walked up the front stoop and went into the house. A minute later, the upstairs blinds were raised.

Marynell may have been getting older, but that didn't take anything away from her wits. She was on to me quicker than a snowboarder on untouched powder. "Why this sudden interest in my neighbor?"

"I've got my reasons."

I thought of how obsessively attentive Roman Judge had been at the party. How he had quickly ordered my first drink and then repeatedly asked me if I wanted another. Was he the one that roofied me? If so to what end? Were those his red boxers in my bed?

Marynell was speaking. "I think the author's OK. It's the one around back I wonder about."

"Who?"

"His renter."

"You mean Jason Click? I thought he did you favors."

"He does, but that doesn't mean he don't give me the heebie-jeebies. If he wasn't religious, I'd be worried." The words were barely out of her mouth when the side entrance to the garage next door opened and Jason Click walked out carrying a shovel. My eyes followed him as he disappeared around the back.

And then the door opened again. And durn it if Judy's Cecily didn't come walking out and follow Jason around the back.

FORTY-THREE
Marynell

Marynell sat in silence, her head throbbing so hard she couldn't see straight. Her life had spun out of control. She'd suffered her share of tough luck over the years. Almost starving to death during the first year in Alaska when a storm left them housebound for weeks. Nearly going broke when they first opened the Powder and having to sell most of their possessions to keep it going. Never being able to give Cappie a proper funeral, her final resting place somewhere near the top of this planet. Losing Clive after sixty years of marriage. She'd accepted all those things and bounced back as best she could. But those horrid people wanting to take her home, along with her chickens, was more than her soul could bear.

Her eyes traveled around her small house, the place where she'd shared so many years of hard work and hard play with her husband and her daughter. They were here during the quiet times, before Aspen became too fashionable for its own good, when people loved it for its beauty and the challenge of the outdoors, when cowboys rode their horses into town from the surrounding ranches and tied up in front of the Jerome or the Ute City Banque. The townspeople had been in it together and looked out for each other and each others' businesses. Back then, people pitched in during emergencies and brought hot meals to their neighbors in hard times. But most important, they loved Aspen and worked to keep it the unique place it was, dusty streets and all.

But as the saying goes, all good things come to an end. The streets got paved and the first traffic light went in. Tom the butcher closed his market after a big chain store opened a few blocks away. And then construction started, monster houses replacing small ones, edifices that resembled hotels scarring the mountains. Most the people she knew had died off or sold out. Or been driven out by the likes of those cold creatures inhabiting the house next door.

It was bad enough that they were living in her world, but now they wanted to appropriate her life, take her land and her home. The very thought was eating her from inside. And that's what they wanted, wasn't it? For her to get sick and die or go away so they could buy her house and turn it into a mausoleum and get rid of the chickens who'd been laying fresh eggs for breakfast since she could remember.

Her headache was getting worse. The word splitting came to mind, because it ran straight down the middle of her forehead. Finally, it got so bad where she couldn't take it anymore, and she decided to call her doctor. Dr. Renee Patchett had been hers and Clive's doctor for over twenty years, ever since she took over her father's practice when he retired. Born and raised in Aspen, Dr. Renee was a native who understood the needs of her once small town. Not like the newbies who'd allowed the hospital to be bought by outsiders and turned it into a medical corporation. People who weren't so lucky to have Dr. Patchett told her it sometimes took a month to schedule appointments these days. Who schedules getting sick anyhow?

She started to dial the doctor's office when she remembered it was a Sunday. So she hung up and called Renee at home. She knew both numbers by heart.

"I'm sorry to bother you on a Sunday," Marynell said when Renee picked up. "But I have a fierce headache and I'm wondering if you can prescribe me something for it. It's probably stress, but the pain is sure real."

"Of course, Marynell. I'll phone it over to Russell right away. But be careful with the meds until you see how they affect you," the doctor warned. "Are you sure you don't want to give any more thought to a service animal like we talked?"

"More than certain. Clive and I had our share of animals over the years. I'm done with picking up dog dung," she laughed. "I got enough with the chickens."

Marynell hung up and put on her winter gear and heavy boots in preparation for the five-block walk to the pharmacy.

Her pace was brisk despite the oxygen backpack, and she wondered if people thought she was crazy to walk the snowy streets at her age. But she'd been walking snowy streets for as long as she could remember and she wasn't about to stop now. She only hoped there'd still be snowy streets long after she was gone.

FORTY-FOUR

Greta

After leaving Marynell's, I drove to the county building hoping to find Elsa Blanding. The offices were weekend quiet, but a woman working at one of the desks told me I could find Elsa at the hospital. She very graciously put a call in to Elsa on my behalf, telling her that there was someone inquiring about the hand. I was surprised when she hung up and said, "Elsa says to come on over to the hospital."

Feeling both pleased and surprised, I jumped back into the Goner and hightailed it across town to the hospital. I'd spoken to Elsa briefly at a few events in the past, but that was about as far as our familiarity went. I did know her reputation as coroner and medical examiner was impeccable. She was rumored to be a party girl, but I couldn't see where that mattered as long as she did her job.

When I got to the hospital, I was directed to an operating theater in the back apart from the others. Elsa came out to greet me dressed in scrubs. "I'm sorry to have to meet like this, but I'm in the middle of an autopsy and slammed for the rest of the day. Ski season, you know. If you want to dress the part, we can talk while I work. I warn you, it may be a little gross if you're not used to it."

I accepted the challenge and her white-robed assistant led me to a room filled with standard medical wear. I donned the requisite clothing, pulled the blue booties over my boots and followed the assistant into the operating theater. Having fallen victim to several orthopedics repairs myself during my career, I was familiar with the stark white room and the stainless steel furniture. The only difference was there was a dead, naked, middle-aged male on the operating table instead of a living, breathing skier. It's a good thing my job has hardened me to gore, because this gentlemen's chest was open, the sternum pulled apart. A blood-tinged circular saw on the steel table beside Elsa told the story.

She nodded and turned her attention back to the corpse.

"Like I said, I'm sorry to have to meet like this," she said, cutting into the chest as casually as if she were preparing a roast for dinner. "I'm on a time schedule here. Apparent heart attack on the mountain, but I need to verify it really was a heart attack and not anything else. With these big money policies, the insurance company wants to rule out any outside help in easing the victim along, if you know what I mean."

She stopped cutting and pointed a surgical knife at me as she spoke. "And believe you me, it happens more often than you know. It's easier to get away with a little foul play here because the first thought is to place blame on exertion at high elevation. There was this guy who was in his late sixties who seized up and folded over right in the lift line. He was way overweight and with a heart condition. Most MEs would just write that one off, but I wanted to be thorough. In doing the autopsy, I found bundles of NSAIDs in his system which can be deadly to a guy with his pre-existings. The life insurance policy was for ten million and who do you think it was assigned to?"

She didn't wait for me to venture that guess, but continued talking as if we were taking tea as she pulled the dead man's heart out of his chest. She held it out in front of her and studied it.

"Second wife. Yep she was getting it all. His estate was going to the kids, but she was the sole beneficiary of the life insurance policy. Her boyfriend was the one most devastated when their plan failed. The wife claimed ignorance and he ended up doing ten years. Of course, the policy didn't pay and she wisely decided not to fight that. She ended up moving back to Shreveport to look for another sucker."

She dropped the heart on a scale. "Nah, this one is definitely a massive coronary event. Just look at this scarring. A miracle he lived as long as he did."

She put the heart into a bag and directed her attention at me.

"Now I understand you have some procedural questions for me?"

"Procedural questions?"

"Aren't you the reporter from the *Times*?"

"No. I was a friend of Evie Kearney and I'm here to ask some questions about the hand I found."

"You're not a reporter?" she said in an 'ohmygod' sort of way.

I shook my head.

"Damn," she said.

We were sitting in the office Elsa kept at the hospital. Like the operating room, it was white and spartan, but there were shelves lined with medical books bearing titles like *Diagnoses from the Dead* and *Forensic Autopsy*. Bringing her into the realm of normal was a drawing with crayon stick figures taped to the wall behind her. A stick figure wearing neon green clothes and a blue shower cap over long yellow hair held up a stethoscope. It was captioned, 'Aunt Elsa.'

"My niece," she explained when she saw me looking.

"Budding artist," I said.

"Kid'll be lucky to pass Kindergarten first time round," she replied. I got the feeling she wasn't joking.

She had changed from her scrubs into street clothes and was wearing jeans and a mohair sweater. Elsa Blanding was young for her job and, even more surprising, stunningly beautiful. Her blonde hair was tied into a ponytail and her emerald green eyes were accented by a thick stripe of eyeliner. The image she presented was as far from a person dealing in her trade as anyone could ever imagine.

"I'm sorry for dragging you into the operating theater like that," she said. "For some reason I thought you were the press, and I always like having a little fun with them." Her laugh had the slightest tinge of cruelty to it. "Sometimes we end up wiping them off the floor."

"What I've seen on patrol has left me immune to it."

"So you want to know about the hand from Gulch Creek? You found it?"

I nodded. "My dog and me. Dan said you've already verified it belonged to my friend, Evie Kearney."

"Yes, we got the prints back pretty fast from my friend at the DMV. I don't have any connections at CBI so we'll still have to wait for DNA."

"Dan said you're fairly sure her hand wasn't gnawed off by some animal, but was cut off by a knife."

"I'm not fairly sure. I'm certain. First off, it would be very odd for an animal to chew off a hand. An entire arm, yes, but a hand, very rare. This hand was definitely cut off at the wrist with some kind of blade, most likely a knife," she said as if I needed more convincing. "Although hacked off might be a better description. It was a pretty amateur job."

Her eyes rolled round to the other side of the office before she returned her gaze to me.

"How close were you to the victim?"

"Very close."

"Then I'm sure Dan already told you this," she said going into professional mode, "but from the lack of rigor mortis and the way the blood clotted we can assume the victim was alive when it was cut off. The condition of the hand is consistent with . . ."

If I'd been in a boxing ring, my head would have snapped backwards.

My entire body went numb. Elsa Blanding was still talking, but I wasn't hearing a word. Blood was swimming in my ears as I fought to stay upright in my chair. As difficult as it was to learn that Evie had been murdered, to learn she was still alive when she was mutilated was even more horrifying.

I dialed back into the conversation just in time to hear her say, "What's more, I can tell you when that hand came to me it hadn't been separated from its owner for very long. Couple days at most."

"Couple of days? Couple of days?" I repeated louder. I did the math. I found the hand on Thursday which was three days ago. If the hand had been cut off two days before I found it, that added up to five days. "But that could mean . . ."

The coroner nodded her head sadly and finished my sentence for me. "That she was alive five days ago."

Those last words landed with a thud. That meant Evie had been alive while we searched for her a month ago and could have still been alive when we stopped searching. Could have been alive the day I found the pack. Death had found her no more than five days ago. Death. That was a euphemism. Murder. Evie had been murdered around five days ago.

"And Dan knows this?" I demanded.

"The sheriff? Of course. I told him yesterday. He didn't tell you?"

FORTY-FIVE
Greta

I left Ella Blanding's office numb beyond words. My anger toward Dan defied description. He had known everything Elsa just told me since yesterday. For some reason, he'd chosen not to share that Evie might still have been alive when I found the hand. Suddenly I understood what is meant by seeing red. I was seeing scarlet.

Traffic into town was jammed up at the roundabout and I sat in the Goner immobile, unable to purge Roman Judge's book from my thoughts. It was set in a remote location. The villain was a guy who had everything and kidnapped to fulfill his fantasies. He kept his victims alive, so he could come back and use them at will. When he tired of them, he stabbed them and cut them into pieces.

So much of Evie's disappearance mirrored Roman's book it was eerie. It made me wonder if the author was involved. His writing certainly showed he had the mind for it. Or what about Jason? It wouldn't be the first time some sicko hid behind religion. Had he given me the book as some kind of a tease? Or worse, what if the two of them were some kind of demented team?

I parked in my usual illegal spot in front of the sheriff's office, daring them to give me a ticket. As in the county building, there were very few people there on a Sunday. Just lots of empty desks behind glass windows. A deputy let me in and I found Dan in his office devouring a massive burger and an equally large pile of fries.

"Oh that's real good for you," I quipped, working hard to contain my ire. "I'm sure your doctor is loving this diet."

"Don't you ever work any more?" he asked. But he must have felt guilty, because he put the hamburger down.

"I'm taking a little sabbatical. I'm doing some more research about Evie." I was about to hit him with what Elsa had told me, but at the last second I decided to hold on to that wild card. "I need to know what in hell is going on up Gulch Creek. I have a right to know that."

Without answering me, he picked up the phone. "Jim, can you come into my office?"

A minute later Deputy Sheriff Roark presented himself in the office. He was all coolness, clean-shaven and wearing a freshly pressed uniform. His green eyes glowed from beneath a duck-billed hat. His face turned quizzical when he saw me sitting in the leather chair in front of Dan's desk. He nodded and his eyes darted from mine to Dan's.

"Greta wants to know what's happened with the search up Gulch Creek," he asked.

I chimed in. "What I really want to know is why you aren't up there right now?"

Roark directed his response at Dan. "As I wrote in my report, we were in the field all day Friday and Saturday, three teams of two with cadaver dogs. We covered more terrain than expected, much of it in level two avalanche danger. I'm sure you're aware of the alluvial fan in that area," he emphasized. "We didn't come up with a thread of clothing, never mind a body part. The dogs did uncover a deer skull and an elk skeleton. The team went back in this morning, but the avalanche danger is so high that I called them back. I don't see avy risk changing much tomorrow, so I'm thinking of diverting them to Independence to search where Greta found Evie's pack."

Having filled Dan in, he turned to me, his eyes respectful in his handsome face. "I'm sorry about cutting you loose the other day, Greta. Really. And I'm sorry for pulling the teams out today, but I can't put my people at risk. We'll continue searching when conditions get better."

I knew what Roark was saying was totally reasonable. Avalanche danger was huge. And while that alluvial fan in the Gulch Creek Valley hadn't slid in years, when that mother lets go, it's an event. But I still couldn't hold my frustration back.

"Yeah, I get it. But you're wasting your time up Independence. You should be looking up Gulch Creek."

Roark looked at Dan and raised his hands in a helpless gesture.

"Thanks, Jim. You can go back to what you were doing," said Dan, dismissing him. Jim tipped the brim of his hat and walked out of the room.

"Greta, I seriously hope you're not thinking of going back out Gulch Creek. It's snowed another two feet since Thursday and the conditions are the worst they've been in twenty years. There's already been four major backcountry avalanches in the past month and two deaths. I want to keep the number at that. I don't want you out there risking your life. It's not worth it. Jim's team will go back in when the risk is lower."

"What if she's alive out there somewhere?"

His face filled with astonishment. "What in hell makes you say that?"

"Just a feeling I have. I want to be there when they go back in."

"Greta, it's best you and your dog stay out of the way. Floyd doesn't always play nice with other dogs."

That much was true. Floyd didn't play nice all the time, but I didn't play nice all the time either. But I didn't feel like telling Dan that. Just like I decided not to tell him I knew the whole truth, that Evie'd been alive when her hand was cut off. I respected that avalanche danger was highest in the afternoon, and that any foray into Gulch Creek would have to wait until tomorrow morning.

I got up to leave, wondering what in the hell I was going to do to keep myself distracted for the rest of the day. Then I remembered I still had a couple of chapters to read in *The Only Way Out*. I figured I'd go home to see how it ended.

FORTY-SIX

Judy

Cecily turned up late again, full of apologies. And once again she was flushed in that way that made Judy think that she'd come from lovemaking. But dressed in her shapeless clothes and with her ruddy complexion even redder than usual, it didn't add up. Still, the woman was acting oddly lately. Something about her had changed though Judy had no idea what.

The two of them sat together reviewing the final surprise party plans. Everything was in place, from toga rentals to the menu. Entirely pleased with herself, Judy e-signed the final contracts. If anything, she had overperformed her wifely duties. Of course, she never could have done it without Cecily, so she gave the girl a cash bonus and sent her on her way. Judy was still in the booth reviewing the final menu when she heard the rumble of the garage opening. She knew Paul was in town running errands, so it had to be Gene.

He was catching her off guard. It was barely one o'clock, and she hadn't expected him until much later. He and Roman were supposed to ski all day and then après ski with the Texans. Gene was so predictable it made her nervous when he wasn't. She hated to think how it could have ruined the surprise party if he'd walked in while she and Cecily were working on it. That would have been terrible. Not to mention how terrible it would be if he ever walked in during any of her other extra-curricular activities.

She heard the mudroom door open and close followed by the heavy tread of Gene's boots coming up the steps. She switched the laptop page from the party menu to a home furnishings website she kept open for just such emergencies.

Gene came in wearing a huge smile. He walked over to give

her a hug and peered over her shoulder at her computer. The screen displayed a selection of 800-count linens. "I'm thinking of refreshing the bedding in the guest rooms," she said perfunctorily, giving him a brief smile before turning back to the computer.

"Oh, I thought you'd be working on my party," he said.

"You know?" Judy countered, truly disappointed. She had worked so hard to keep it a secret, because she knew how pleased he would be to hear the roar of surprise when he walked into the club. She was no slouch when it came to earning her keep. Keeping Gene happy always came first.

"Of course I know," he replied. And then: "You'd be surprised at what I know."

His words sounded ominous and lingered in the air long after he disappeared down the hall into the master suite. A sick, sinking feeling came over her, her stomach falling like on the first dip of a roller coaster. She tapped aimlessly on the computer until she heard him coming back down the hall. He had changed from his ski clothes into jeans and a Hooters T-shirt Roman had given him as a joke.

She greeted him with a tight smile hoping to hide her anxiety. His earlier smile had faded, and his expression had changed into a leer. "C'mon, my sweet," he said in a voice that was too measured, too calculated. "I've got something to show you."

Her blood turned ice. *I've got something to show you.* Those were Paul's exact words only hours before. Stop it, Judy, she told herself. You're letting your imagination run away with you. Gene had been out skiing with Roman and the Texans when she and Paul snatched their early-morning rendezvous.

He took her by the hand and led her down the hall to their bedroom. The shutters were open and the room glowed bright in the afternoon sun with Aspen Mountain unfolding directly across from them. He pulled her toward the bed and tore the duvet cover back. Judy gasped to see a pair of red boxers crumpled at the foot of the bed.

"My scarlet woman," he said. "Not only scarlet but careless. You know there are security cameras at all the entries. What you didn't know is from time to time I monitor them on my watch."

Her rendezvous with Paul came back to her in a flood of memory. Being on her knees in the mudroom, a slave to him amid the piles of coats and boots and equipment. But today wasn't the first time they'd made love there. Or the front entry. Or the kitchen. She wondered how long Gene had been spying on her. How long he had known.

He pushed her face down onto the bed without warning, the act filled with intentional cruelty. She was wearing leggings beneath a loose-fitting sweater and he yanked the leggings down to her knees, exposing her naked buttocks. He climbed on top of her with his knees on her shoulders and pushed her face into the pillow so she could barely breathe. She didn't know if she was better off to accept what was coming or to fight him. She had opted to accept what was coming when she heard the door open and another person entered the room.

"I'd love to ride her rough," Gene said in a hostile voice, "but she's far too valuable."

Then something pricked her exposed ass and seconds later the world went black.

FORTY-SEVEN
Greta

I turned the last page of *The Only Way Out* and let out a tortured sigh. The last victim of the psychopath got hold of her captor's instrument of torture and turned it on him, killing him. End of story. Except she's alive and trapped in a cabin in the middle of nowhere. Roman left the reader to imagine what would happen next. No wonder the book never got published. 'That's cheating,' I shouted aloud, sending Floyd scurrying up to the loft.

I put the book down. A noise in my head started screaming, 'Evie'. I tried muffling it by visiting Everest base camp and staring up at the top of the world. But my head was spinning so hard that everything was a scramble. A centrifuge swirled in my brain with scenes of finding Evie's hand to meeting with Elsa Blanding to my anger with Dan and my frustration with Roark.

And then the maelstrom came to a halt. My memory traveled back to the night I found Evie's pack and later emptied it onto my living-room floor. I sifted through its contents once again in my brain. Warm clothing, first aid, survival gear, bungy cords, compass, maps, food, water and more. Everything you could need for survival. But it was a jigsaw puzzle with one missing piece.

I searched and I searched until finally I found the missing piece way deep in my grey matter.

Her Leatherneck knife.

Evie always carried that knife with her, 'as much for the corkscrew as anything,' she would joke. The knife wasn't there when I inventoried her pack. Had it been with her when she was taken? Had her captor turned her own knife against her and cut off her hand? I pictured the remote cabin in Roman

Judge's book and the victim cuffed to the wall. Then I heard Evie telling me you only need to get raped once. That you have to look out for yourself. And then I realized that Evie's captor had not cut off her hand. Evie had done it herself.

Which meant she was probably alive when Floyd found her hand. Which explained why he'd been so difficult about getting into the car. Wherever she'd been and whatever she'd been through, her survival instinct had prevailed and she had freed herself. If Elsa Blanding was right that the hand had been cut off around two days before she examined it, then today would be day five. Was it possible she was still alive somewhere out there?

I read a story in the *Daily* last summer about a survivalist who was discovered in a remote cabin up the Castle Creek Valley. He'd been living there undetected for ten years. He hadn't done anything illegal, except poach forest service land, but the very notion that someone could live off the grid like that really caught my imagination. The irony was even though the Castle Creek Valley was fairly well traveled, he'd been invisible. Gulch Creek was more remote making it even more invisible.

I pictured the vast terrain of Gulch Creek and the thousands of acres crossed by single-track roads leading to abandoned miners' shacks. For the most part it remained wild, uninhabited forest land. It would be a formidable challenge to find someone in that wilderness. Except I had one advantage. Floyd the wonder dog.

It was early afternoon which made avy danger ridiculously high, so even I wasn't foolhardy enough to go into that valley now. But the skies were clear, and you can learn a lot from the air.

FORTY-EIGHT
Greta

From the cockpit, the white-capped peaks bristled the horizon like pointed meringues. The motor of the single engine hummed as much as a prop plane can hum. Winks was at the controls with his large hands wrapped around the wheel, beyond comfortable in his element. If I wasn't so driven by my mission, I might have put more energy into admiring him as well as the surrounding beauty. But my full attention was focused on the terrain below.

"Are we headed in the right direction?" he asked.

"Spot on," I replied.

We were flying at low elevation over the winding road into the Gulch Creek Valley. Everything was white even where the plow had passed the night before. Snow melts quickly on frequently traveled roads like Castle and Brush Creeks. But Gulch Creek sees little traffic and holds its snow white and blanket like, long after the other roads are cleared.

The terrain below us was raw, with unpaved miners' roads making barely visible slits in the snow. I directed him to fly low over the parking area where Floyd had gotten into it with the cadaver dogs. It was completely deserted, but you could see miles of yellow crime scene tape poking through the snow in a comical stream from the parking lot through the meadow.

"Now follow the valley north-east about a mile," I said.

Winks banked the plane ever so slightly and straightened it to fly across the flat valley floor. The terrain to either side was rugged mountain, thick with pine and fir trees. I asked him to fly higher and he went up, riding the thermals coming off the snow on the sunny day.

We passed over a deserted miner's cabin snuggled in the woods, its roof studded with gaping holes. Uninhabitable. My eyes stayed fixed on the woods, searching for any hint of a structure where someone who wanted to stay off the grid might hide. Aside from that one beaten-down shack, all I'd seen was snow and trees.

We neared the end of the valley where the peak opened into the alluvial fan, its slopes cleared of trees from avalanches years past. But my interest wasn't there. My interest lay on the other side. I instructed him to fly to where the yellow tape disappeared into the woods. He circled around and revisited the terrain we had previously passed over. My eyes surveyed the forest below us, searching for something that might be inhabitable, but I saw nothing other than trees, rocks and snow.

Winks had met me at the private ops terminal two hours earlier, the tarmac so weighty with private aircraft it looked like a used plane lot. I'd remembered Winks' offer to take me for an aerial tour sometime and retrieved his card from the pocket of the black slacks I'd worn to the party. He'd answered my call so quickly it was almost like he'd been waiting for me. Remember the wedding ring, I told myself.

When I explained that I wanted to go up Gulch Creek, he informed me that the G5 he'd flown in on would be inappropriate for my purposes. That was no news to me. I'd already known that to get close in we would need a small plane.

"Can you fly a single engine prop?" I'd asked him.

"Like a kid rides a tricycle," he'd replied.

We'd met at the airport an hour later, him showing up in a borrowed Escalade. And now we were flying over Gulch Creek in a rented Cessna, searching for a needle in a haystack. Or as Dan Nichols might say, a needle in a snowstorm. The rental was not small change I might add. With fuel and all, it was going to make a huge dent in the Everest fund. But I couldn't live with myself if I didn't do everything possible to find Evie.

As we circled around traces of yellow tape, I pinpointed the arrowhead rocks that had been my landmark. Oddly enough, the crime scene tape didn't go anywhere near them. The rocks were a couple of football fields to the east of where the tape circled into the woods. Which meant Roark's teams had been wasting their time since day one.

"It's no wonder they haven't found anything," I said aloud. "They've been looking in the wrong place."

Winks was quiet, his focus intense at such low elevation. The sun was slipping behind a peak and casting the valley into shadow. Daylight was growing weak, and the sky was blackening to the north-west under the weight of a storm.

"Can you go over those arrowhead rocks and stay as low as possible?" I asked him. He turned back again, flying as low as he safely could. I scanned the terrain and saw nothing. No cabin, no roof, no shelter of any kind. Maybe Roman Judge's book had fed my overactive imagination and this was all a folly. An expensive one. It was looking like I'd blown a chunk of Everest money for nothing.

"Greta, hate to say this," said Winks, confirming my fears. "It's time to take her back in. That storm won't be long coming and we're getting low on fuel."

"One more pass," I pleaded. He humored me and went back around again. Keeping my eyes focused on the trees below, I recalled my fellow patroller Meghan swore by St. Anthony when looking for the impossible. My mother hadn't raised us with any religion, and I wondered how the saint felt about agnostics, but I figured it couldn't hurt to try. "C'mon St. Anthony. If there's something out there find it for me," I prayed aloud, narrowing my eyes in a last desperate search.

And as mystery novels, mythology and Shakespeare have it, the solution is found in the last pages. I spotted a miniscule clearing and saw something that caught my interest.

"Winks, another pass," I pretty much ordered.

He went around a last time and sure enough St. Anthony had delivered. About a thousand vertical feet up from where Floyd had disappeared into the woods was a crude 'X' in the snow. It was broken in places by snow cover, but it was either a bizarre natural phenomenon or it was intentional.

"Up higher," I commanded. Winks started to argue, but I doubled down. "Go up!"

He gave me a sideways look and took the plane back up the side of the mountain while my eyes stayed riveted to the ground. And then through a crack in the densest cover of the deep woods far above the 'X,' I spied a glint of metal. And then it was gone.

"Do you see that?" I asked him.

"See what?"

"There was something moving back there." I pointed. "Back in the woods. And did you see that timber 'X'?"

"I didn't see anything," he said, his eyes following my pointed finger. "Which doesn't necessarily mean there's nothing there, but my eyes were on the horizon."

"Can you fly lower again?"

"OK, but last one," he said, looking out at the threatening clouds.

"Last one," I promised.

He complied and though the flash of metal had disappeared, I noted where the crude 'X' was in the waning light. As we flew back across the valley, I wondered once again why the yellow crime tape was nowhere near the arrowhead rocks. Roark had clearly made a mistake, and my anger spiked over the missed opportunity to set him on the right path from the beginning.

Wink tipped the plane upwards over the higher mountains, and we headed back toward the airport. He made a perfect landing, the wheels touching the tarmac just as the last light ebbed from the sky.

We were standing in the parking lot after I'd signed over a substantial chunk of the Everest fund for the Cessna rental, hoping it would prove worth it. The storm was blowing in seriously with the wind whipping our faces and huge dark clouds hanging overhead. Snow was starting to fall, the flakes turning yellow under the overhead lights.

I was working out my next move, and that move meant going back to Gulch Creek in the morning.

"I can see those wheels turning," he said. "What are you thinking?"

"I'm thinking about that 'X.'"

"That 'X' could be a weird coincidence. Falling branches or dead wood. The way clouds resemble images. I've seen them enough from the pilot's seat."

His skepticism didn't bother me in the least. "It doesn't matter. I'm going to check it out anyway."

"You're going to what?" His voice was filled with true concern. "Do you mind if I ask when you plan on doing that?"

"First light tomorrow."

"Alone?"

"I can't risk taking anyone with me. But I have Floyd."

"Look, Greta," he said gently, "this storm is supposed to be big and the snow is going to be deep. It's not a good idea going out there alone. You never know what you might find out there beside the avalanche danger." He lowered his head on that beautiful thick neck. "I'd volunteer to come with you, but I've got to fly the doc out in the morning. He's got a heart transplant scheduled in Texas."

"How do you schedule a heart transplant?" I asked. "Don't you need to have a donor?"

"They're expecting one tomorrow. A young woman in a car accident is brain dead, and they'll be taking her off the respirator in the morning."

The snow started coming down thicker. "What happens if you can't get out?"

"Then they'll wait to pull the plug. But I've already checked the weather like any reliable pilot should," he replied. "The storm clears up around three a.m. Unless things change, we're wheels up as soon as the airport opens."

I pondered the dichotomy of waiting for someone with bad luck to die in order for someone else to live. It occurred to me how people with substantial means have such a better shot at staying alive. It seemed that advantage tipped towards the wealthy, even when it came to organ transplants.

"Well, I gotta go," I said, and that was the truth. I needed to get home to prepare for the morning, not to mention make the dreaded call to Neverman, informing him that I wouldn't be in again. We shared an uneventful goodbye and I headed back to the Goner. I was brushing snow off the rear window when he surprised me from behind, wrapping his arms around my waist.

"OK if I call you next time I'm in town?"

"You know, I noticed that ring on your left hand the other day. I don't think it's a good idea."

His face fell flat. "You know, I should take that ring off one of these days. I'm a widower. My wife died a year ago of breast cancer, but I've been having a hard time." Then he smiled a warm and only slightly ironic smile. "Besides, it's been helping to keep women away until I'm ready. I'm feeling kind of ready."

What could I say? I spun around and we shared a pretty important kiss. "I'd love it," I said. Then I extricated myself from his arms and got into my car. He got into the Escalade and waved goodbye, and we drove off our separate ways.

FORTY-NINE
Gene

Gene sat in front of Judy's laptop wearing a pair of rubber gloves he'd found under the kitchen island sink. He keyed in her password and opened her Gmail account. He read through her latest emails without seeing anything of consequence. Some online order confirmations, an invitation to lunch with some local women, junk mail for wine clubs and gym memberships. Then he smirked with satisfaction as he landed on the email he was looking for. Manager@bugaboo.com.

He opened it and read through the email chain. It went back and forth with plans for the Ides of March party. The most recent exchange confirmed the menu of smoked salmon and caviar to start, followed by filets and crab legs. Served with sides of roasted Brussels sprouts, his favorite. He nodded with approval though she was really overspending. Taittinger champagne? Really? Evidently, she thought he was made of money. Still, it would have been a great party. Sad to miss it.

He moved the curser to the reply icon and typed:

> Roger, I am so sorry, but something has come up forcing me to cancel the party on the 15th. Please keep the deposit with my apologies. I really appreciate all your help. All best, Judy.

He reread his note and pushed send.

Next he hit compose. A blank page came up, and he typed in his own email address as recipient. Geneboy@me.com. Then he invented the email his wife would send to him.

> Dear Gene, I am so sorry to do this in such an impersonal way. You are a great guy and have always been a

wonderful husband to me. But the truth is, I am in love with Paul and what's more I'm carrying his baby. We are leaving Aspen to start a new life together. By the time you read this I will be gone. Please know that I did love you in the beginning, but the passion I feel for Paul is overwhelming and we need to be together. I won't ask you to forgive me, but I hope the day comes when you understand. I wish you all the best, Judy.

He reread his email. Satisfied he'd covered all the bases with what he'd written, he pushed the send button. Then he took off the rubber gloves and put them back where they lived under the kitchen sink.

A minute later, Paul Glendale walked into the room.

"You call for me?" he asked Gene.

"I need you to do me a favor. Can you pick up a friend of mine in front of the Mountain View condos and take him down to Glenwood? I told him you'd be happy to do it." Paul looked irritated, so Gene reached into his pocket and pulled out a wad of cash. Just like this asshole, he thought. Pay the guy a fortune as property manager and he not only fucks my wife, he gets pissy about running an errand. Gene peeled off three hundred dollar bills and held them out in front of him. "Fair enough?"

Paul's attitude changed visibly. He took the money from Gene's outstretched hand and stuffed it in his pocket. "Happy to help out," he said. "I was thinking of watching the game, but I can tape it."

"Do you mind leaving right away? He's got a rendezvous in an hour, so he's in a hurry." He scribbled a number on a card. "Give him a call when you're out front."

"No problem," said Paul. "Looks like you're stag tonight."

"And happily so," Gene replied with a smile as he watched his property manager's eyes sweep the kitchen looking around for his wife. Did this guy think he was a total idiot?

FIFTY

Greta

I stopped at the Hick House on my way in from the airport hoping to find Dan. He was out of uniform, drinking a beer with his eyes glued to the Nuggets game. The cleaned bones of half a barbecued chicken sat on the plate in front of him.

"Poor chicken never stood a chance," I said, taking the stool beside him. He wiped his mouth with his napkin to catch any stray barbecue sauce and then gave it another swipe just to be sure.

"Hey, Trouble," he said, going for my braids, but I was a step ahead of him and flicked them over my shoulders. "To what do I owe this honor?"

"How many times have I told you it bugs the crap out of me when you call me 'Trouble'?"

"I've lost track. Somehow you just bring it on. Can I get you something?"

"Yeah, I'll take a draft." He signaled to the bartender. I waited for my beer before getting down to the reason for my visit. "Dan, I didn't tell you this before because I was so pissed, but I saw Elsa Blanding this morning."

"You did." It wasn't a question. It was a statement. His tease of a smile went flat. "I suppose she told you everything."

"She did. And she not only told me about that hand being freshly cut off, but she told me that you knew yesterday." I took a long draw of the beer and waited for its anesthetic properties to lessen my ire. "I didn't bring it up earlier because Roark was around, and he and I don't exactly see eye to eye. But Dan, why didn't you tell me?"

Dan didn't lose any time explaining. "Greta, the reason I didn't tell you is I knew if you knew that Evie was alive when her hand was cut off, you'd be out there looking for her. I don't want you out there looking for a lost cause. Besides it's dangerous. You heard Roark. They've been out there searching since you found that hand and they've turned up nothing. In fact, searching for anything in conditions like this is not only dangerous, it's insanity. I want you to promise me you're not going to go out there on your own."

"I can't promise that, Dan," I said, taking another sip of beer. "And Roark's been searching in the wrong place by the way."

"How do you know that?" he asked.

"A little bird," I said honestly.

"Greta, stop it. It's damn dangerous. This is exactly why I didn't tell you. I figured you'd think exactly what you're thinking. And while we always treat a body part as a possible life to be saved, it's my call as to risk of life. And I'm keeping my men out. You know as well as I do, if she's out there, she's a popsicle. I want you to promise me you won't go looking for her."

"I told you, I can't promise that."

"Then I'll have to take steps to stop you."

"Such as . . ."

"Such as positioning a car at the trailhead."

"It's open space. You can't stop me."

"It's a possible crime scene. Yes, I can."

It was then I realized how serious he was about keeping me out of Gulch Creek. Almost as serious as I was about going. I raised my beer glass with one hand and crossed my fingers behind my back with the other.

"All right, I promise," I said, staring him in the eyes to placate him. "As long as you promise to send your people back in when it's safe."

"I promise," he said.

"That's all I can ask for," I said, turning my hand to look at my watch. "Well, gotta go. Early day at work."

I put my unfinished beer down on the bar and walked out just as the Nuggets scored a three pointer and the crowd let out a roar.

FIFTY-ONE
Dan

Even though he probably shouldn't have, Dan ordered a third beer. Hell, he was out of uniform. He felt like a total jerk about not telling Greta the whole truth as he knew it. His fear for her held his tongue. He knew exactly what her reaction would be and he was right. Wanting to go out and search by herself. What did she think this was anyway? The movies? Where they all come in and find the missing girl right before the closing credits. Well, he had news for her. Real life didn't work that way.

He had been just as shocked as Greta to learn the short window of time since Evie's hand had parted from her body, but unlike Greta he knew there was little hope Evie was alive out there. Or anywhere. If she wasn't victim of the cretin who had cut off her hand, she was a victim of the elements and that was that.

When he told Greta it was too dangerous for her to go back out Gulch Creek, avalanche danger wasn't his primary worry. A couple of days ago a detective from Crested Butte called investigating a missing person, a young woman who disappeared last autumn after heading out on an afternoon hike. It had come to the detective's attention that the missing woman had worked in Aspen the winter before. He wondered if maybe she'd blown Crested Butte and landed back in Aspen.

"I'll check around and get back to you," Dan had told him.

"Thanks. I just wanted to run out the Aspen connection. You never know. These girls go off on their own into the wilderness without thinking of what can happen out there."

"Ten four on that one. I got one of my own going on, but we found a body part so mine's a criminal now," Dan had confessed.

The call had rattled Dan. There was something too coincidental about that missing woman in Crested Butte. And then there was the young woman who'd disappeared without a trace while snowshoeing up Ruedi Reservoir a year ago. But people in the mountains went missing all the time. Sometimes it took years for their remains to turn up. Only last year some hikers on Burnt Mountain stumbled on the remains of a woman who'd been missing since 2014. Same story with the guy whose body was discovered in a gulley last summer after missing over ten years. He'd slipped off the trail and bumped his head. End of story. Sad as the outcome was, it felt good to bring some closure to his wife and two kids on that one. And sadly, some disappearances were suicides. He really couldn't recall any homicides in recent times. Thing was, you never knew until the body came home.

What bothered him was that the missing Crested Butte woman with Aspen ties and the Ruedi snowshoer and Evie Kearney all smelled the same. Three young healthy athletic women vanishing into the elements not to be seen again. Could there be a link? That was the true reason he didn't want Greta going out Gulch Creek by herself. But he knew if he told her of his suspicions, it would have made her all the more determined, so he kept them to himself.

The whole thing left a bad taste in his mouth. However, the taste wasn't bad enough to deter him from eating the slab of chocolate cake the bartender had just set in front of him. But it was bad just the same.

FIFTY-TWO
Greta

Stan came running toward me waving a large envelope. It was clear he'd been watching for the Goner for some time. I didn't feel like socializing, that was for sure, but it was kind of hard to pretend I didn't see him. Besides, I owed him one. I stopped and rolled the window down.

"Got a minute?" he asked, his breath forming clouds in the glow of the headlights.

"Yes, but only a minute. I really have to get home before Floyd eats the couch." Which wasn't a lie. "What's up?"

He handed me the manila envelope through the open window. It was thick and weighty as a book. "I thought you might be interested in this. Go home and read it and then give me your take on it."

I promised to take a look as soon as possible and then drove away, flipping the envelope onto the passenger's side to be read when I got a chance. If there was any reading to be done tonight, it would be finishing up *Macbeth* for next week's class. And I didn't have time for that either.

Floyd was waiting at the door and flew past me into the woods. He gave me that damning stare as he took a long piss. This was getting to be a regular thing. "I know, boy, I know," I called out in an attempt to sooth him. "It's been one hell of a day. I'll make it up to you, I promise."

I left the door ajar and started a fire in the Franklin. Then I filled Floyd's bowls with fresh food and water. Floyd came back and went straight for his dinner, devouring his food in three quick bites.

I grabbed myself a beer and settled in the Barca. It was then I remembered that I'd left Stan's manila envelope in the car. My stocking feet were warming in front of the fire, and the last thing I wanted was to pull my boots back on. But after thinking about what Stan had done for me the other night, reading his document was the least I could do. I slipped back into my Sorels and went out to get it.

I sat in the Barca and stared at the envelope for a long time. It wasn't until my beer was almost gone that I opened the back flap and pulled out the paper-weight sheath of document. It turned out to be an absurdly generous offer from a developer for Stan and Gwyn's real estate. The buyer outlined how he was going to turn the street into a luxury retreat. The price he was offering almost bowled me from my chair.

No wonder Sam's kid was back at me for the A-frame. Some developer wanted the entire street. For beaucoup bucks.

FIFTY-THREE
Greta

I dined on Triscuits and cheese, treating myself to a bag of Cheetos for dessert. Last supper dining. Then I started preparing for the morning. My favorite pack was lost up Independence, but I had more than a few spares, and I picked out one of the larger ones to bring with me. I filled it carefully, going down my winter checklist item by item. Extra clothes, extra food, extra water, handwarmers and extra gloves and socks. Matches. First aid kit. Shovel. After finishing, I double-checked my list and was glad I did. I'd almost forgotten my avalanche beacon. An avalanche beacon can mean the difference between life and death in the backcountry. I grabbed it from its hook and changed the batteries to make sure they were fresh. Then I laid it on the floor in front of the door to make certain it wouldn't get left behind.

Satisfied that all was in order, I climbed into the loft and settled into my down comforter, listening to the fire crackle as it consumed the last of the logs in its fight to stay alive. My thoughts turned to me and Evie and Judy and the friendship we'd shared. We'd been three lost souls when we met, that was for sure. Each in her own way. All three of us wanting to fit in somewhere. I found my place and I'd thought that Evie and Judy had found theirs.

I loved those two women like the sisters I never had, and it broke my heart when the two of them fell apart over Gene. I'd always thought we'd be a trio until the bitter end. But there was no sense in worrying about that now.

I fell asleep thinking of all the good times.

FIFTY-FOUR
Judy

Judy cracked her eyes open; at least she thought they were open. She couldn't know for sure because she was immersed in inky black without even a pinpoint of light. She had no idea where she was, but wherever it was it sure was cold. The tip of her nose told her so. But strangely enough she didn't feel cold. Her hands were in mittens and she'd been wrapped in a down comforter. She tried to sit up, and felt something restraining her right arm. Her left hand went to her wrist and her stomach contracted as it met a thick metal cuff. Upon further investigation, she realized it was connected to a chain.

Searching for calm, she replayed her last memory. Gene had come home unexpectedly and dragged her into their bedroom for sex. Someone else had come into the room and then . . . unconsciousness.

Oh, Gene was pissed all right and this was her punishment. Locking her up in this windowless cell. She tried to think of where she could be and then it dawned on her. The wine cellar. Of course, that's where she was. He was punishing her by locking her in the wine cellar.

She worked on coming up with some reasonable explanation for what he had seen with Paul, but after giving it more thought, realized she was pretty much screwed. He'd come down to get her out of the cellar after he calmed down, but then what next? Would he throw her out? Most likely. Maybe Paul would stay with her and they could run away together as she dreamed. And then she realized that was folly. Paul would never settle down.

Still, Gene locking her up like this was unconscionable. She decided to scream though the likelihood of anyone hearing her was low. It was a Sunday and the housekeepers came on Monday and Thursday. Paul would be out skiing. Though it wouldn't hurt to try.

"Gene," she howled. "Gene. You come and let me out right now!" She continued screaming until her throat was raw and she was exhausted. She was still drowsy from whatever drug he'd given her and she fell back asleep.

The next time she woke, gray light was coming in through a window and she saw that she wasn't in the wine cellar after all. She was in a log cabin, the kind you might pass on a trail in the woods. As the room lightened into dull morning, she could see there were two windows in the cabin, only one was boarded up. The cot she was on was bolted to the same wall as the heavy chain around her wrist. The room was cut in half by a makeshift wall. She shuddered and not from the cold.

She tugged at the chain and it moved. Upon further investigation, she found it was attached to a track that was also bolted into the wall. She slid the chain to the foot of the bed and discovered a cache of supplies, plastic jugs of water and a bin filled with dry food. There was a makeshift toilet as well that emptied into a metal trash can. Though she was frightened, there was some relief in seeing the provisions. They meant whoever brought her here did not intend to kill her.

Whatever drug she'd been given made her thirsty, so she drank some water and sat there contemplating her situation. She wondered if Gene knew about the child. She thought of the pregnancy test in the trash beneath her bathroom sink and hoped he hadn't found it. But he never touched anything on her side of the bathroom, and Gene rooting through the trash didn't seem likely. Emptying the trash was the housekeeper's job.

She wondered why he had brought her here and imprisoned her like this. They had been together over ten years and she thought he loved her. Or loved her enough at least to not harm her. But taking another look around told her she was deceiving herself. This sure seemed like a drastic punishment for being unfaithful.

This was the stuff of a horror movie.

FIFTY-FIVE
Greta

Day five

I was down from the loft well before dawn and the house felt colder than ever. Floyd took his time following me, clearly not happy with the unusually early rising. While he ate, I made a strong coffee and put it in a traveler for the trip. I double-checked the gear I'd put together the night before and loaded it into the car. Then I wrapped the avalanche beacon around my neck and grabbed Floyd. A minute later we were side by side in the Goner, heading down the road in the dark.

It was perfectly still and the sky was clear, the stars sharp points above me. Winks had been right about the storm breaking up before morning. I drove through the deserted town, breathing in the calm and trying to pat down the nerves boiling within me. Had I taken leave of my senses thinking Evie might still be alive. Was this my imagination gone haywire and whatever was left of her was buried deep in the snow, not to be found until spring?

I did the math again. It had been five or six days, depending, since Evie and her hand had parted ways. A stretch for survival in the elements under any circumstances. Worse when maimed. But Evie was just the type to survive—which was why I had no choice but to go look for her.

There was no service up Gulch Creek, so once I hit town I made a couple of calls, despite the early hour. My first victim was Singh. I was hoping he'd muted his cell and my call would go to his voicemail, but evidently he left his phone on at night. He answered on the third ring.

"This better be important," he grumbled in a voice choked with sleep. There was a pause as he checked his caller ID.

"Greta? Is there any reason in particular that you are calling me pre-dawn."

"Yah, I figure I have a better chance of survival disturbing *you* at five in the morning than disturbing Neverman. I need you to tell him I'm not coming in again today."

"You're kidding, right? He was smokin' pissed yesterday when you were a no-show. You left us kind of short as a matter of fact. Broke the record on AFKs." Another fucking knee. Patrol lingo.

"I'm sorry. I really am. But this is more important. I'm heading up Gulch Creek with Floyd. I think Evie might be alive out there. I saw a shack from the air and I've got to check it out. Tell Neverman I'll be back tomorrow."

"Greta, have you lost your mind? Evie's been dead over a month. Going out there by yourself is dangerous."

"Assumed dead. There's no body."

"A chewed-off hand isn't enough proof?"

"Yeah, well, that hand wasn't chewed off by any wild animal. It was hacked off by the human kind. And not too long ago." I didn't bother to tell him that I thought the human animal was Evie herself. Way more info than he needed.

This was news to Singh, as it would be to most everyone we know. I could picture him sitting up in his bed, running his hand through his shiny black hair as he chewed this around in his mind. "All the more reason not to go. I forbid you to do it."

"Singh, I didn't know you cared."

"Honestly, Greta. You can't do this. It's suicidal."

"Probably not as suicidal as telling Neverman I'm not coming in. I have to, Singh. She was my best friend."

Knowing me well enough to know he'd never be able to talk me out of it, his voice turned gentle. "I'll let Neverman know. I hope you find what you are looking for and even more I hope I see you at work tomorrow."

"I'll be there. If I still have a job," I joked and signed off.

Then I made one last call. To Marynell. I wanted to let her know what to do if things didn't go right.

FIFTY-SIX

Greta

I was totally in my head as I drove towards Gulch Creek. Sure, I was taking a big risk heading into avalanche-prone territory, but the risk was calculated. Most avalanches don't take place until the sun warms those layers of snow piled up like sheets of plywood on ball bearings. That wouldn't be until after noon, and I hoped to be out of Gulch Creek by then.

And after all, isn't it a risk just getting out of bed?

Back when I lived in Milwaukee and there were still newspapers, I read a front page story about three women being crushed to death when an empty window washer's scaffolding fell from a high-rise building and landed on their car. The car wasn't even moving. It was standing still. You can't get much less risky than that.

Or those thousands of people who went to work in New York City on a beautiful September day in 2001, thinking about where they were going to have lunch or what they were going to buy their niece for a wedding gift. They weren't doing anything that might be considered remotely risky, and we all know how that day ended.

No, the risk I was taking today was small compared to the very risk of being alive.

My phone rang just as I turned onto the road up to Gulch Creek. I couldn't imagine who would be calling at this time, but a victim of my own curiosity, I glanced down at the screen. My heart skipped an odd beat upon seeing 'WINKS PILOT' on the display. No need to wonder if I answered.

"Good morning," he said in his Southern-tinged accent.

"Aren't you supposed to be taking off this morning?"

"Been pushed back. Weather's all good, but damn if my

pre-flight check didn't turn in a mechanical, and they have to Fedex in the part. Turns out we're not leaving until tomorrow."

"What about the emergency surgery?"

"Guess she'll just have to hang in there for another day."

"I'm sorry to learn that, Winks," I said, my thoughts with the person waiting for a transplant.

"So . . . you still planning on that damned fool's mission of looking for your friend?"

"Yep." My one-word response pretty much said it. Not only did I not owe him an explanation, I was beyond giving one out.

"May I ask where y'all are now?"

"Just heading up to Gulch Creek. Where else would I be?"

He answered my question with one of his own. "Would you be opposed to a little company?"

The trill of excitement that surged though me was like being told I won the lottery. Or you made the cut for Everest. Or you found a place to live in Aspen. I didn't even consider playing it coy.

"Are you kidding me? I'd love company."

"Well, then why don't you come and collect me. I'm at private ops. I'll go out there with you. It'll be a chance to get to know each other better."

"I'm not going to sugar-coat this. It's going to be a slog and you're going to need gear."

"I keep all-weather equipment in the plane. Cross-country skis, snowshoes, clothes for extreme temperatures. Remember I was special ops. Be prepared."

"Isn't that the boy scout motto?"

"I was one of them too."

"Well, it would be nice to have a scout along," I said as I hung a U-ey and headed back towards the airport.

FIFTY-SEVEN
Evie

Evie knew that it would soon be dawn, not that it made any difference. She watched through bloodshot eyes as the first crack of day crested the small opening of the snow cave. She was lucky to have found a south-facing aspect where any day's warmth might work its way in. The opening had been wider when she first built it, but she'd shored up the entry with snow to make it more protective against the elements—and intruders. She peered out the opening just in time to see the first rays of daylight unfold in the valley below.

Day five. She inventoried what was left of her food supplies and wondered why she hadn't provisioned herself better when she left the cabin. Whoever knew she would still be out here after five days. She picked up a water bottle and after breaking through the ice took a precious sip. When the sun got higher, she would fill the plastic bottle with snow and place it outside the cave where the spring sun peeked through for a couple of hours. She wasn't actually thirsty, or hungry for that matter, but she knew in order to survive it was essential to stay fed and hydrated.

She examined the stump of her right arm. It was tightly wrapped in medical supplies from the cabin. It was a good thing she was left-handed or she would never have been able to cut her right hand off. All in all, she'd done a good job, but the gauze was starting to seep and the smell of the fluid was not good. Blood poisoning or infection, she wasn't sure which. How long could she last like this? Maybe another day. Two at the most. She shivered more from the knowledge of her critical situation than the cold. Or was it fever causing her to shiver. She looked back up the mountain toward the prison she'd escaped from.

She'd managed to climb out the window just before they came back. Careful to cover her tracks, she'd hidden in the woods near the cabin at first. You should have heard the chaos explode when they discovered she was gone. Her escape had taken them totally by surprise. Of course, it had taken them by surprise. Who else, other than Aron Ralston, cuts off a limb in order to escape. An animal caught in a trap that's who. And she'd been exactly that. An animal caught in a trap. The only difference was they didn't want her for her fur. They wanted her for another commodity.

They'd searched for her for hours, coming within feet of her hiding place inside a cluster of trees more than once. Lucky for her it was snowing so hard that visibility had been close to nil. They'd searched until dark and left among a chorus of blaming voices.

"Don't worry," she heard one of them say. "She'll be dead by morning."

She stared from the snow cave to the flat floor of the valley. Where in hell was Greta anyway? Why hadn't she figured it out when Floyd came back with her hand. When that dog poked his nose into her cave, Evie had cried with happiness thinking her ordeal was almost over. She had given Floyd her hand, certain that when Greta saw it, she'd bring help. That had been three days ago and nothing.

She thought of how she had cared for that severed part of her, tenderly carried from the cabin inside her coat, kept just inside the cave entrance in the hopes of preserving it to be reattached after she was found. She looked back at the oozing stump. Reattached to what anyhow? Way too late for that now.

And while she'd been lucky thus far, if someone didn't find her soon, she would freeze to death. She recalled the Jack London short story, *To Build a Fire*, when the protagonist died after being unable to light a fire in the freezing Artic. She wondered if freezing to death would be like it was in the story, when he just went to sleep. Her class had read the story in seventh grade and she'd written a book report. That was the year they lived outside Georgetown and her parents enrolled her in a traditional school. It was her favorite year of adolescence, going to school with normal kids who lived in normal houses and ate meals with food bought at a grocery store. Not food that was home-grown or trapped or stolen when necessary.

But unlike the man in the Jack London story, she wasn't succumbing to sleep yet. She was a fighter.

She figured it had been about a month since Gene kidnapped her on the pass. She had fought him hard, losing her pack as she tried to ski out of reach, but whatever was in that needle of his made all fighting moot. She had awakened in the cabin all alone, dopey from the drugs, handcuffed to the wall and still wearing the same clothes she'd had on when she was taken. There was food and water within reach and some kind of chemical toilet, and though it was cold in the cabin the bed had plenty of down sleeping bags to keep her warm.

Three days had passed before she heard the growing sound of an approaching motor. It didn't have the high-pitched whine of a snowmobile, so she figured it to be a Snowcat. A man wearing a black ski mask came into the cabin and wordlessly replenished her food and water, and took her human waste away. At first she feared she'd been kidnapped to be some kind of a sex slave, but she'd dismissed that thought after the first visit by the masked man. He hadn't talked to her, much less touched her, but he'd left her some romance novels to while her time away when pale light came in the window during the day. The windows made freedom seem so close, yet it was far away, any chance of escape restricted by the tight cuff keeping her bolted to the wall.

This went on for weeks. The man came and brought food and emptied the toilet. She tried to engage him in conversation, but he never spoke, leaving her new books each time. Her eyes never left him when he was there. She was memorizing every aspect of him, looking for any hold in the process which might help her effectuate an escape. She would try to engage him in conversation, but he refused to talk to her, remaining mute each time he visited.

Her fear numbed and she whiled the days away reading the glop he'd brought her and using every clue she could to figure out where she might be. The sounds of animals and the wind told her she was in the wilderness, but as to where was a question still to be answered. There was little to do and the worst part after a while was the boredom. That and missing Buzz. She wondered if he still loved her and if he had ever come around to believing she knew nothing about those damn boxers.

Any complacency with the situation came to an abrupt halt the day a doctor came along with the food guy. He never said he was a doctor, but he didn't have to. He'd taken blood, prodded her and poked her in the kidneys, listened to her heart. And then as the two men were leaving, she heard a single word pass between them.

Tomorrow.

Tomorrow. The word had resonated as important and she would never forget the voices that said it. She had no idea why she was being kept there, she certainly wasn't valuable for any kind of ransom, but she knew her time for their purpose had come. That's when she decided to resort to the last possible means of escape.

She had been contemplating this escape since she was taken and had wimped out each time. Now her mind was made up. She knew what she had to do. She'd tried breaking her hand to slip out of the cuff in the early days, but the cuff had been engineered to prevent escape and was a sleeve, longer and thicker than the bracelet kind you see cops carry on TV. Even if she could break her hand, it would have been impossible to pull it through that sleeve.

No, there was only one way out. She would have to cut off the hand. She still had the Leatherneck knife that had been hidden in her boot the day she was taken. When she first woke up in the cabin alone, she had the presence of mind to slip it under the thin mattress of the cot thinking it might come in handy. She needn't have worried about hiding it, because they'd never taken off any of her clothes and she was still wearing the same boots she was captured in. And her captor never got close enough for her to do him any harm, even if she had the courage and the opportunity.

She knew every single thing within view in the cabin. There

were some towels folded on top of a small table beneath the farthest window. He would hand her one to wipe the grime from herself during his visits. The shelves below were covered with a flap, so she had no idea what they held. But she hoped there might be some other useful items for first aid. She stared down at the hand that had served her so well for gripping ski poles or rappelling down cliffs or touching the face of a lover. She thought of how Aron Ralston had cut his arm off after it had been pinned under a boulder for days. She'd been cuffed for far longer than that.

She'd met Aron once in town. He was a real risk taker, but if he could do it, she could do it. He walked away from his arm, but she would take her hand with her. Her mind made up, she took off a sock and cinched it tight below the cuff to cut off the circulation. She waited for the hand to get numb and then, clenching her teeth so hard she nearly cracked them, she went to work.

It's amazing how the fear of death or torture can override pain. When she thought she might faint before finishing the job, she told herself that people seek pleasure and flee pain. Pleasure is freedom. Pain isn't losing a hand. Pain is not knowing what's on the other side of tomorrow.

Once her hand was severed and her arm was free, she held it over her head until she was able to wrap one of the towels around it to staunch the flow of blood. Then she pulled the flap back underneath the table to see what else there was of use. What she saw put fear into her unlike any she had experienced thus far, and she knew why she had been taken.

The shelves held medical supplies and surgical tools. She couldn't understand why anyone would be operating out here in the wilderness until she looked on the bottom shelf. Even with her cast iron stomach, she had to work not to vomit when she saw the styrofoam coolers labeled 'HUMAN ORGANS.'

And for the first time she saw what was on the other side of the wall that divided the cabin. It was an operating theater complete with unlit lights and a generator. A pile of neatly stacked clothes in the corner told her she wasn't the first.

She rummaged through the supplies and found a rubber

tourniquet to staunch the flow of blood. There was antiseptic too and she poured some over the wound, grimacing in pain at the sting of the medicine on her raw flesh. Then she wrapped her stump of an arm in gauze, using her teeth to pull it tight. Her pain was overridden by what she had avoided. She thought of stories of men in war and the torments they'd been able to survive.

More than anything she knew she had to get out of there fast, to put as much time between her and them as possible. She foraged through the clothing from the women before her, layering up as much as she could. Her backpack was long gone, lost up Independence Pass during her struggle with Gene, but she found another one in a cabinet. She helped herself to a water bottle and the food supplies they'd left her. It all made sense now. Of course they would want a healthy, well-fed donor. Then she took a fleece jacket and another hat from a separate pile of clothes. Oh my God. How many victims had there been? Her arm was throbbing and she searched the supplies for some painkillers, but the bastards weren't kind enough to keep those around. She imagined the patients weren't going to have any need for them after their procedures.

She found a small plastic shovel, an essential item in mountaineering, and some matches. She rooted around in a drawer and was surprised to find a lighter which she put into the bag as well. The last thing she did was tuck her loyal Leatherneck knife back into her boot. It had served her well.

She tried the door. There was a keyed deadbolt and it was locked. The windows were sealed as well. She picked up a folding chair and started slamming it into one of windows. It was grueling work, but adrenaline kept her going and finally it shattered. Then she dragged the thin mattress from the cot and laid it over the shards of glass in the window frame. She threw the pack out the window and gave the room a last once-over to see if there was anything of value she may have missed, Her eyes fell upon the chemical toilet. She sure wouldn't be needing that anymore. She pulled it across the room and emptied her shit onto the ground in front of the door.

Then she climbed out the window.

FIFTY-EIGHT

Greta

The road was tricky but the Goner with her heavy tires and industrial weight was up for the challenge. She plowed effortlessly through the six inches of snow from the night before, her headlights leading the way through the dark. Despite the formidable challenge of my mission, I felt light, relieved to have Winks by my side. His hands were ungloved, and I noticed he wasn't wearing his wedding ring anymore. I wondered if that was some kind of signal. But even toying with romance at a time like this was absurd. We were in an unsure situation where who knew what might wait ahead. Still, it felt good that he was here.

I parked at the snowbank where I'd parked my two earlier visits. The mound had grown so monumental, you could no longer see the other side of it. For a change, the Goner didn't sputter as I killed the engine. I took it as a good omen.

I hopped out of the car and went around back to open the hatch. Floyd jumped out and busied himself prancing among the drifts while Winks and I prepared for our sortie, strapping essentials like snowshoes to our packs and layering up our outerwear. It wasn't until we'd ticked off all the boxes that we clipped into our skis.

I turned the avalanche beacon around my neck to transmit.

"Last chance to bail," I said, hoping he wouldn't take me up on the offer. He seemed taller than before, the fur-rimmed hood of his down jacket adding a few inches to his height. He pretended to think for a minute and then gave me a wry smile.

"Long overdue for a good workout," he replied.

We set out across the field, our skis cutting through the untracked snow. Dawn had not quite cracked yet, and the gray that spread before us was so low it felt more like a ceiling than the sky. We made our way cautiously through the meadow staying close to the yellow crime scene tape so as not to stray too far off the target, quietly aware of the alluvial fan with its avalanche danger that lay up valley to our right. As we skied along the yellow line, I was well aware of the gravity of what we were undertaking.

"Man, spare no expense on tape," Winks said, breaking the silence and thus the tension.

"County funded," I shot back.

If I had any reservations about Winks being up for the task, they were quickly put to rest. He proved quite fit and we made the first mile in no time at all. We hadn't skied much farther when the yellow tape tapered off into the woods. Dawn had broken, the sun illuminating the terrain and the visibility was good. It didn't take a minute for me to verify what I'd seen from the air.

"See, they weren't searching in the right place at all," I said, looking uphill. "Those arrowhead-shaped rocks aren't anywhere in sight. They didn't go far enough."

"Wonder how they missed that," Winks said.

"I don't know, but when we get back, I'm giving Roark a piece of my mind." I thought of telling him that Roark had refused my help from the beginning, but decided to let it go. There was no fixing it now.

We pressed forward at a good pace with snow-covered peaks rising to either side of us and Floyd leading the way. We skied quietly, my eyes fixed to my left the entire time, looking for my landmark. After traveling another couple of football fields, the arrowhead-shaped rocks finally came into view, two sentries keeping watch over the valley.

Floyd sat down and held his ground as if he remembered. "This is where Floyd ran into the woods," I said. Then I swept my arm to point further down the field. "And he came out somewhere up there."

Floyd was sitting obediently at my heel. With Evie's sleeping bag long gone, I had brought something else to put him on the track. I reached into my pack and pulled out the sweater I'd poached from her pack the night I found it. I held the sweater to Floyd's nose.

His nose went up and he sniffed at the air in the same way he had the day he found the backpack up Independence. His nostrils flared in search of scent, and he started quivering as something registered in that dog brain of his. He turned his head toward me looking for his release, every ounce of him shivering impatience as he strained to stay still.

"Something out there's got his attention," I said to Winks.

And before I could say 'Vas-y,' Floyd took matters into his own hands. Or paws I should say. He took off running for the woods and disappeared. I shouted after him, ordering him to stop, knowing all along that it was futile, that once he got an idea in his mind there was no bringing him back. I skied towards the woods with Winks right behind me. Through the barren Aspens, I could see Floyd moving uphill.

"Floyd, come back," I commanded one last time. He stopped and glared down at me, letting me know that if I wanted him, I was going to have to come to him. My attempts to follow didn't get me very far before tree roots and fallen pine branches made it impossible to navigate any farther on skis. I stood there frozen while Floyd held his stance above.

"Looks like we're putting on snowshoes," said Winks.

I gave Floyd the evil eye. "I knew I should have taken him back to the shelter while I had the chance."

Winks and I changed out of our skis for snowshoes and started the uphill climb while Floyd sat stone still watching us. But the moment we drew within reach of him, he sprang into action and started leaping up the mountain again. It was hard work to keep up with him, the game stacked in his favor, his webbed paws far better equipped for the uphill mission than our clumsy snowshoes. Every time I ordered him to stay, he obeyed until we got near him. Then he would take off running again. I was sweating and straining for breath and suspected Winks was feeling the same, if not worse, coming from Texas and not accustomed to the higher elevation.

We'd climbed around 1,500 feet, the equivalent of half of Aspen Mountain, when Floyd stopped sprinting. When we caught up to him, both Winks and I were gasping for air.

"Go ahead, boy," I commanded once we'd caught our breath.

This time, instead of climbing higher, he held his ground, his muzzle swaying back and forth. Then he turned toward something that had his attention and began cutting sideways across the mountain.

I followed after him with Winks following me. But this time whenever we caught up with him, Floyd would sit petulantly until I gave him his release. Then he would sprint forward another twenty yards and sit again.

"I don't know what this game is," I said, thinking he might be intimidated by Winks. Or a little jealous. "Let me go ahead with him alone."

While Winks waited behind, I followed Floyd, stumbling through the woods on the racquet-like shoes as quickly as I could. Floyd kept moving until we reached a small clearing where he stopped and pawed at the ground. I looked down and noticed some branches lined up in what appeared an intentional manner. Then I saw a second line intercepting it. We were standing at the 'X' I had seen from the air.

Floyd started moving again, dancing ahead of me, begging me to follow him. It was then I heard Winks calling out from behind. I turned to see him standing where I'd left him, pointing uphill. I ordered Floyd to stay, trudged back through the woods to Winks.

"Hey, I think there's a cabin above us. Up there. Can you see it?" he asked. My eyes followed the trajectory of his gloved hand, and just ever so visible through the woods, I could see the black tarp of a roof. My heart thudded with anxious excitement. OK, maybe terrified excitement. That had to be the place where I'd seen the flash of metal from the plane.

"Let's go check it out," he said.

"Right. Just let me get Floyd."

But when I turned around Floyd was nowhere to be seen. Damn if he hadn't run around a bend and disappeared from sight. I called to him and he reappeared momentarily before disappearing again. "Let me go get him," I said to Winks. "I'll be right back."

I traced my steps back to where I'd left Floyd, the snowshoes sinking with each step. I followed his tracks around the bend and found him in a cluster of trees with his tail straight out like a hunting dog. "What's the problem, boy?" I asked.

He whined and refused to move. I plodded to where he was entrenched and got my answer. Hidden below the cluster of trees was the opening to a snow cave.

FIFTY-NINE
Neverman

"What do you mean she's not coming in again today?" Neverman huffed, his wind-burned cheeks flushing red with anger. Singh actually cringed. He was used to Neverman's flare-ups, but he'd never seen his boss this angry. "What exactly did she say?"

"I just told you. She said she's going out to Gulch Creek to search for Evie. I told her she was nuts but she wouldn't listen. Somewhere in that scrambled brain of hers, Greta thinks Evie's alive somewhere out there."

"She thinks what . . ." Neverman could feel his face turning purple as his blood pressure rose higher. He had never told anyone he had high blood pressure, a matter of personal pride, and it was pretty well managed by meds. Until times like these. He could feel his will overriding the twenty milligrams of Valsartan he took every morning. "What did she say exactly?"

"Only that she saw something from the air, and she was going there to look for Evie. And she said not to worry. She has Floyd with her."

"Does she have any idea what the slide risk is out there right now? What the hell good is Floyd going to do if they're both buried. Does she think since she's already survived one avalanche she's bulletproof? It's not goddam lightning. It's snow and it can strike twice."

Neverman could never forget the time Greta skied out of bounds to save a friend, and a slide had been triggered above her. It took her friend out, and would have taken her out too, but for her ski pole sticking out of the snow. That and having the presence of mind to make an air pocket in front of her face before the snow closed over her. She'd dodged the bullet that time, but there were no guarantees that her luck would hold again.

Neverman was putting in a call to the sheriff's department when a cold blast of air blew into the shack. He looked up to see Buzz walk in and grab a donut from the ever-present pile in front of the radio room. He started to take a bite and stopped upon seeing the raw looks on Singh's and Neverman's faces.

"What's happened?" he asked cautiously.

"Shit for brains Westerlind is at this moment somewhere up Gulch Creek with her dog in search of Evie," said Neverman tersely, listening to the empty sound of the phone ringing. "By herself. She's got it in her head that Evie's alive somewhere out there."

The donut fell to the floor.

Just when Neverman feared the call would go to voicemail, Dan Nichols picked up the call. "Mike?" he answered, calling the patroller by his seldom used first name. The two men touched base with regularity about issues that were shared by the county and the ski company.

Neverman wasted no time getting to the point. "I need to know if you have people out Gulch Creek looking for the body belonging to that hand?"

"Not today. Avy danger is too high. Roark pulled everyone from the field."

"Did you know the unsinkable Ms. Westerlind is out there on her own as we speak."

The sheriff s response was angry. Or was that fear Neverman was hearing? "You're shittin' me. I told her in no uncertain terms not to go out there."

"Yeah, well she listened, didn't she?"

Buzz paced behind Neverman listening, his head in his hands. "She's alive, she's alive," he kept repeating. Then he suddenly stopped pacing and announced, "I'm taking one of the snowmobiles and going out there."

He was almost out the door when Neverman grabbed him from behind. "No *you're* not going out there," Neverman commanded. He paused and then added, "*We're* going out there."

SIXTY
Greta

I stuck my head tentatively into the opening of the small cave. And when I say tentatively, I mean really, really tentatively. Animals hibernate in caves like this one, and I didn't want to surprise anything that didn't want to be surprised. The space was little more than a scooped-out hole and brighter than you would expect because of its southern exposure. And then I came nose to nose with another human being and jumped back in shock.

Though her face was barely visible, there was no doubt it was her. She was wearing a nest of clothing and huddled against the back of the cave. Her auburn hair was matted and oily and stuck out from a filthy wool cap. Her eyes were shut, and at first I couldn't tell if they were closed in sleep or the other. I'm not really a praying person, but I said a quick prayer nonetheless.

"Evie?" I said softly.

The eyelids separated ever so slowly. They were red-rimmed as if someone had taken an ink pen to them and her irises were a cloudy seaweed in her sunken cheeks. But she was alive. Alive! It took her time to focus, but when she saw it was me, she straightened up ever so slightly.

"Where the fuck have you been, Westerlind?" she said in a weak voice. "I'd have thought you would have figured it out when I gave my friggin' hand to your dog."

"Well I'm standing here now, aren't I?" I replied, averting my eyes from her stump of an arm, hating myself for not putting things together sooner.

"A little slow."

"But not too late, I hope."

"Not too late for me," she said. "Do you have any water? Hard to get much from the snow."

I was so relieved to see her, I hadn't thought to ask her what she needed. I opened my water bottle and slowly poured water into her open mouth. She took a few swallows and then fell back upon the wall of the cave.

When she spoke next, her voice was so weak it was difficult to hear her. "I escaped. I've been here all along, right here under their noses. Must think I'm dead. Stupid fucks." She crooked the finger to draw me near. "I heard the Snowcat come last night. They must have brought a fresh one."

"Fresh what?"

"Fresh victim."

"Greta!" I heard my name coming from around the bend and moments later Winks' parka-clad body came into sight. Floyd jumped to his feet and started barking. Winks stopped in his tracks and yelled to me, "You find anything?"

"Yes, it's Evie. She's here. She's alive," I shouted excitedly. "I need you to go for help and I'll stay here with her."

"Wait. I'm coming over." He marched towards us, a big bear in a parka moving across the mountain. Floyd stopped barking and started growling.

"Floyd! Stop! What is wrong with you?" I commanded. He shut up and whined.

"No, no help yet," Evie managed in a voice little louder than a breath. "I'm good for now. Hungry and cold, but I'm OK really. I've lasted this long. I can hold out a little longer." I offered her more water and she took it, half of it spilling from her mouth. She wiped it away with her only hand, the handless arm motionless at her side, the gauze dark and stained black.

"That Snowcat last night probably held my replacement. It'll be coming back soon so they can harvest her."

"Harvest her? Harvest what?"

The pause was interminable. Finally, she gave a one-word answer. "Organs."

At first, I couldn't process what she was talking about. Why would anyone be messing with organs in the mountains? Were they going to have some kind of mountain concert? And then the curtain rose and my jaw dropped open.

"Did you say organs? As in human?"

She nodded weakly. "The cabin where they kept me is up the other side of that rock platform," she said, pointing to the outcropping a couple hundred yards above us. "Hurry, you have to do something before they come back. And they will. Soon."

Winks was drawing near, chunks of snow flying off his snowshoes with each step. I found myself once again reassured by his presence, especially in light of what Evie had just told me.

Winks stopped just shy of the snow cave, huffing from the effort of the hike. "What's going on?" he asked, looking from me to Floyd who was pacing anxious circles in front of the cave.

"Evie's here and she's alive. She thinks there's a woman being held captive up in that cabin you showed me."

"You're saying she's alive in there?" he asked. "With one hand?"

"I told you she's a survivor," I said, choking up with righteous tears.

A look of enlightenment came over his face just as a distant mechanical hum pierced the calm. In fulfillment of Evie's prediction, it was the sound of a Snowcat. I've been around enough of them to know. Floyd's ears perked and then flattened against his head.

And then Winks pulled out a gun. I wasn't surprised to see it. He was the kind of guy you figured carried all the time, and at that exact moment I was thinking it would come in handy when we got to the cabin. But when Floyd saw the gun, he started snarling which was unusual for him. I've heard him bark and growl, but snarling meant something more threatening. Like when he challenged the cadaver dogs.

"Floyd, stop. It's OK."

Floyd knows what OK means and hearing it come from my mouth was enough to calm him down some. But that didn't stop his nervous prancing, and I realized he was trying to block Winks from coming any closer to the cave. I grabbed him by the collar and held him.

"Let me take a look at her," said Winks. "I've done medic's work in the field." I moved out of the way and he stuck his head into the opening. It was at that moment things turned surreal. "There you are," he said to her. "You've given us quite a bit of trouble."

The scream Evie let out was an animal sound unlike anything I'd ever heard before. The echo of her scream hadn't yet died down when the air reverberated with an equally horrific sound, the pained howl of a male human. Everything happened so quickly my heart came to a momentary stop. Then it started beating again, pounding my chest like it wanted to leap out as I watched Winks come to a stand and move away from the cave.

Floyd was barking non-stop and the natural world was utter chaos. Wink's gun slipped to the ground and his hands went to his neck. Blood spurted between his fingers, which were wrapped around the hilt of a Leatherneck knife.

He pulled the knife from his throat and his eyes went wide, his head swaying unevenly as blood pulsed unchecked from the wound. Then, like a tree giving way, he crashed face first to the ground. The snow beneath him turned cherry red, like syrup poured over a snow cone, as he bled the rest of the way out.

Evie's good arm was on the mouth of the cave and she pulled herself out. Then she knelt beside him, staring down with a hate-filled face.

"I'll never forget his voice saying, 'tomorrow.' He was the one who brought me food."

SIXTY-ONE

Greta

Oddly enough, my first thought as I watched the red stain grow around retired AF pilot Winks Denmark was it was a good thing I hadn't gotten any fonder of him. But there was no time for that kind of idle thought. Not when there were more pressing issues to be attended to.

Evie was leaning over the body, staring at it. For a moment I thought she was going to spit on him. She slumped against the entrance to the snow cave. "He's evil personified," she said.

"He didn't seem that way at first. He sure had me fooled."

"Oh, that piece of shit too." Evie thumbed her only hand toward the corpse. "I wasn't talking about him. I'm talking about Gene. He's the one behind all this. I always knew he wasn't a good person. I just didn't know how rotten he was. He's foul from the inside out."

"Gene!" I wanted to be in total shock, but Evie had warned against him long ago. Not quite the way it was coming down, but she had always maintained there was a cruel side to Judy's husband, a man who for all appearances was just an easy-going guy. Well, turned out he wasn't so easy-going after all. He was easy-taking.

One of the toughest challenges to our friendship was the night Judy told us she was marrying Gene. Though I was a bit skeptical, I was happy for Judy because marrying someone with money was what she wanted. Evie's response was almost hostile.

"You're not really going to marry that asshole?" she'd said. "You're selling out for money. You know, rumor has it he got his start dealing coke. And rumors are usually based in truth. If that's the kind of person you want to spend your time with, I don't know if I want to spend my time with you."

"I'm marrying Gene and that's it," said Judy.

"You'll regret it some day," was all Evie had said. She hadn't even wished her luck.

From that day forward we were no longer a trio.

Frail as she was, Evie kept talking. "You've got to go up there, Greta, and see if you can help whoever they brought in last night."

"How do you know they didn't kill her last night?"

"Because there's a window of time for organ transplants. They have to wait to operate until the last minute so they can fly the organs out while they are fresh."

"But we need to get you to a doctor," I pleaded. If Evie didn't get medical attention soon, she could be dead. Even if I left to find help now, I was still a good three hours from cell service. Evie was real and could be saved. What was up above was an unknown.

"Greta, you've got to go up there. I couldn't live with myself if someone died because you were saving me."

That was Evie. Thinking of others till the bitter end. But the more I weighed the situation, the more dangerous it appeared. I'm good with search and rescues and finding avy victims. But stopping known killers was way beyond my skill set. That was a job for the police, not ski patrol.

I bent over Winks and picked up his gun. I could feel the power of it, the weight in my hand. If I went up to the cabin, at least I would have a weapon to protect myself. All I would have to do was squeeze the trigger. The thought of taking another human's life was horrifying to me, no matter how lowly the person. I wasn't sure if that was a line I could cross.

I put the gun into my pack as gently as possible and hoped a slip along the way wasn't going to blow my head off.

"All right, I'll go check it out," I said, adjusting the straps on my pack. "You sure you don't want me to get you help."

"Dead sure," she said

"Wish you'd come up with a better choice of words."

I shouldered my pack and started up the hill with Floyd at my side. According to Evie, the cabin wasn't more than a few hundred yards above us. Fueled with adrenaline and fear, the climb went a lot faster than the slog up to Evie's snow cave had been.

I climbed onto some dry, south-facing rocks and brooked the ridge without any trouble. I found myself on a piece of land with forest grown to the very edge. I walked through the pines, my ears so dialed in that the crack of every twig made me jump out of my boots. The dull sound of the Snowcat was still in the distance, but there was no doubt it was growing nearer. And then I saw a cabin nestled deep in the trees, so camouflaged it would be invisible if you weren't looking for it.

The eerie part was how much it resembled the cabin my imagination had drawn of the cabin in Roman's book. It was an abandoned miner's shack, a small squat refuge with a low roof and an off-center door. Two small windows sat shoulder high. But this cabin had one window with glass panes and a second one boarded up with plywood, which must have been the window Evie smashed to climb out.

It came as no surprise that the door was locked. I tried pulling the plywood off the boarded-up window, but the nails were pounded in too securely. I needed a tool. I walked around the cabin and found an open shed with a shingle roof in a stand of trees. In the snow was the imprint of a Snowcat which explained the flash of metal I saw from the plane yesterday.

There was a tool chest in the back where I found a hammer. I took it back to the cabin and rolled a log in front of the boarded-up window. Standing on the log, I used the peen end to pry out the nails. It was hard work and the nails came out slowly, but one by one they let loose, and after freeing two dozen of them the plywood fell to the ground with a crash.

I peered inside the open window and was shocked to see a replica of the cabin from Roman's book down to the corner cot, the bins of supplies and the chemical toilet. Like in the book a partition blocked the far side of the room from sight, so the victim couldn't see what was in store for her.

There was only one difference between this cabin and the one in Roman's book. Roman's cabin didn't have Judy in it.

SIXTY-TWO
Marynell

Marynell's visit to the pharmacy yesterday had given her a whole new outlook on life. For a day anyhow. Whatever it was that Renee prescribed really took the headache away, and she'd enjoyed catching up on gossip with the pharmacist, Russell, who always gave her a local's discount. They had known each other a long time. She'd left the pharmacy with her spirits soaring and a renewed faith in humankind. But that was yesterday. This morning, after Greta's call, she wondered if she could ever drum up that euphoria again.

She'd been angry at Greta at first. Not for calling at five a.m., Marynell was always up by five, but because ignorance is bliss. And Greta had chosen to deprive her of her ignorance. But as the hours passed and she had time to think it over, her anger lessened. She should feel privileged that Greta considered her a good enough friend to be the one to contact her brother if all didn't go well.

She fidgeted with the handle of her teacup and tried to stop worrying. Worry was a wasted effort that did no one any good. She didn't expect to hear from Greta any time soon, so there was no sense in worry. Not yet anyhow. She did the calculations. If you allowed time for Greta to make the trip to the end of the Gulch Creek Valley, and hours for the search and then the ski out, she didn't expect Greta to be in cell-service range much before late afternoon. She told herself to keep worry at bay until then. Then she prayed, Please, Greta, don't make me wait too long to know you're safe.

A loud crash coming from the front of the house startled her back into the world and she got up to investigate. The heat of the sun had loosened a slab of snow on the roof causing it to slide off and land right in front of the window. The slab was so large it blocked her view of the street. This sort of thing was a rare occurrence. The snow usually melted off the roof slowly, but the recent storms combined with the day's warm temperatures had brought the snow down in one large parcel. Right on top of the daffodils who had started peeking out their shy noses a week before. If she were younger and had anything near her earlier strength, she would be out front right now shoveling the snow off the precious buds herself. But she wasn't younger and she didn't have her previous strength.

Marynell was working to come up with a solution when she heard the sound of a snow shovel next door. She peeked out the side window and saw the Bible thumper shoveling the walk alongside the writer's house. He was always asking her if she needed help with anything. She decided this time not to be shy.

She pulled on her boots and coat and that damn oxygen pack. Then she went out back and called to him from the stoop. When he didn't answer at first, she walked through the yard to get closer. It was then she noticed that he was wearing headphones. No wonder he didn't hear her. She stepped up to the waist-high fence between the properties and started waving her arms. When he still didn't see her, she bent down and made a reasonably-sized snowball. She let it go, hitting him square between the shoulder blades.

That got his attention. He stopped shoveling and pulled out his earphones. He looked ready to be mad, but when he saw Marynell his face softened. "Sorry, Mrs. Hennings. Listening to the gospel of the Lord. It blocks out just about everything else."

"It sure does," said Marynell generously. She'd pretty much given up on God since Cappie's death. "Jason, I wonder if you could do me a favor. A big old chunk of snow fell in front of my window and I wonder if you might shovel it off for me."

"Happy to help, Mrs. Hennings. I'll be over as soon as I finish this."

She thanked him and went back into the house. It wasn't long before she saw him walk around the front with his shovel. She lit the fire under her kettle for another pot of tea and put together a paper plate of cookies to give him for his troubles.

By the time she returned to the salon, her view of the street was clear again and the daffodils seemed to be safe. He was just leaving, and she tried waving him to the door to give him the cookies, but the headphones were back on and he was one with the Lord again.

And then she saw a woman appear from around the back of the house. She'd seen the woman a couple of times before. Though her plain face was nothing to speak of, it was a kind one. When Jason saw her, he took off his headphones and an ear-to-ear smile broke his serious face. They spoke briefly and then she went back down the walk and he returned to his shoveling. Marynell wondered if her odd neighbor had found himself a girlfriend. She rapped on the window until she got his attention and went to the door with the cookies.

"Something for your troubles," she said, handing him the paper plate.

"Oh, Mrs. Hennings. It's no trouble at all. Do unto your neighbor and all."

"Yeah, well, I'd like to do onto my neighbor on the other side," she quipped.

"Huh?"

"That was a pretty girl," she fibbed, changing the subject. "I've seen her come and go a few times."

"Well Mrs. Hennings, I've been courting her. For the Lord. She usually comes to see me before work, but her boss, Judy, told her she needed her early today, so we didn't have our chance to meet this morning. But turns out when she went to work her boss wasn't even there, so here she is after all. Lord works in mysterious ways, because now we can share some scripture. That is if I don't get called out on search and rescue."

"I didn't know you did S and R," said Marynell. "You thinkin' there will be some slides today?"

"Are you kidding? With this kind of hot, cold snow cycle you can bet there will be all kinds of avalanches in the back country today. Just look at what slid off your roof. I'm only hopin' there's no one stupid enough to be out there when something lets loose."

"What about Gulch Creek?" she asked.

"Especially Gulch Creek. Only a crazy person would go out there. That fan is totally primed to let go."

She thought of Greta out there searching for some cabin that may or may not exist much less have Evie in it. Honestly. "You know of any abandoned miners' shacks up in Gulch Creek?"

"I think I've hiked or skied just about every inch of this valley and I don't know of any up that way. That doesn't mean they aren't there," he added.

"Jason, can you do me a favor? Can you let me know if you hear of anything happening out there? I know somebody who might be cross-country skiing out there today."

"I sure will. But like I said, anyone skiing out that way today is either shortchanged in the brain department or looking for a fast track to the hereafter."

As he walked away, Marynell suddenly turned light-headed. The feeling was so strong, she had to go back inside to sit down.

SIXTY-THREE

Greta

The sight of Judy in the cabin put me into another zone. I was prepared to find a kidnap victim, but nowhere in my darkest imagination was it going to be one of my best friends. But there she was, chained to the wall just as Evie had been, her breath coming in a deep and drugged rhythm, dead to the world in the metaphorical sense. The thought that Gene could have anything to do with this was overwhelming.

I walked over and stared down at her. The set-up was exactly as Evie described. Judy's wrist was encircled by a thick cuff that looked like something from a medieval torture chamber. The room was cold, but not unbearably so. She was covered with a mound of blankets and her hands were in gloves. More important, there was a hat on her head. Of course they would want to keep her warm. So much healthier to keep the blood flowing to the organs. I couldn't even believe I was thinking this stuff.

I tried shaking her to wake her up and got a mumbled response. I tugged at the chain, just because, and could tell it was solidly secured both to her wrist and to the wall. Beyond solidly. No wonder Evie had resorted to cutting off her hand. It would have taken a small bomb to loosen that chain.

I investigated the side of the room behind the partition. Here was where reality split from Roman's story. In *The Only Way Out* this side of the cabin was a kinky torture chamber, all the fittings intended for sex. This torture chamber was furnished with a stainless steel operating table and shelves loaded with medical equipment and surgical tools. The nausea that struck me was almost disabling. This can't be happening, I told myself. This is some macabre dream and I'm going to wake in bed and be glad it was over. I pinched myself hard, but the operating table was still there. And so was Judy.

I tried waking her again, and this time she moaned in her sleep and tugged at the wall with her chained hand. Her eyes cracked open the tiniest bit and then opened wider when she saw me kneeling beside her. They circled around the room before settling back on me.

"Greta?" she said, groggily. "What are you doing in the wine cellar?"

"Judy, we are not in your wine cellar. Now wake up." Her eyes grew wider as some comprehension set in. "Do you remember how you got here?" I asked.

She paused to gather her thoughts. Her confusion started to clear, and she sat upright on the cot and stared at the manacled hand. "Oh my god, it was Gene. He drugged me and the next thing I knew, I woke up here in this . . . cabin. I dreamed I was in the wine cellar." She tugged on the chain and her face tightened upon realizing exactly what it was. "Where in the hell am I? Where's Gene?"

"I'm not going to take time to explain," I said, wanting to save her from the hysteria that would certainly follow knowledge. "Let's just say we've got to figure out a way to get you out of here. I don't have to tell you we're both in danger."

I pulled up the cuff and jiggled her wrist. As I already knew from Evie, there was no way that cuff was sliding off. It was locked by key, though, and I wondered if the key was somewhere on the premises. I went back into the surgical area and started searching through some drawers stacked on the shelves. In the bottom drawer, I found a keyring with a half dozen keys and hoped I'd struck the mother lode.

I went back to Judy who was still loopy from the drugs. I tried matching up the keys with no luck. Judy's eyes closed and she lapsed back into semi-consciousness. I decided it was better to leave her like that for the time being since there was nothing she could do to help me or herself. In fact, there was nothing *I* could do to help me or her. Not while that steel cuff was around her wrist.

I explored my options. The first was to leave Judy and go for help, but it would take hours to get back to the car, much less drive to someplace with phone service. The odds of getting help to her before the Snowcat arrived were slim. Even now the distant rumble was growing less distant. I thought of how Evie had maimed herself to escape and thought of the surgical tools just beyond me wondering if I could cut off Judy's hand to save her life. That solution rested briefly in my mind before the gruesome nature of it forced it back down. I was at an impasse as to what to do. I felt completely helpless.

Floyd was outside whimpering and trying to jump into the open window. When I stuck my head out to silence him, the rumble of the Snowcat told me there wasn't much time before it would be here. I had to make a decision quickly. I could jump out the window and run for safety or stay here with Judy. I took Winks' gun out of my pack and curled my hand around the grip. I looked at my dear friend, happily oblivious in sleep, and decided not to run. I was going to stay with her and defend us.

Sensing something terribly wrong, Floyd started pacing beneath the window and whining even louder. I was trying to send him off to save himself when a wild thought occurred to me. Maybe, just maybe, after learning the latest about the hand, Roark and the search teams had gone back to Gulch Creek. The possibility was a longshot, but from where I stood, it was the only shot I had. I thought of the clothes I'd left buried in the meadow from Floyd's training. They were still there beneath a couple of feet of snow. I took off my gator and rubbed it over my face and neck. Then I rubbed it in my armpits for good measure and tossed it out the window to my Labhound.

"Floyd, vas -y," I commanded. "Go find my things."

He gave me a look that said, 'You've got to be kidding.'

"Yes, I'm serious. *Vas-y.* Go find my buried things." He challenged me one last time, lying down in the snow in front of the windows and locking eyes with mine.

"I mean it, Floyd," I said. "Now."

He gave me a hopeless last look and picked up the gator. Holding it in his mouth, he trotted down the mountain without looking back. I wrapped my hands around Winks' gun and sat down next to Judy to wait.

I'm not sure how much time passed before the Snowcat rumbled into the grove and pulled into the shed, but it was bowel-grinding. I was frightened out of my mind, my heart pounding so hard it was a miracle I hadn't passed out. The primal instinct of self-preservation must have been keeping me conscious. My entire nervous system was overwhelmed with fear, my lungs so dry it felt like the air sacs were sticking together. After all this time claiming I didn't know fear, I was learning what it was. And it sucked.

Winks' gun was in a death grip in front of me, clenched tight in both hands.

The sound of agitated voices came through the open window followed by the crash of someone throwing the plywood I knocked down against the cabin. The door rattled, and then I heard the deadbolt turn in the lock. I held my breath and waited.

The door opened and to my utter surprise Jim Roark walked in. He was wearing winter gear, his green eyes intense beneath a wool knit cap. My initial response upon seeing him was relief. That he'd somehow learned we were here and had come to save us. Had Floyd somehow found him and led him here? I started to ease my grip on Winks' gun, and that's when Dr. Emmanuel walked in behind him. The renowned transplant expert from Judy's party. My heart sank as I realized why Roark hadn't taken the search up to the arrowhead rocks. He was one of them.

SIXTY-FOUR
Roark

Twenty minutes ago Roark had been at the controls of the Snowcat with the doc in the seat beside him. They had left their vehicle in the locked shed on Gene's parcel a few miles back, the shed with about a hundred 'Private Property' signs warning of electric shock. The road they were navigating was so hidden you'd never find it unless you knew it existed, which was exactly the terrain that suited them.

It was probably a good thing that Gene was taking a pass on this one, Roark thought. Gene was seldom there for the harvests anyhow, didn't have the stomach for it, and it would have been extra tough with his wife being the donor and all. That's what Roark called them. Donors. They had no other identity in his mind. Donors to his bank account. Thanks to the donors, he'd already squirreled away several million dollars. After such a run of good luck, they'd agreed to close shop after this last one. But this one they just couldn't pass up. The payout was huge. The wife of a Saudi billionaire needed a new heart, and he was willing to pay a ridiculous sum to save her.

Of course, none of the beneficiaries knew where the organs were coming from and they didn't ask. All anyone knew was that Dr. Emmanuel's success rate beat all the odds and that's what mattered most. And why wouldn't his surgeries be successful? He had the healthiest, best-matched donors going.

Roark was working border patrol in San Antonio when he first met the doc at a holding site for detainees. Just like Roark, the doc was beyond disgusted with all these illegal aliens coming over the border to mooch off the US. When the doc suggested he could actually put the wetbacks to good use, Roark thought he was talking about jobs. When the doc explained what the good use was, he was totally down with it. What better way to be useful US citizens.

They started with kidneys. It was a lucrative business, but it was nearly impossible to find a suitable place to operate and, besides that, the donors weren't all too healthy. Then the doc came to Aspen looking for a second home, and Gene was his realtor. Sensing a kindred spirit, he talked about transplants and the shortage of suitable donors.

The rest was history. Gene's initial fortune had come from dealing drugs, so he was no stranger to causing a death or two. And the timing for the partnership had been optimal. Gene was digging his way out of spec property losses during the recession, and he was eager to find a new source of income. Otherwise, he might have had to return to the drug trade, a business he'd grown to find distasteful.

Fast forward. The doc bought a home in the West End and Roark went to work in Pitkin County as a deputy sheriff. He had no problem getting the job after having worked border patrol. And what better place for them to set up business than in one of the wealthiest places in the world. An ideal place to meet billionaires happy to pay big bucks to save their loved ones. Millions for a single organ. And since a single body could yield a heart, a couple of kidneys, a liver and lungs, if they scheduled things right one donor could save more than a few lives not to mention score them big bucks.

Business had been booming from the beginning. There was no shortage of wealthy people waiting for a donor. Like the Saudi who wanted the heart for his wife. When Evie turned out to be a perfect match for the Saudi wife, Roark planted those boxers in her bed, hoping they would produce the exact response they had. Cause a fight that would drive her from her house and her boyfriend. She was easy pickings after that, always out somewhere on her own. But in truth, she'd given Gene one hell of a fight, squirming out of her pack and trying to ski away.

It defied imagination that she escaped the operating theater. Jesus, what kind of sicko cuts off their own hand. They were shitting their pants when Greta's dog turned up with the hand, but after five nights alone in the elements, they figured Evie to be a popsicle by now. And if somehow she wasn't dead, Winks would find her. Winks'd take care of things and there would be all the more profit to be had. Two donors instead of one. Lemonade from lemons.

That nuisance patroller sure was tough to shake off, and he was going to be glad when they were finally rid of her. He'd even gone up the pass looking for her the night she found the hand. When he couldn't find her, he'd stolen her car hoping she would do them the favor of freezing to death. When that didn't work out, Winks roofied her at the party hoping that might keep her out of the way, and Roark had planted the boxers in the A-frame to yank her chain even more.

Judy and the boxers? A little joke for Gene's benefit. As for the adulterous property manager, Winks had taken care of him. That guy's car slid off a cliff with him in it, and it would be a long time before it was found, if ever.

But back to the donors. The doc was fast in and out and they needed to get the organs delivered to the jet pronto. With four hours for a heart to stay good, they had to stick to a strict schedule. The kidneys and liver had a longer life span, up to a couple of days, but you still didn't want to sit on those too long either. It would be a shame to waste them.

To keep the timing tight, Winks would meet them at the cabin and they'd ride back down together with the payoff.

That was the plan. But standing in the cabin doorway staring at Greta with a gun, he could see that had all changed now.

SIXTY-FIVE

Gene

A week of new snow followed by a cloudless sky makes for perfect spring skiing, and Gene and Roman were taking advantage of it. They were riding the mid-mountain chair and basking in the sun and enjoying the mild spring temperatures. They had started out late this morning since Paul hadn't been around to shovel the walk, so Gene had to do it. Although they'd missed making first tracks through the virgin powder, there was still plenty of fluff left in the trees. And when they tired of that, they could always ski the corduroy of the groomers that made anyone look like a pro.

A pile of slush had collected on Gene's skis, so he banged them together to knock it off, dumping a pile of wet snow onto a skier below. The skier looked up and flipped Gene off with a gloved hand. Gene ignored the gesture and pulled up his sleeve to check his watch. He figured the Snowcat to be well on its way to the cabin by now. The plan was for Winks to neutralize Greta whether they found Evie or not. And her dog. Gene liked animals, so he felt kind of bad about the dog, but it had to be done.

According to his calculations, any minute now Roark and the doc would be showing up for the harvesting. They'd take what they could from the girls and dispose of what was left in the usual way, down a long abandoned, bottomless mine-shaft. Then they'd drive the Snowcat with its payload of chilled organs back to the shed and head straight for the airport. Off they'd go into the wild blue yonder. Soon people would be talking about Greta the same way they talked about Evie, wondering what had happened to her in the wilderness. As for Judy, he'd already covered her disappearance with the email.

"Doesn't get much better than this," said Roman, raising his face toward the sun.

"Nope. We are lucky guys," Gene concurred.

Yep, we sure are lucky, Gene thought, especially when you make your own luck. Roman had no idea how much luck he'd brought Gene. When they first became friends, the author had given him a signed copy of his first book, *The Only Way Out.*

"This is a collector's item, guaranteed," Roman had laughed in a self-deprecating manner. "Couldn't get a publisher to touch it, so I published it myself. It sold all of two hundred and thirty-six copies."

Gene had taken out his wallet and handed Roman a twenty. "Make that two hundred and thirty-seven," he'd said.

Gene had been mesmerized by the book about a psychopath who kept women as sex slaves in a remote cabin. Without knowing it, Roman had given him something of far more value than the twenty-dollar cover price. He'd given him a template for his future business. Only Gene's victims would serve a far higher purpose than that of a sex slave. They would serve his checkbook.

When he and the doc and Roark set up shop, they copied the layout of the cabin verbatim from the book, food and water in reach of the victim, chemical toilet, a cleverly hidden solar disk for heat, a location so far from anything that victims could scream their brains out and no one would hear them. And a single handcuff keeping the victim trapped but still able to feed herself and take care of her bodily functions assuring she would stay healthy.

Having Roark on the team was the real godsend. The guy was a master at breaking and entering. He could gain entry into doctors' offices in seconds and quickly access the medical records of potential victims, giving them everything they needed for the perfect match from blood type to allergies. And if Roark ever got caught in one of the offices, he could always play the 'checking out a false alarm' card. That was the beauty of having a sheriff's deputy on the team.

There were organs out there on the black market, but delivering organs that were a perfect match from healthy 'accident victims' was key when it came to the big bucks. And as long as you sold the 'accident' line to the consumer, they didn't ask questions they didn't want to know the answer to. In over ten years they hadn't had one problem.

Until Evie. She sure threw a wrench into the works by escaping. Granted, they had kept her in the cabin way longer than they intended, longer than anyone before, but she was a perfect match for the Saudi oil baron's wife. And price was no object to the Saudi, so they had kept Evie out there marinating. By now Evie was a wasted commodity, frozen to death in the wilderness. By the time anyone found her body, if anyone ever found her body, the operation would be dismantled and the cabin burnt down, courtesy of Roark. But incredibly, the Saudi project hadn't turned out to be a total waste. As things turned out, Judy was a perfect match for the Saudi's wife too. What were the odds that both Judy and Evie shared the same blood type as well as being the right fit for the Saudi princess.

Gene was glad to be closing shop. With real estate booming again and the big bucks back, he didn't need the extra income anymore. And with one less mouth to feed, not to mention a hell of a lot less to pay out for Judy's maintenance, it was going to be easy sailing for him from here on out. He was already primed to go after a few of the younger girls on the scene. The Russian babes who'd been hanging around town were particularly attractive and highly skilled, he'd been told.

"Penny for your thoughts," Roman said, breaking the silence.

"You wouldn't want to know my thoughts," Gene laughed, shaking his head in disbelief that a writer of Roman's caliber couldn't come up with something more clever than a stupid cliché.

SIXTY-SIX
Neverman

They were traveling at an unsafe speed, the wind cutting their faces, and their lips frozen into grimaces as they struggled to keep the snowmobiles under control. If they'd been able to take their eyes from the trail, they would have appreciated the view of Castle Creek Valley rolling to the west and the rugged Continental Divide to the east. But they didn't dare take their eyes off course or they might self-destruct. Sixty miles an hour wasn't anywhere near the hundred miles an hour the vehicles were capable of doing, but pushing it any harder on this terrain would have meant disaster.

Neverman had taken the lead from the beginning, taking them around the back of the gondola onto Richmond Ridge. From there they could cut down the back of Little Annie's on Aspen Mountain and through the Castle Creek wilderness into the most remote part of Gulch Creek. Gulch Creek was relatively untraveled, one of the last outposts of wilderness in a valley invaded by humans, but Neverman knew the area well. That was where he would go when he wanted to escape construction and his fellow sapiens. It was his place to be truly alone.

For the first couple of miles there were reminders of civilization, houses where millionaires, or more likely billionaires, had built edifices in their own private piece of the valley, sanctuaries complete with Snowcats and all-terrain vehicles for transport down the driveways in the winter. They flew past the mansions without looking up and followed the timber line down obscure roads denuded by miners during the silver days. The trail plunged them further into the pines.

They eventually passed a tenth mountain division hut, where soldiers had trained for winter warfare in the Alps during the second world war. The hut had been converted to a refuge for wilderness use during the winter, and they would have knocked a backcountry skier off the trail if Neverman hadn't hit the brakes. Motorized vehicles were verboten in this terrain, but Neverman didn't have the time or concern for rules at present. Of course, the guy flipped them off as they ripped past him. Neverman would have done no less to anyone destroying his backcountry peace.

They pushed the snowmobiles through ever-changing terrain, dipping in and out of glades and meadows, climbing and descending, every fiber of their bodies on alert to control the monster machines beneath them. When they passed through avalanche-prone areas, they distanced themselves from each other in case there was a slide. Neverman chastised himself for starting on this quest without bringing so much as an avalanche beacon or a shovel.

But Neverman knew every second was crucial. The day was growing warmer and avalanche risk would be getting high soon. No one could say when a certain aspect might slide. Maybe never, but the risk was so bad, he just couldn't believe Greta's naivete in venturing into Gulch Creek under these conditions. She was headstrong, to be certain, but putting her life on the line over some dead-end search was just plain insanity. She had clearly taken leave of her senses in this ridiculous odyssey for a lost friend.

Not that it was any of his business, but it was time for Greta to accept that the woman was dead for Christ's sake. When this was over, she really needed to consider seeing a therapist. But if Evie somehow turned up alive, which would be the longshot of all time, Neverman might start believing in God again, like when he was a kid in Rockford, Illinois and went to the Episcopalian services on Sundays with his parents. Actually, you don't stop believing in God. You segue. He still prayed when he was in danger. And he was praying now. Maybe he was the one who had taken leave of his senses.

They'd been pushing it for well over an hour, and his hands were frozen stones from gripping the handlebars, when they finally started ascending the back side of the Gulch Creek

Valley. They crested the trail and reached the saddle of the mountain. For the first time since leaving the patrol shack, he came to a full stop.

"There's an obscure miner's trail here where I used to motocross back when I liked making a lot of noise," he said to Buzz over the sound of their idling engines. "I don't think anyone else knows this route, but it will take us down to the Gulch Creek Road near where the plow stops.

"It's a steep descent though, so be careful," he warned.

Buzz, whose pale face beneath the goggles had turned the color of a raspberry, leaned forward to look down the incline. A man of few words, he gave a frozen thumbs up. They put the snow machines in gear and kept moving.

As they navigated the last stretch down to the valley, Neverman's mind looped back to the night of Judy and Gene's party. As much as he tried not to, he couldn't shake the memory of how good Greta's arms had felt around his neck. It had resurrected something inside him he hadn't felt since Dotty Redding had kissed him behind school when he was thirteen. It was so simple and so pure and so memorable.

He felt that way about Greta's touch. Did he and Greta share some unnamed bond? Was it coincidence that they were both children of the Midwest who had never even seen a mountain in their lives until they came west and fell hard? No matter their differences, he knew the mountains meant the same to both of them. The mountains were everything.

Like so many of the guys he knew here, he'd married and divorced not long after he landed in Aspen. Met a local woman at a party and she so bewitched him, he swore it had to be rabies. They got married and what had started out as 'I can't live without you' turned to 'I hope I never see your stinking face ever again' three short years later. On both their parts. He'd been blissfully single ever since. His marriage had taught him all about love turning to hate. But was it possible hate could turn to love? He'd never actually hated Greta. He just hated how aggravating and stubborn she was.

And beautiful. Not only in her looks.

Neverman's musings stopped as they popped out of the

woods onto the road exactly where he had said they would. Even though the road had been plowed, there was plenty of snowpack for operating the snowmobiles and they pushed the machines over the level turf. Before long they were flirting with a hundred miles an hour. The pure speed and the bite of wind in his face made Neverman forget momentarily why he was there. He was overwhelmed by adrenaline, the rush of speed, the blur of the terrain, the power of control. Just like when he skied, the narcotic of challenge made him feel the wonder of being alive.

They stopped when they got to the end of the plow line and spotted the Goner, the old Jeep looking ominous in her solitude. Neverman noticed two pairs of ski tracks leading from the car into the valley alongside the tattered vestiges of crime scene tape. He pointed them out to Buzz.

"She found someone stupid enough to go with her?" he asked.

"Evidently," said Neverman. "Stupid as us anyhow. Let's see where they went."

Buzz gave him another thumbs up and they revved up the engines and started across the valley, staying near the tracks and the crime scene tape, ever aware of the alluvial fan looming ahead. The tracks disappeared after a while, filled in by blowing snow, but the yellow tape took a turn and climbed into the mountainside behind them. Neverman stopped the snowmobile and dismounted, through the deep snow to the edge of the woods. "There are no ski tracks going in here. Where in hell did they disappear to?" he asked aloud.

But Buzz wasn't listening to him. He was staring at an animal digging for something not too far in the distance.

"Neverman," he called, pointing straight ahead. "Isn't that Floyd?"

SIXTY-SEVEN
Greta

"Well lookie here. Isn't this convenient?" said Roark, doing a quick survey of the room. He noticed the gun in my hand and his head whipped around again searching for something. Or someone. "Where's Winks?" he demanded.

"Winks had an accident," I replied, raising the gun higher and trying to hold it steady. Seated on the floor next to Judy, I dug my feet into the floorboards. "Stay there."

"Greta, you can't shoot me," he said matter of factly as if I wasn't holding a gun on him. The doctor hovered his sorry ass behind Roark for safety. Judy stirred on the cot. Roark took a step towards me.

My grip on the gun tightened. Unlike my brother, I'd never fired a gun and didn't really know how. But I was aware of the final consequences of such an action. I didn't know if I could murder someone, even such a despicable person as Roark. He took a step closer and held his hand out for the gun. By the time Roark took his third step, I had a change of heart about killing someone. These circumstances were extraordinary. I stopped overthinking it and pulled the trigger, waiting for the sound of gunfire to fill the air.

When nothing happened, I learned I had been wrong about something. Winks *had* left the safety on. Roark reached out faster than a downhill racer skiing ice and grabbed the gun from me. Within seconds I was face down on the ground with Winks' gun at the back of my neck. There was a sharp yank at my wrists as Roark bound my hands behind my back with plastic cuffs. Then I felt more cuffs pulled tight at my ankles above my boots.

"Now I'm going to ask again, where's Winks?"

I continued my game of cat and mouse. I couldn't tell him more about Winks without revealing Evie's hiding place, not to mention he'd be pretty pissed at what he found there.

"Winks decided to leave. He said to tell you he'd meet you back at the car," I grunted through clenched teeth, saying the first thing that came to mind, hoping it would buy me some time. Time for what I wasn't sure.

There was no telling what was to come next. But one thing was looking fairly certain. If no one came to our rescue, neither Judy nor I were getting out of there alive. In light of what I already knew about his intentions, the thought of Roark shooting me was becoming the most attractive option. I closed my eyes and put myself in another place. I was skiing the dumps on Ajax, my mouth fixed in an ear-to-ear smile. The run was steep and the powder was deep and it was ecstasy.

Roark and the doctor retreated behind the wall where they spoke in low tones, but not so low that I couldn't hear.

"Do you really think he left?" Roark drawled. "Why would he give her his gun?"

"That begs a larger question. He's already stashed a huge nest egg, and we've all agreed this is our last event. Maybe he was hoping she would take us out of the equation."

There was silence as they both rolled that thought around in their febrile minds. No honor amongst thieves. Or murderers.

"What do you think we should do?" Roark asked.

"We should do what we came to do. And we have a plus one this time. More profit. The plane's ready and waiting to go." The doc.

"Without a pilot?"

"I know of half a dozen guys in town who would jump at the opportunity to fly the G. We'll make some calls when we get cell service. We can just load the cargo on as usual. No one ever questions anything we do at private ops. I've got TSA in my pocket, especially after last year's Christmas gift."

Roark was silent for a long time, and then I heard him say, "Well let's get to it then. We need to be out of here before it gets too late. I say we do the patroller first, because we want to take that other heart very last."

"All right," came the smooth Latin voice. "Bring her over and I'll shoot her. You do something about the cold coming in that window."

A moment later, there was the sound of nails being pounded as Roark put the plywood back in place. I could hear the sound of metal on metal coming from the other side of the screen as I pictured the doctor laying out his surgical tools. I squeezed my eyes tight not knowing if 'shoot her' meant a gun or a syringe, but I hoped whatever it was would be swift and painless.

Judy was coming to again and let out a deep moan. I managed to raise my head high enough to see her. Her eyes were open and when she saw me trussed like a pig going to slaughter, they shivered with fear.

"I'm scared, Greta. I'm so scared," she said, and then she started softly crying.

This wasn't the kind of situation where I could offer any words of encouragement. "Me too, Judy. Me too," was the best I could do.

Roark came around the partition and picked me up, throwing me over his shoulder like I was a sack of laundry. I tried to struggle, but he was strong and I was helpless. He carried me around the partition into the operating theater. A plastic curtain had been draped around the operating table and a dozen instruments were laid out on a stand. Dr. Emmanuel had changed into surgical gear and the entire area reeked of antiseptic. Roark slapped me face up onto the operating table which hurt tremendously because my hands were behind my back. But the pain was trumped by fear at the sight of the doc holding the mother of all syringes in his right hand.

Roark stood beside him, now wearing scrubs over his coat. Instead of avoiding his eyes, I stared him down, thinking if he was going to do this, he was going to have to remember me. It saddened me I wouldn't have a chance to say goodbye to Toby, but I was glad that he was married with the baby on the way so he wouldn't be alone.

My final thought was I would never climb Everest.

SIXTY-EIGHT

Greta

When Neverman and Buzz burst in the door of the cabin, they already knew the layout of the room. After Floyd had led them from the meadow to the snow cave, the barely conscious Evie filled them in on all the details. She told them that I was at the cabin and that she had just heard the Snowcat pull in. Buzz couldn't take his eyes off Evie's bandaged arm the entire time. Seeing the bloodied stump where her capable hand had once been nearly caused him to lose it. Buzz wanted to kill someone, and Evie told him that if that was what he wanted to do he needed to get up to the cabin fast.

The two men left Floyd with Evie and crept quickly up the hill. They had no idea who would be in the cabin; they only knew that Gene was somehow involved, as well as the dead guy whose body they dragged away from the mouth of the snow cave so Evie wouldn't have to suffer looking at it. They followed my steps into the woods and saw the hidden cabin with the Snowcat parked outside. Neverman started running and burst through the unlocked cabin door, his eyes going straight to Dr. Emmanuel who was standing over me holding a hypodermic needle. I watched Neverman fly across the room with his arms out like a comic book hero and smack the needle from Emmanuel's hand. Then he gave the doctor a swift fist to the abdomen, and the man doubled over in pain.

In the meantime, Buzz had clearly lost touch with his feminine side and was pummeling Roark. The sheriff's deputy was a much bigger guy and would have had the advantage, but Buzz had anger and adrenaline on his side, landing punch after punch on Evie's behalf. I had never seen Buzz so angry. He was prehistoric man against a mastodon, a gladiator in the

Coliseum, Mike Tyson in the ring, meeting every one of Roark's blows with two of his own.

Neverman had retrieved the syringe from the floor and had the doctor on the ground with his knee in his back. He knew all about injections from years of administering ketamine to injured skiers. He rammed that needle into the doctor so hard, I swear he hit bone. Then spying the open bottle on the stand next to the operating table, he jumped up and prepared another injection.

In the meantime, Buzz and Roark were still going at it. Roark had gained some advantage, and I watched helplessly from my supine position on the table as he smacked Buzz on the jaw so hard his head snapped back. The next thing I knew, the two men were on the ground and Roark was pounding Buzz with a relentless fist, hitting him so hard I could hear his nose break. And then Neverman was on the scene, standing calmly above the two men with the needle poised. When Roark pulled his arm back to deliver another blow to the disabled Buzz, Neverman saw his opportunity and jabbed him in the ass. Roark whirled around to confront his attacker, but before he was able to do anything, he slumped to the ground.

There was a moment of blessed silence. And then Buzz pulled himself to a sitting position with a loud moan, blood pouring from the broken nose. "The keys," he sputtered. "We have to find the keys."

He got to his feet and started rifling through Roark's jacket, unearthing a set of keys from one of the inside pockets. He went over to the now wide awake Judy, and after some trial and error, managed to free her from her medieval restraint.

Neverman stood beside me on the surgical table, holding the knife that the doctor undoubtedly planned to use on me.

"Actually, Westerlind. I kind of like you like this," he said, before going to work on my bonds.

I actually snarled at him.

With the doctor and Roark both unconscious, Neverman and Buzz left me to watch over them while they went down to get Evie. This time there was little doubt that I would use Winks' gun on either of them if need be. Which was unlikely because their hands and feet were secured by plastic handcuffs also retrieved from Roark's jacket.

Judy sat on the cot rubbing her numb wrist, and alternating between rages of crying and anger, unable to believe she'd married a monster who had sentenced her to death.

It wasn't long before the guys came back. Buzz was carrying Evie over his shoulder while Floyd hovered close behind. Evie had lost consciousness along the way which was a good thing. We were going to drive the Snowcat down, and Buzz loaded her carefully onto the bench in the back, taking care to place her arm where it wouldn't be jostled along the way. He climbed in next to her and gently stroked her head. A trembling Judy slid in on her other side.

We were leaving Roark and Dr. Emmanuel in the cabin and would arrange for the authorities to get to them whenever. I was wondering how they would feel when they woke up trapped in the same place they'd trapped their victims.

"Maybe we'll wait a few days before phoning it in," Neverman said, only half joking. Well, not even half.

I climbed into the front next to Neverman and have to admit, I'd never been fonder of him in my life.

"Hope I remember how to drive one of these things," he said messing around with the starter. "Drove a Cat my first couple of years here. Grooming. Worked all night by myself. I thought it was the best job on earth at the time."

After some finagling, he got the machine going and we started the slow trek down the road following Roark's earlier tracks. "Quite a shit sandwich you got yourself into, Westerlind," he said.

I had no viable response, and besides, I didn't feel like speaking. I had been as close to death as I ever had, and the manner of death would have been beyond unpleasant. My pulse was still trying to find normal though I wasn't completely sure if my heart was pounding in post-traumatic stress or from my newfound appreciation of Neverman.

"Thanks, Mike," I said finally, not feeling the need to add 'you saved my life.' And Judy's. And if her luck held, Evie's. I hoped he knew that was implied in my thanks.

He turned his head slightly and gave me a warm, but cynical, smile. "Mike?" he said slyly. "Does that mean you plan to make good on your promise?"

"I have no idea what you're talking about," I said, truly mystified.

"You really don't remember, do you?" The cynical smile turned into a teasing grin before progressing to a shit-eating grin. "The night of Judy's party, you called me from your home and told me you were naked and you would be waiting for me in the downstairs bedroom."

My face turned red hot. I didn't remember the call, but that explained why I woke up naked in Sam's bed.

"I was roofied that night," I said, turning my eyes forward, unwilling to meet his. "I can't be held responsible for my actions."

This time he laughed aloud, a deep belly laugh that was cut short by an ominous crack from outside. The sound was similar to the charges we set for avy control after a big snow. But those blasts are followed by an echo of quiet, like the boom of a canon. This sound was growing louder, like a locomotive coming our way. Neverman put the Snowcat into a higher gear and pushed the lumbering giant forward as fast as he could.

"Avalanche," he said, his hands gripping the steering wheel with all his might. "Hold tight." And then all the windows went white as a slab of concrete slammed us sideways and the Snowcat flew off the trail.

SIXTY-NINE

Gene

Gene's life was in ruins, and he was scrambling to put together his survival package. He would only take one bag and not his Tumi or Vuitton. Nothing that might grab attention. He went down into the ADU where his traitorous house manager had lived and grabbed a canvas tote from the closet. Paul sure wasn't going to miss it.

He carried the bag up to the master bedroom and started filling it with essentials. His watch collection, each watch valued at more than $10,000, the Audemars Piguet worth $60,000 alone. A small sack of diamonds (oh Judy would have had a shitfit if she'd known about them). A couple hundred thousand dollars in cash. Some toiletries, a change of clothes. He thought of the red Ferrari under a protective tarp in the garage. Useless to him now. The last thing he packed was his gun, a Colt Python, hoping he wouldn't have any need for it.

Roman's phone call had just rocked Gene's world. The author had called innocently enough to share the news about a major slide in Gulch Creek. Apparently Roman's renter, the religious nutjob whose name Gene couldn't ever remember, had been called out on search and rescue. There were reports of a Snowcat being buried, seen by a small craft pilot who just happened to be flying overhead.

"Don't you have some property up that way?" Roman asked.

"Just a small piece with a storage shed," Gene replied blindly, his mind already sorting through the situation. Who was in the Snowcat when the slide hit? Roark and the doc had to be inside, but had they harvested the donors? No matter the answers, he'd be in a heap of shit when they recovered that Snowcat since it was licensed to an LLC in his name.

It was a good thing he had spread money in numbered

accounts around the world. He had money in the Caymans, some in Andorra, even some in Liechtenstein. He'd have to be cagey to get to it, but even if he couldn't get his funds, there was always the Basquiat hidden behind a wall in his crummy rental apartment in Gibraltar. Unbelievable what the black market paid for that kind of crap called art.

But first he had to get out of the country. Fast. Maybe they wouldn't figure out his involvement at first, but when they did his passport wouldn't be worth jack shit. It would be flagged and his movements would depend on dealing with lowlifes who took cash with no questions.

He'd always known he should have gotten himself a false passport, but he'd been lazy about it. See what happens when you procrastinate, he lamented. In the space of one day he'd gone from being a man who was about to be fully retired to a man on the run. His life was ruined. If only he'd gotten that second passport, things would be so much easier.

And then it occurred to him there was a solution to his passport dilemma. A simple one. Just thinking about it made him calmer, and he wondered why he hadn't thought of it sooner. And as soon as he secured the passport, he knew exactly where he would be heading. South of the border to pay his amigo Eduardo in Monterrey a visit. Eduardo had connections everywhere.

He called for a taxi. Then he walked for the last time out the front door of his multimillion-dollar house with the priceless view. He sat down on a step with the duffel bag in his lap and waited to be picked up.

SEVENTY

Dan

Dan's heart hadn't hurt like this since the day his mother died, when his dad called to tell him she'd had a heart attack and was gone like that. That was twenty years ago. He'd just received word that Greta's car had been recovered from the parking area at the head of the Gulch Creek Valley. The slide hadn't gotten that far, that would be a thousand-year event instead of hundred, but the possibility of anyone further into the valley surviving really would have been beating the odds.

Now he had to share the devastating news with Marynell.

She watched him pull up and was waiting for him in the foyer. "More on the chickens? Or maybe they just want me to turn the house over to them straight out," she said, holding the door open.

"Got some bad news, Marynell," he said, taking off his hat as he walked into the small foyer. As always, the house had an appealing smell, that of baked goods, but there was more than that. The smell of a well lived-in home. Of a life. Of the past. "Why don't you sit down."

Marynell took the news about the slide more calmly than he'd have thought. He told her there were search efforts underway, and she'd asked him to go next door to get Jason. "He's on search and rescue."

"Don't you think he'll be out at the slide, Marynell?"

"I want you to go and see," she commanded. "He promised me to let me know if anything happened out that way and I haven't heard from him."

"All right," said Dan, getting up and going for the door. He knew damn well most of the search and rescue teams were out in the field looking for that Snowcat, that time was of the essence, but he didn't want to argue with her. Things had been tough enough for her lately.

SEVENTY-ONE

Gene

Gene stood in the basement storage room of Roman's house, staring down at his writer friend who had now moved on to the final chapter, his last page turned by a bullet to his head. He closed the storage room door and locked it. By the time they found his ski buddy's body, Gene would be long gone.

He went back upstairs into the office and found Roman's passport in his unlocked desk. Their resemblance was so close someone would really have to be looking hard to realize that Gene wasn't the guy in the photo. The key was to always lock eyes with the examiner, much like a magician does to deceive the audience. He stashed the passport and Roman's wallet with his license and credit cards into his jacket pocket.

Now that he was Roman, he figured it was best to get moving fast. Roman never talked about family, so he wasn't worried about someone calling in the next couple of days looking for him. Like just about everyone in Aspen, Roman would take off from time to time without telling anyone, so it would be a while before he was missed.

His plan was to drive Roman's car down to Monterrey. He wasn't concerned about carrying money and a gun across the border. You only got checked leaving Mexico. Never going in.

Gene had just taken the keys off the hook when he saw the sheriff coming up the walk. His breath caught in his throat. What in hell was that about? Had someone heard the gunshot and reported it? He had only fired one round, and it was in the concrete-lined basement. It would have made the kind of sound a person wonders if they heard and then forgets about. He couldn't believe the cops were coming to investigate.

He ducked behind the kitchen door and closed it. Through

the crack in the door, he could see the sheriff peering into the darkened foyer through the door's window. Then he started rapping on the glass. The noise grew louder and more urgent as he heard the sheriff shout, "Anyone here."

Gene reached into his tote for his gun. His first thought was to shoot the sheriff and take off, but he realized that would be a long, painful, and losing battle. You can't shoot a cop without spending the rest of your life looking over your shoulder. And he sure couldn't live with that. Then again, he couldn't live with confinement either. He held the gun at the ready, pissed that his plan would have to be scuttled.

And then miracle of miracles, he heard the shrill voice of Marynell Hennings calling from next door. Gene didn't need to see the old gal to picture her on her front porch shouting, the ever-present oxygen on her back.

"Not there, Dan," she ordered, "Jason lives in the ADU around the back."

The sheriff made an exasperated gesture and walked alongside the house toward the alley. Gene could hear knocking again coming from the back of the house, and after a while the knocking stopped and the big lawman came back up the walk. Gene kept his place in the shadows and watched the big man walk back to the miner's shack.

"No one there, Marynell," he heard the sheriff say. "I told you he'd be out in the field."

Gene started to breathe regularly again. Thank God he had been patient and not acted irrationally. Otherwise, he could have been in a high-speed chase right now. He waited until the sheriff's vehicle pulled away, and then went into Roman's garage. He climbed into Roman's fifteen-year-old Subaru and threw the tote with all his worldly possessions into the back. As he headed out of town, he wondered why a rich guy like Roman drove such a piece of shit. Then he thought better of it. The car certainly wouldn't draw any attention crossing the border.

SEVENTY-TWO
Greta

It was pitch dark in the Snowcat, but even in the dark I could tell we were on our side because I was in Neverman's lap. Which I wasn't sure was a good thing or a bad thing. And Floyd was on top of both of us. The interior lit up as Neverman turned on his phone's flashlight. I could see the window on his side had shattered and most of the skylight was gone, but luckily the slide had packed the snow around the cab of the machine in a way that kept the inside of the cab clear.

"Everyone OK?" he asked. Though we'd taken quite a ride, we'd taken a soft landing, presumably propped up by snow.

"I'm good," said Judy.

"I'm good," said Buzz.

"I'm good," I said. My dog whimpered beside me. "Floyd too."

"What about Evie?" he asked.

"She's still passed out, thank God," said Buzz, softly touching her cheek with his fingers.

Neverman tried making a call which we all knew wouldn't work, and it didn't. He assessed our situation. "Well, we're good for air for a while," he said, trying to lighten the situation. We all knew he was just trying to make us feel better. We were in pretty deep, both in snow and in danger. "I guess the only thing we can hope is that someone comes for us. The good news is I can pretty much guarantee that the cabin and the two guys in it are toast."

"Yeah, but they may be taking us along with them," said Buzz dourly.

"Buzz, did you bring a beacon?" Neverman asked suddenly. There was dead silence followed by: "We left so fast I forgot."

"Crap, me too," said Neverman.

"I brought mine," I said, wrapping my hand around the cord hanging from my neck. "So there."

"Is it on transmit?" he asked.

"It sure is."

We lay like that for a couple of hours, me pressed against Neverman like a 3D jigsaw puzzle and Floyd resettling himself periodically along my side. In the back, Judy was on top of Evie who screamed in her sleep whenever anyone touched her crippled arm. Luckily Buzz was on the bottom. It would have been harder on them if his weight was on top.

We turned on our flashlights intermittently, trying to make light of a very dark situation with occasional stories or jokes. At first in a situation like this you're glad to be alive until you start to think about it. I wondered how deep under we were. An alluvial fan holds a tremendous amount of snow and we could be twenty or thirty feet down. Among other things I wondered about the structural integrity of the Snowcat and how much pressure it could take.

"I wonder how long before the phones run out of batteries," said Judy.

Neverman had a swift answer for that. "We'll run out of air before the cells lose their battery life. That is if we keep them warm."

"My phone is back in the cabin," I lamented.

"Greta, your phone is buried for good, so get over it," Neverman said. "And we should all stop talking to save oxygen." He didn't mention CO2 which I knew would get us before lack of oxygen did. Neverman would know about that too.

I went back to thinking of my brother and then Everest. Sometimes I could hear Judy crying softly in the dark. Every once in a while, I could feel Neverman's hand brush my cheek and it eased the anxiety a bit.

Another hour passed and I started wondering how soon it would be dark up above us. Then all bets on rescue could be called off. It was cold, but not terribly cold because all our bodies pressed together threw off heat and, besides, we were dressed for winter. I could feel Neverman's hand on my leg and hear his intake of breath. I could also tell the carbon dioxide level was rising because I was getting drowsy. Even worse I was getting a headache. The window of time before we all succumbed was getting smaller. Maybe another hour. Two at most.

I figured we were going to die and I decided I had no regrets. Not since moving to Aspen anyhow. And the warmth of Neverman next to me was reassuring, making me feel I wasn't going to leave this world alone and unloved. Whether it was true or not.

An hour must have passed before I heard a tapping sound. It was mild at first, and I thought I might be hallucinating, but then I heard it again. And again. It started getting lighter in the Cat and for the first time I thought we just might make it. Then there was the sound of voices followed by the sound of shovels and I knew we were going to make it. A minute later, the door above me opened.

I was staring at the beaming face of Jason Click.

"Praise the Lord," he shouted.

"Praise the Lord," we shouted back.

SEVENTY-THREE
Gene

Gene got to Eduardo's following a twenty-hour marathon from Aspen to Monterrey in the Subaru, stopping only for gas, supplies and to piss, paying in cash and never exceeding the speed limit. The border crossing had been uneventful, him looking the custom's official in the eye, and the man flagging him through with a bored hand after he said he had nothing to declare. He carried no cell phone, and he hadn't wanted to run the risk of buying a burner, so he arrived at his friend's hacienda unannounced. The guard at the gate had taken his name and made a call. To Gene's relief, a moment later the gate swung welcomely open.

Gene and Eduardo became partners back when Gene was getting his start in the drug business in the eighties. They were dealing coke back then, and they had a lucrative franchise going in the south-western states. The business had been a bit more lucrative for Gene, who had skimmed a percentage off the top, unbeknownst to his partner. But with the risks he was taking in the US market, he felt he deserved it. The two had parted ways amicably when the border tightened and Gene decided to go legit, putting his money into Aspen real estate.

Eduardo had welcomed him with open arms, and over dinner, Gene explained to his former partner that he was in a situation where he needed a new face and passport. Eduardo asked no questions, and after some bartering, Gene parted with $100,000 cash, his Audemars Piguet watch and the key to the Gibraltar apartment where the Basquiat was hidden. In return, Eduardo would fly him by private jet to Incheon, Korea where he would be transported to a waiting fishing boat bound for to the paradise of Jeju Island. There he would be given a new face by one of the most accomplished plastic surgeons in the trade and a new identity by a world-class forger. Eduardo's meth connection in Korea would take care of everything. His connection used to deal in opium, Eduardo explained, but the market demand for meth had changed their business model.

And so barely a day later, he was on an old fishing boat chugging south toward the South China Sea. It was explained to him that since he wouldn't want to deal with any authorities until he got his new papers, the long trip would be primarily by night. He settled into his spartan quarters below deck and stretched out on the bunk, feeling safe for the first time in recent history. By tomorrow night he would be on Jeju Island eating kimchi and flirting with the local women. He would stay on the island until he got his new face and it was safe to leave. Maybe he'd pick up a little business in the drug trade in the meantime to make up for his recent losses.

He was exhausted from his long trip, and the rocking of the boat lulled him to sleep.

He was awakened by an abrupt shutdown of the engines and the sound of an approaching boat. He was barely breathing as he heard the craft pull alongside. Were they there looking for something? Him? Then he heard the gobbledygook of raised Korean voices and the sound of footsteps on the deck above. He stayed below and was relieved when he heard the sound of the other boat pulling away not long afterwards. He stayed in his bunk waiting for the captain to start up the fishing boat's engines again.

When the engines remained quiet fifteen minutes later, he decided to go topside to see what was going on. The captain spoke a little English, so he hoped he would be able to explain the problem. But when Gene got up top, he was surprised to see the boat brightly lit with no crew member in sight. He walked onto the bridge, which was deserted, and saw an envelope with his name on it taped to the ship's wheel. He recognized Eduardo's handwriting and swiftly tore the envelope open, reading the words inside with shaking hands.

THIS IS WHAT HAPPENS TO PEOPLE WHO CHEAT ME.

Then his eye went to the horizon where he could see running lights of a boat approaching at high speed. His innards went slack when he saw it was a patrol flying the colors of the North Korean flag. He had been abandoned in North Korean waters. He didn't know what happened to undocumented visitors violating the maritime boundary that separated the two Koreas, but he knew it couldn't be pleasant. People disappeared into the North Korean labor camps and were never heard from again. He wished he had his gun, gifted as a final gesture to Eduardo. He fell to the deck cursing as the North Korean vessel pulled alongside and discharged a dozen uniformed soldiers onto the fishing boat with their rifles drawn.

SEVENTY-FOUR
Dan

Two days later

Dan parked on the street in front of Marynell's house. He could see Greta was already there, the Goner crunched in the driveway behind Clive's dead truck. His watch told him it was 10:15. The animal control people weren't due until 10:30. His stomach growled, not from hunger but from unpleasantness. He was sick in his heart at his mission, making it all that more difficult for him to tend to it personally.

Clutching the paperwork, he got out of the sheriff's vehicle and started up the walk. No sense in prolonging the inevitable. Out of the corner of his eye he could see a tall figure standing in the fishbowl window next door. That guy sure wasn't taking any chances on not getting rid of those chickens. He wondered at the type of human being who took pleasure in the misery of another.

Greta was waiting at the door to let him in, an odd smirk on her face. He was expecting something more hostile considering his mission. He wondered if this was her way of coping, kind of like laughing at a funeral.

"Hey, Dan," she greeted him.

"Howdy, Sheriff," Marynell echoed from her seat on the couch in the window. Her embroidery was in her lap and she was smiling too. There was a tray of cookies on the table. For the first time in practically ever he had no appetite.

"I'm sorry, Marynell, but as you know, Animal Control will be here at any minute. They've guaranteed your chickens will be relocated to a farm and kept there for eggs. No need to fear for them. They will be well taken care of."

"Oh, I don't know about that," said Marynell.

"I swear to you they'll be looked after."

"No, I mean about them being relocated."

"Marynell, we've talked about this. This order I'm carrying says they have to go."

Marynell stood up and pulled the oxygen tank onto her back. "Follow me," she commanded. She led him through the small house and out the kitchen door, across the yard to the barn on the alley. Then she slid the door open with a sly smile and stood aside. Dan looked mystified and walked into the barn. He came back out a second later, his massive gut jiggling in laughter. Marynell slid the door shut behind him and they walked back to the house, Dan laughing the entire way.

When they got inside, he took a cookie from the tray.

Ten minutes later a county vehicle bearing the logo of the animal control unit pulled up behind the sheriff's car. Dan met the animal control officer halfway up the walk, a dark-haired man in this thirties with a gorilla tattoo climbing his neck like King Kong. "Hey, Travis," he said, tearing the order in half. "Guess we won't be needing you after all."

Travis raised his hands in a 'whatever' gesture. "If you're saying it's so, I guess it is."

Travis ambled back to the truck and was pulling away when the door to the fishbowl flew open and Hayden came running down the steps with his own copy of the orders in his hand. Hatless and in his shirtsleeves, he hadn't even taken the time to put on his shearling coat.

"Those chickens are supposed to be taken off this property today," he shouted, pointing at the truck to stop, his face red in frustrated fury. He waved the sheet of paper in the air. "I have the order."

"There's been a change in plan," Dan responded. "If you'll follow me."

Dan led the seething man around the side of the house to the barn. Greta and Marynell came outside to watch. Dan slid the barn door open and waited. Hayden stormed inside and was back seconds later with six squawking chickens nipping at his heels, each of them sporting a red bib that read: SERVICE ANIMAL.

"Prescribed by her doctor," Dan said.

"What the fuck," he sputtered. "She'll hear from my attorney. And she's going to hear about that encroachment too."

"If you're talking about the property line," Greta said, just waiting for the perfect moment, "my attorney took a look at the parcel map and according to the most recent plan, you're on a couple of feet of her property instead of her being on yours."

"That's impossible," Hayden sputtered.

"No, it isn't. We brought a surveyor in. This entire area was laid out in a grid in the 1880s and in fact your driveway is on part of her property. Talk about encroachment. She could make you tear it up."

When Greta had called Barry Levin about her latest problem, she told him Marynell's story. Levin had volunteered to take on her case pro bono. He even got a surveyor who owed him a favor to draw up a survey. With Hayden standing there huffing, Greta added, "Called your bluff."

Hayden stomped the ground hard and stormed wordlessly back to his house. He hit black ice on his walkway and landed on his butt in a puddle of melted snow. When he jumped back up, his pants were soaking. He stomped up the stairs and pulled the blinds in one of the big windows. Dan found himself thinking of Rumpelstiltskin. Greta and Marynell witnessed the entire thing trying not to laugh.

"Guess that shows him," Greta managed to say.

"Yep," said Marynell. "If that's how he acts over the chickens, I can't imagine what he's going to do when I get the pig."

EPILOGUE

Well, we got to ski a few more days before the virus reared its ugly head, forcing the mountain to shut down on the Ides of March, the day Judy had planned to celebrate Gene's birthday at the Bugaboo. All things aside, due to Covid, Gene wouldn't have been having that surprise party anyway. Not that I would have felt bad for him. Gene was living proof that evil exists in our world. Exemplified by the murder of his friend, Roman Judge, whose body poor Jason Click had the misfortune to discover in the basement after searching the house when he hadn't been heard from for days.

I wondered where Gene spent his sixtieth. Hiding somewhere, no doubt, while every branch of law enforcement in the state, and possibly the country, was searching for him. It's unnerving knowing he could be out there somewhere, but I'm pretty certain he'll never dare show his face here again. As is Judy. She's more worried over what happened to Paul, though after reading Gene's email on her computer it's pretty much a forgone conclusion. But she's in remarkable spirits about being pregnant, though she's not sure how she's going to support the baby after it's born.

Evie's had a rough go of it, but she's been fitted with her prosthetic arm and in her usual stoic way already has it mastered. She and Buzz are getting married, and he dotes on her even more than ever. If we're ever allowed out in public again, we'll celebrate like we used to.

In yet another letdown, my Everest trip cancelled because of all the travel restrictions, so that will have to wait until . . . whenever.

But on the positive side, the Greenes turned down the developer's offer for their house, so the heat's off me losing my A-frame. And Toby's back in the States. Quarantined with his new wife and baby, but home safe just the same.

* * *

In the few days of work before the lifts closed, things went back to business as usual between Neverman and me, almost. The underlying tension has morphed into something other than dislike. There's something simmering beneath the surface though neither one of us wants to admit it. But if I had to take a lie detector test, I would have to confess it was kind of nice being squished next to him in the Snowcat.

In fact, that's why I'm kind of excited to be meeting him in an hour. We're going to skin 3,000 feet to the top of Highlands with Floyd along as chaperone. I mean, why not? With this quarantine and all, we're still free to enjoy the outdoors. Once we hit the top, we'll come back down the steeps and float through the deeps together, making love—to the mountain.

Acknowledgements

Thank you as always to my agent, Helen Breitwieser, at Cornerstone Literary Agency, who is an amazing advocate and friend who has tirelessly championed my books. And to my editor at Severn House, Laurie Johnson, whose support and insight has been instrumental in honing these pages. And to proofreader, Anna Harrisson, whose professionalism and attention to minutiae, as well as adjusting my timeline errors, helped bring this book to near perfection. And to Pitkin County Sheriff, Joe DiSalvo, for his expert advice and input on what course law force might take when a human hand is found in the wilderness.

Lastly, extra appreciation to Aspen Ski Patrol and all ski patrollers everywhere for keeping us safe on mountain.